BRIDGE OF ETERNITY

VELA SERIES
BOOK ONE

AMELIA COLE

For Content Warnings please see my website at www.ameliacolebooks.com

To my mom,
For your unwavering spirit to help others

The large fields produced no grain
The flooded fields produced no fish
The watered garden produced no honey and wine...
 - From "The Curse of Akkad," written circa 4,000 BP,
Enheduanna, Priestess of Ur

    "The wisest astronomer living cannot tell us how far the stars reach...for there is no getting to the borders of space."
      -Agnes Giberne

CHAPTER

ONE

The wiry man slid the precious item across the splintered countertop.

"This was not easy to find," Jamil said. "That'll be a hundred."

"A hundred? It was fifty last time," I groaned.

His stony-eyed gaze didn't waver. He knew my livelihood depended on that charging cord since the current one for my laptop had decided to radiate a burning plastic smell instead of actually charging my battery. I'd pay any price for it, but that didn't mean I'd go down without a fight.

"So much for the friends and family discount," I said, slapping the cash on the counter.

The store owner patted his chest and took the money. "I am touched you think I am your friend, Ella."

Jamil placed the money inside the metal lockbox alongside other bills from various currencies. The price hike was to be expected. In this region of Syria, roads were often either closed or too dangerous to travel, and an Amazon locker delivery would be two weeks out, if not longer, which meant weeks without my computer to work on editing and sending photos.

"And my mail?" I asked.

Jamil shut and locked the lid. "Ah yes," he said, disappearing into the back room. I turned around to wait, resting my elbows against the edge of the store's counter. Various types of papers, pens, and pencils, as well as a few souvenir items, lined the crowded store shelves. It was all a front, of course; Jamil's real income came from procuring goods not readily available here.

Two men entered wearing crisp white button-up shirts, dress coats, and black slacks. Their massive forms blocked the afternoon sunlight from entering the convenience store. I eyed them warily, adjusting my hijab by tucking a strand of hair under the silk covering. They hovered by the entrance, and the bigger of the two flicked a postcard of the Palmyra ruins and Bosra amphitheater.

The second one muttered something under his breath, turning to speak to his companion, and I spotted the unmistakable bulge of a pistol under his coat.

There was no way these guys were tourists.

Thankfully, before I'd had time to consider bailing and get my letter, Jamil emerged from the back carrying two envelopes. I shifted to face him, keeping the other guys in my periphery. Jamil held out the mail to me, and I reached to take them.

"Ah ha," he said, holding them just out of my reach. He held out his left hand and raised a bushy eyebrow.

"Dammit, Jamil," I said. However, the oppressive presence of the two shady-looking guys and my anxiousness to leave the store stilled the protest on my tongue, and I simply grumbled as I handed over more money.

Jamil gave me the letters and stuffed the twenty in his other pocket. Then, seeing another customer approach a rack of t-shirts at the opposite end of the store, he sauntered over to assist him. I moved to the far end of the shop, seeking a corner behind a shelf of canned goods for privacy.

I held up the first envelope. It was addressed from The Washington Post and had been mailed six weeks ago. I ripped it open.

Dear Ms. Eleanora Dawson,

You are cordially invited to the United States Society of Journalism banquet dinner. As a nominee for Outstanding Journalist Photography, it would please the Society if you would attend to receive your award. Your invitation includes a plus one. The award ceremony is scheduled for October 20th at the Roseland Ballroom in New York City.

Sincerely,

Virginia Roushald USSJ Vice-President

I crumpled the letter and tossed it into the trash bin. What a joke. What would I tell them? That I'd eaten nothing but flaming hot Cheetos and sour Skittles for three days while sleeping in the back of Taamir's station wagon. Or maybe a funny anecdote about how I'd endured bigoted comments for weeks when I'd followed soldiers who had forgotten all their manners. Oh, or the story about how I'd taken pepper spray straight to the face when a Syrian police officer mistook me for a drug dealer, which, to be fair, he *did* catch me handing an informant money, and then how afterward I'd violently vomited for an hour. Bet that one would go over well with the audience all sipping on their lobster bisque and champagne.

Capturing photos to document and bring to light the struggles people around the world faced was my reward, not some framed plaque.

People in this region of the world were suffering. Every day, the conflict destroyed businesses, tore families apart, or disrupted their way of life. So how about they spend money on planes to ship medical equipment and food instead of a banquet dinner full of expensive champagne and half-hearted speeches?

I tossed the invitation in the trash and looked at the next envelope. The corners were dog-eared, and the stamp—a pair of golden bells — was peeling up at the edges. In beautifully handwritten cursive was my name and addressed to my Damascus mailbox. I'd never asked, and probably didn't want to know how Jamil forwarded it here.

In the space where the sender's address should have been was a sticker of two golden metallic swans, their long necks curved into an elegant heart. I tore it open, ripping the matching gold sticker on the flap. The envelope's lining was a lighter shade of gold, and I pulled a sturdy piece of card stock from it. The paper's border was embossed and smooth under my callused hands.

It was a wedding announcement.

Cara was getting married. A tightness grew in my chest. This was too soon, wasn't it? I swore she and Shawn had only been together a year. The invitation stated the wedding would be at our parents' house in Sacramento in three months. My thumb stroked the thick, textured card stock, filled with emotion that my younger sister was getting married before me. I'd resigned myself to the fact that I wasn't cut out for married life or a relationship. The best chance I'd had was last Summer, and that had not ended in a happily-ever-after, more like a slam the door, throw away the key kind of way.

Besides, as cliché as it sounded, I was married to my work. I shoved the letter into my satchel. I'd look it over later in my hotel room, preferably with a bottle of Arak.

I tucked the invitation into my bag, preparing to leave. The two men had moved to the front of the store and leaned over the counter. They spoke in hushed, hurried tones to Jamil.

All color had drained from Jamil's face, and worry pinched

the skin between his eyebrows. He kept bobbing his head in quick nods as they spoke, and a sheen of sweat reflected off his forehead. Clearly, they were negotiating the price of something. I gritted my teeth.

Bet they get a discount.

I hitched up my shoulder bag, exited the shop, and went onto the busy street. People passed by with their arms burdened by bags from the neighboring businesses. The vendors' voices echoed off the stone buildings as they called out their wares for sale.

I glanced at my watch. Taamir was supposed to be here to pick me up.

The sun blazed overhead, dust swirling from the multitude of passing cars as I stood on the curb. I pulled the satin cloth over my mouth and nose to keep from breathing the dust and to further hide my face. Unfortunately, a lone woman tended to draw more looks than if I were escorted.

Growing impatient, I shifted my weight and stared down the street.

The store's bell clinked to my right, and from my periphery, the two men stepped out of Jamil's store. Without hesitating, they turned to their right and vanished around the corner of the building.

The bell clinked again, and Jamil exited the store. He quickly locked the door and then shuffled hurriedly toward the direction the men had gone.

My pulse quickened. Jamil was always up to something. But I'd never known him to leave the store for *any* reason, ever. Partly because he lived in the apartment upstairs and partly because of the security cameras he'd oh-so-not-secretly hidden everywhere in his shop.

So, what could these guys possibly have that would force him to leave? Jamil had tipped me off to a few leads that had paid off. A refugee family that had consented to let me visit their home and take photos. A rumor about a stray dog that a group of teens had found in a collapsed apartment building and befriended. I'd made bank on photos from that one.

My relationship with Jamil was tenuous. Even so, I liked the guy and would hate if anything happened to him.

Abandoning the curb and my wait for Taamir, I approached the corner of the block. Two rust-covered cars sat broken in the alleyway between the buildings, and men's voices carried toward me, speaking Arabic. I sidled over to a pile of cardboard boxes that sat next to an overflowing dumpster.

I pressed my back against the brick wall and caught Jamil's voice in the mix.

Thirty feet from where I hid, the two men stood facing each other with their backs toward me. Jamil hunched and lifted a large wooden crate into the back of an old flatbed truck. The second man secured a tarp over it with two bungee cords. Jamil stared at the ground as the first man approached.

I held my breath, listening.

"...they increased the security around the site," Jamil said. "Two of my most trusted men were arrested."

"Mr. Kane understands the risk that was placed on you to acquire this," the first, bigger man said. "And since he is feeling generous, he permitted me to pay you double to replace the resources you lost." He handed Jamil a bulging envelope. "He will likely require your services again and prefers to keep those under his employment content with their agreement."

I quickly wiped my sweating palms on the thighs of my jeans and slowly reached for the camera in my bag.

Steady now, Ella.

I'd spent enough time in places I shouldn't be, following the wrong people to know it was a matter of time before I'd witnessed something I shouldn't. And my number must've come up because today was that day.

Photos like these would bring a bidding war from the presses I worked with. However, if there was a chance that these were stolen munitions, my photos would mean an attack could be diffused before it ever happened. Lives could be saved because of them.

I knew other photographers who had connections to Syrian police, the US military, and another who had a cousin at the CIA. Giving them copies *would* be the right thing to do, as much as my bank account would disagree.

My finger continuously pressed on the camera, and I prayed the sounds of the car's engines from the street behind me covered up the button's light click.

Jamil looked at the envelope, his eyes darting quickly to the big man's face. "Yes, of course," he stammered and hugged the envelope.

The first man walked to the driver's side door while the second strode past a cowering Jamil and whispered something. Dark rings of sweat-stained the pits of Jamil's shirt. He lowered his gaze to his fidgeting hands and nodded. The second man gave a tight-lipped grin and slapped Jamil on the back. His small frame recoiled from the impact, causing him to stagger forward a step. The second man climbed into the passenger side of the truck. A starter whined, eventually rumbling the tired engine to life. Jamil turned and climbed the rusted metal stairway to his apartment upstairs.

I spun before darting to the front of the building. I skidded to a stop on the sidewalk and spotted Taamir's faded blue Volkswagen, with its yellow hood, sitting idle in front of the store.

What was I doing? Was I actually considering following these guys? This was *so* out of my job description. Photojournalists were supposed to observe, capture, and report. Not act like a wannabe Charlie's Angel spy and chase after suspicious thugs.

I *should* tell Taamir to take me home.

I s*hould* stick to what I knew and had literal skills in.

Skills that—in my twenty-six years of life — had kept me safe, kept me *alive*.

For starters, I didn't have a weapon or hand-to-hand combat training besides the semester of fencing I'd taken as an elective in college. I had nothing to protect myself with except my Nikon.

I chewed my bottom lip, hesitation tearing me in opposite directions.

Maybe my camera was all I needed.

Was I prepared to live with myself if there was a slight chance that I learned of an attack that I could've somehow averted? If innocent people died, people that would still be alive if I'd only swallowed my fear and *hadn't* played it safe, how could I ever get over that?

My gut solidified the decision even as my mind told me otherwise, still berating me with the plethora of reasons this was a very, *very* bad idea.

"Fuck it," I muttered under my breath. I looped a thumb under the strap of my bag and stepped off the curb.

I wrenched open the passenger side door to Taamir's car, my head buzzing with the realization this was happening.

"Hey, Taamir," I said, my hands shaking as I fastened my seat belt. The flatbed pulled out of the alleyway behind them and turned right in the opposite direction. "So, I need you to follow that truck," I said, pointing behind them. "I need to see where it's going."

"Ms. Dawson," he said, his English tinged with an Arabic accent. "I apologize greatly for my being late. Unfortunately, my daughter lost her favorite shoe, and I had to go to three stores to find her a new one. I want to make it up to you by inviting you to dinner with my family tonight."

I wiped the sweat from my brow, looking at the middle-aged man's bearded face. His eyes watched me expectantly. His weekly dinner invitations were drifting into daily territory, and I wasn't sure how much longer I'd be able to come up with excuses to get out of them. I rested a hand on his shoulder and chewed the inside of my cheek. "Dinner sounds...great. Now, we really need to go."

He flashed me a beaming smile before grasping the shifter on the steering wheel and putting the car into gear. He gunned the engine, weaving around the pedestrians. I sat up tall in my seat with my fists clenched. Our odds of catching the truck dwindled with every passing second. I could make out the green roof of the truck's cab three cars ahead. We needed to keep a safe distance but not fall too far behind, or we'd risk losing them in the traffic. Dozens of alleyways intersected the road, and they could turn down one and disappear at any moment.

The crowded tan and whitewashed stone buildings loomed over them. On this side of town, many had crumbling rooftops and broken windows. The walls that once surrounded peoples' rooms were flayed open, exposing the building's entrails to the world.

The car in front of us stopped, and its one working brake light flashed as a person climbed out of the passenger door.

Taamir's hand laid on the horn, blasting it loudly before swerving hard around the stalled car. *This* was why I loved Taamir. Well, that and his — don't ask questions when I ask you to do weird and sometimes dangerous shit — attitude.

The Volkswagen's engine strained as Taamir cranked the wheel to the right, positioning us behind a dented brown station wagon. I leaned out the window, clutching the scarf over my face. My eyes stung from the powdered dust stirred up from the car's tires in front, and I peered through the haze. Finally, I spotted the truck and watched it turn to the right.

"Slow down," I said, popping my head back inside the car. "Up ahead. Pull over to that building."

Taamir did as instructed and shifted the car into the park beside a four-story apartment building. "Wait here for me," I said, reaching over the opened window to grasp the only working door handle. "You know what to do if I'm not back in thirty minutes."

Taamir nodded and tapped on his Rolex—the one I'd gifted him when they'd started working together. Over the past two months, his assistance allowed me to take enough photos to earn me triple what it was worth.

I shoved open the door, pulling my shoulder bag over my head. The car door hinges protested as I slammed it shut. I stepped over the gray-colored roof tiles and crushed plaster that littered the sidewalk, my bag gently bumping against my hip. Although this area was less crowded than the business district, a few people passed me chatting with each other as their children eyed the street vendors wafting mouthwatering-smelling food.

At the corner of the building, I stopped and casually glanced around. The narrow road the truck had turned down was a street leading into an enclosed parking garage. The truck idled in front of a large metal overhead door to my right, thirty feet away. A man dressed in camouflage pants stepped out of the metal side door.

I pulled my camera out of my bag. Putting it up to my eye, I zoomed in on the man and snapped pictures. He carried a rifle and a bulletproof vest, but I didn't recognize anything else about him.

The guard strode to the driver's side, and I could see his

mouth move as he spoke to the driver. A second later, he stepped back, waving them forward. I snapped another photo, focusing on the man's face before he turned and re-entered the side door. The truck lurched forward, and the metal door slammed shut behind it. I stuffed my camera in my bag and sprinted across the drive to the man's door. My heart thumped in my chest as I pulled on the doorknob.

Locked.

I pressed my lips together. I needed to find a way inside.

My eyes quickly searched the side of the apartment buildings on either side. A tangled mess of a fire escape hung crookedly from the building to my right. The bottom rung was just out of my reach, so I scrambled onto the roof of a bombed-out car. I spread my feet, crouched, and leaped.

My hands reached out, and the metal clang echoed off the buildings' walls. The bar dug painfully into my palms, and I hissed through gritted teeth, my feet dangling helplessly.

Slowly, shoulder muscles straining, I managed to pull myself up. My fingers clung to the metal grating platform, and I most ungracefully hauled my lower half up, flopping onto my stomach.

I gave myself only a second to rest, then started up the stairs. The bolts securing the metal frame to the side of the building trembled and creaked with each step, and I breathed a sigh of relief when I finally found an open window and slipped inside. The stagnant air reeked of urine and old cigarettes. Once a living room, the space was deserted, except for scraps of newspaper and a dresser missing two drawers. Empty apartments were a common sight as sporadic violence and civil unrest caused more and more people to flee the city.

I hurried to the front door and scanned both ways down the deserted hallway before darting to my right.

Each passing second ticked loudly in my head. I was

running out of time before Taamir would worry. I peered down a set of stairs, saw no one, then took them two at a time. My pulse galloped in my ears as I hurried down the concrete steps. At the bottom landing, I pushed open a metal door, and the stench of car exhaust and charred metal filled my nose.

A handful of cars were parked in the underground parking garage, and the truck was visible in the center. I crouched down behind a newer BMW. The murmur of voices from the middle of the room drifted to me. I pressed my back against the cold metal of the blue sedan and peered over the hood to where I had a clear view of the truck.

The two men from before were standing by the tailgate, and one had their arm slung casually over the tarp covering a crate.

Tires squealed again, signaling a black sedan entering down the off-street ramp. The car stopped, and I held my camera up, snapping pictures. A man emerged from the backseat wearing a gray pageboy hat and a long black dress coat like he'd stepped off the set of Peaky Blinders. Even from this distance, I could see his pristinely clean and polished black shoes.

He strode toward the other two men. I caught fragments of the conversation and was surprised to hear they were speaking English. The heavier-set man from Jamil's store led the suited man to the back of the truck. He pulled off the canvas tarp and displayed the crate, then flipped open the latch and lifted the lid of the wooden box. The instant it opened, a sharp, burning sensation tingled my nostrils, reminding me of a hotel's over-chlorinated swimming pool. The scent had gone as soon as it came, and an amber light bloomed from inside the crate. Slowly, it pulsed, reflecting a golden glow on the men's startled faces before they slammed the lid shut, snuffing it out.

I blinked my eyes, the sweat from my forehead stinging them as it blurred my vision. I used my arm to wipe it away. My brain rushed to make sense of what I'd seen. Maybe it was an illuminated countdown timer to a bomb? The eerie fluorescence of a beaker full of radioactive material?

Maybe I should cut back on the Bond movies.

The man handed the bigger guy an envelope and climbed into the back seat of the gleaming black town car. With the door open, smooth classical jazz played.

The garage slider door opened, revealing the noonday sun outside. The sounds of the street filtered in as the town car drove out of the garage. I squinted, allowing my eyes to acclimate. The metal door slammed onto the concrete floor below with a *bang*. Soon after, the truck's doors shut. I leaned my head to the side, focusing on the truck and the two men sitting in the front seat. The large man examined a hundred-dollar bill, holding it up to the light. The mechanism in my Nikon buzzed as I snapped more pictures. A door behind me, leading to what I assumed was the central part of the building, opened, and I scurried to the front of a parked car.

A dozen men wearing black face masks and armed with assault rifles streamed into the garage. My heart mimicked the thudding of their boots as they ran by.

I needed to get out of here before this whole place went to shit. My eyes searched the garage, desperately searching for an escape.

I heard the soft thump of music coming from the truck, and the two men inside appeared oblivious to the masked men circling it with guns drawn. The concrete floor was cold against my hands as I scooted further back. Then, slowly, I positioned myself directly behind the car's trunk, eyeing the door they'd entered.

A split second later, the soldiers shouted a command to Jamil and the other man to get out. I lifted myself a hair barely high enough to peek over the car and through the rear windshield. If Jamil saw me, I'd lose him as an informant. Worse, if the other men saw me, I'd be dead.

Jamil held up his hands, his eyes wide with fear. He sputtered, pleading with them not to shoot. His driver, however, had different plans, and the truck's engine roared, lurching forward. The big truck smashed through the metal garage door, tearing it like tin foil. It swerved onto the street, horns blaring as it cut off cars. The masked men chased after it, shouting commands to shoot it. I covered my ears from the deafening barrage of gunfire. The group bolted for the door, chasing after on foot for the speeding truck.

I sat motionless in the eerily quiet garage. Adrenaline surged through my veins, forcing me to stand and disappear before the police or more masked men arrived. My leg muscles protested as I extended them from the crouching position. I'd have time to review the pictures later; now, I needed to get the hell out of here and back to Taamir. I tucked my camera in my bag and looked over to the space the truck had been in a minute before.

The small wooden crate lay on the ground.

TWO

I clenched my teeth, torn over what to do with the crate that had fallen off the back of the truck.

I swallowed the lump in my throat, indecision causing me to remain frozen. It'd be so easy just to walk away and let the fates decide what to do with it, or I could call the authorities as an anonymous tip and let them deal with it. I had minutes before the armed men returned.

Even before I'd fully committed to my decision, my feet were already moving. My gaze swept the area, ensuring I was still alone, and my heartbeat pounding in my ears, I cautiously approached the crate. I knelt next to it. The top of the wood paneling had splintered, and the screws on the lock had been torn from the wood, broken by the fall. I pulled my bag over my head, set it beside me, and placed my hands on the lid. The crate was new and smelled of pungent pine. I slid my fingers under the lid and lifted it. Inside, tucked in a bed of straw and newspaper shreds, was a small bronze statue. *What the hell?* I'd expected drugs or stacks of cash, anything but a tarnished bronze statue of a woman that looked like it'd come straight out of the home decor section of Anthropologie. The figure was small, at about six inches, and the woman's eyes were closed. While her facial features had worn away with time, I could see that the artist had carved her lips into a smile as if she were enjoying a nice dream. She was barefoot but wore a flowing dress, and she held in her arms an eight-pointed star enclosed in a ring.

While my left hand held the lid, my other hand hovered inches above the statue. I bit my lip, fighting the urge to take it in my grasp. I longed to touch the figure's smooth curves and its weight in my hand. Instead, I pulled my camera free from my bag and, still propping the lid with my left hand, I focused on the statue with my camera, and after a few snaps, I checked that the camera had picked up enough detail. Somewhere in the distance, a siren wailed, and loud bangs from either a car back-firing or gunshots. I shouldn't stay to find out. My phone buzzed in my pocket, jolting me. It was a text from Taamir.

Five minutes.

I secured my camera in my bag and stood. I frowned, hesitation stilling my feet as I stared down at the statue. It'd be wrong to leave it here, and given the determined group of guys with guns that had swept through here, chances were good they'd be circling back as soon as they discovered the crate was no longer on the truck. With me, however, it'd be safe. The odds were extremely good it was stolen, and with my connections, I could subtly ask and see if any of my contacts knew who it belonged to and return it to its rightful owner.

Choice decided; I slipped my hand under the figure and lifted it from the box. The parts of the statue that were untarnished, the woman's hands, the star, and her legs under the dress gleamed with the coppery finish as I rotated my hand to look at it. A horn honked loudly, interrupting my thoughts, and I slid the statue into my bag's side pocket. My eyes went to the open doorway, and the rusty Volkswagen sat across the street with an anxious-faced Taamir waving from the inside. I crossed the street and stepped around the trunk to the passenger side.

As soon as my door shut, Taamir stepped down on the accelerator. The tired engine sputtered in response before heaving us forward.

Taamir flashed me a toothy grin. "Cutting it a bit close, Ms. Ella?"

"Always do," I replied.

"Did you get some good ones?"

I shrugged. "A few, yeah." Understatement of the year.

"I saw the soldiers leave. No one saw you?" he said and gave me another look.

"C'mon, Taamir, do you really have to ask?" I said, smirking.

He chuckled. "Of course, I do, Ms. Ella. This job means I can support my family. If you die, I have to find a new job."

I shook my head. Taamir was joking, of course. But the truth was, there was a legitimate danger to my profession. I rolled my eyes and stared out the window. "I love you too, Taamir."

The sun had faded to no more than a red ember on the horizon by the time Taamir pulled the rattling car into the driveway of his house. Set on the city's outskirts, the scraggly trees and thorn-laden bushes surrounded the drab concrete block house native to the shores of the nearby Euphrates River. A warm light glowed from the two front windows. Although the house was small—and a thirty-minute drive South of the city— I understood Taamir's decision to make his home here. The larger cities would always be the primary targets of terrorist group activities. Out here was safer.

Taamir put the car in park and switched off the headlights. Since we'd spent the last four months working in a partnership, he'd learned not to ask too many questions. His discretion was one of his most valuable assets. Another reason I paid him double what I should.

"Taamir," I said, my hand going to the lump in my bag.

Taamir's hand hesitated on the door handle.

"I found something in that parking garage today."

He cocked an eyebrow and shifted his weight in his seat to face me.

"Is it dangerous?"

"I don't think so." I pulled the statue from my bag. The metallic glint of the bronze cast penny-colored reflections on the car's dash lights. The woman's features were worn and chipped, but she was still pretty. It'd look nice as a shelf decoration or a paperweight.

"Ya Salam," he murmured, his eyes wide with astonishment.

"I know, right? I don't see any date markings or artists' signatures. It looks old, though. It has to be worth a lot of money if those people were willing to go all Wild West shootout off over it.

"Ms. Dawson, I don't think it was wise of you to take that."

"You're probably right, but I couldn't just *leave* it there."

Taamir furrowed his eyebrows, his gaze moving from the statue to my face. "What will you do with it?"

I'd pondered that exact question the entire car ride out of the city and still didn't have a good answer. The truth was, I hadn't thought about anything when I'd taken it. I'd acted on the overwhelming impulse that I *needed* it.

"I know some people," I said. "I'll call them tomorrow. See if any museum break-ins or auctions had deliveries go missing. Then I'll do what I can to return it to where it's supposed to be."

Taamir frowned. "Whoever stole it will come looking for it."

I cleared my throat and tucked the statue away again. "That is a possibility."

He studied me, and for the first time since we'd been

working together, I saw genuine fear on his face. "My car is well-known in town," he said. "As is my contract with you."

Guilt coated my tongue. "I'm sorry and understand. Do what you think you must."

Taamir took risks driving me to active insurgencies because he believed in my actions. He was far from a coward, but he also wasn't stupid. Besides, he had a wife and kids to think about.

He chewed the bristly mustache above his upper lip. "Perhaps, now, it is a good idea for my family to visit my wife's parents."

I nodded.

"But from now on," he said, his face grim. "I suggest you only take photographs."

My lips curved into a crooked smile. "Agreed."

CHAPTER

THREE

The unforgiving summer heat had already stripped the grass of all its color. It crunched under our feet as we walked toward the house, and wood smoke drifted through the night air. Away from the dangers of the city, I sighed, slowing my pace, and craned my neck up, gazing at the milky way, like an ethereal path of twinkling stars smeared across the velvet sky.

"Stay for dinner?" Taamir asked as his hand paused on the front door handle.

My stomach grumbled. I *had* promised him earlier. "Sure, give me a minute to put my bag away and wash up."

Taamir ducked into the low-roofed house. The mumbled sounds of his girl's cheerful greetings came from inside as I continued outside toward the back, following a worn stone path that encircled the house.

My apartment had once been a livestock shed used for goats, but Taamir had had it re-conditioned into a small house with its stucco siding painted a creamsicle orange with pink spots, thanks to Taamir's budding artist daughters. A jasmine tree grew along its right side, and its sprawling branches arched over the rusted tin roof. The tree's yellow blooms had opened the previous week, and their intoxicating sweet scent lingered around the doorway.

When I'd first hired Taamir, I'd been staying at an apartment complex in the city's north end. But a month later, when a car bomb exploded a street market a block away, the West wall collapsed. All the residents, including myself, were left on the side of the street with garbage bags of our belongings. With limited options as a solitary woman available, Taamir had offered this building, and I'd begrudgingly agreed. I promised him it would only be temporary until I found a new place.

That'd been four months ago.

I'd grown fond of Taamir and his family and the security the rural location provided.

My hand fumbled for the lamp inside the door. I clicked it on, and the single bulb cast a yellow hue around the cramped room. A metal desk sat to my right. The silver paint curled up along its legs, exposing the corroded metal under it. To my left was an upholstered sleeper sofa. Beside it was a small wooden stool I used as a table and desk chair. Although the plumbing drained out into the field outside, there was no running water, and I had to fill buckets from the pump outside whenever I needed to flush or manage a bath. A microwave perched on a narrow windowsill, and a beige, tired-looking fridge sat on the floor. I placed my camera bag gently on the couch, went to the small sink, and splashed water on my face from a pitcher.

I was dying to review and edit the photos from the parking garage. Once I'd sorted through them, and got a better idea of what I had, then I'd reach out to my connections and decide if the other crates I saw were something they should or could pursue, and if not, it'd be off to sell to one of the presses.

I returned to the couch and flipped open the top of the bag

to take out my camera, but my fingers brushed across something smooth.

The bronze statue.

I started to pull it out, but my stomach grumbled, reminding me that the protein bar I'd had at breakfast was all I'd eaten that day. "Manage your self-care, Ella," my therapist's voice played in the back of my mind, scolding me for obsessing over my work and neglecting myself. Jason had been good at fixing me healthy meals, scheduling check-ups, and encouraging me to get massages and spa days.

Come to think of it; he'd been more than attentive to *all* my needs.

I stuffed the statue into my bag, irritated that I'd drudged up my memories of him, and went outside. I crossed the yard to the back door and entered without knocking. The spicy scent of cooked meat led me into the dining room, where Taamir and his two daughters were already seated at the small table. His wife, Larissa, stood at the opposite end of the room, holding a water pitcher. Her arm was missing from her left elbow, and she used the residual limb to steady her daughter's cups while she poured with her right. After filling the last glass, she sat the pitcher down and looked up at where I stood.

"Good evening, Ella," she said.

"Good evening," I echoed the greeting.

Taamir's wife smiled before disappearing into the kitchen.

"Please sit," Taamir said, pointing to the empty chair across from his daughters.

I did as he instructed. Fresh food had been scarce for the last three years. However, the NATO military had worked to lift the siege held by various rebel groups barricading roads and warehouses. In the past month, supplies have finally been trickling into the city. So dinner tonight comprised a platter of lamb kebabs, a bowl of hummus, and freshly baked Manushi bread.

I waited as Taamir said the Muslim blessing. The second after, his daughter's hands snapped out, grabbing the spoonful of hummus and tearing off pieces of the bread. It was the most food I'd seen in months.

I smiled to myself. Taamir's daughters, Maya, age ten, and Rima, age eight, had their mother's long brown hair neatly braided down their backs.

I helped myself to one kebab skewer with dried herbs sprinkled on it. It smelled heavenly. I nibbled on the meat, resisting the urge to gulp it in three bites. The reality was this food was a rare gift. Another attack could mean back to dried fruit and Manushi next week.

I chewed as the family discussed the day's events. The young girls spoke rapidly, vying for their parents' attention.

"Eat your food, girls," Larissa said, then shifted her gaze to me. "How'd it go today in the city?"

I swallowed the lump of pita bread as her eyes glanced concernedly toward her husband. He sat the skewer down on his plate and licked the tips of his fingers before wiping them on the cloth napkin. She had to hand it to him. Taamir's poker face was damn good.

His wife, however, apparently didn't buy the laissez-faire attitude and furrowed her brow. "Girls, you're excused."

The girls exchanged confused looks, stopping mid-conversation. Rima opened her mouth to speak, but Larissa shot her a quick, stern look and held up her hand to silence their protests.

"Come on, Rima," Maya said, resigned, and pushed her chair back. Once the two had left, Larissa's eyes narrowed on Taamir. "Tell me what happened."

I cleared my throat and sipped from the glass of water.

Taamir's eyes burned the side of my face.

My thirst quenched, and the delay expired; I wiped my mouth with the napkin. "I followed some guys I'm pretty sure were up to no good today. They didn't see me, but I got photos of their faces, and I…." I trailed off.

"She took something from them," Taamir finished for me.

Larissa tilted her head, confused. "You *took* something?"

I nodded and held up my hands. "It's nothing dangerous, I promise, but it may be of some value. Until I can be sure, Taamir and I agree you should take the girls up North."

Larissa tilted her head at her husband, and a line formed between her brows.

Taamir held up a hand, his voice pleading. "It'd only be for a few days. After that, we can stay with your parents. The girls would love to see them."

"Just for a few days," I added, looking at Larissa. "I'll check in with a contact of mine and see what they can tell me. And if there's *any* risk, I'll pack my bag and head out. Okay?"

Larissa twisted her mouth in thought. Born and raised in Syria, she knew when to keep her head down. "I suppose my parents wouldn't mind if we stayed for a couple of days."

I let out the breath I'd been holding. I'd made a reckless choice today. One I believed was putting my own life at risk. However, it was not something Taamir's family had chosen.

AFTER DINNER, Larissa phoned her parents. Of course, they were happy to have them come to visit and would leave first thing in the morning.

I'd positioned myself on my couch. My laptop's screen illuminated my face as I began the process of downloading the photos from my memory card. The Syrian military, NATO, and American soldiers had all pushed the insurgent groups to the East of the city. Over the past week, I'd captured dozens of photos of hundreds of citizens, who'd spent two years cut off from the world, and were now regaining freedom. Their faces flashed on my computer screen. Men, women, children. Clothes were dirty and torn, with sharp-edged cheekbones and dull eyes.

The indicator bar on my computer displayed the download was half complete. I rested my face on my hands. Throughout the years, I'd taken thousands of pictures, capturing the faces of people worldwide who were at the mercy of conflict, rebellions, and natural disasters. Still, it wasn't enough. The innocent still suffered, and evil triumphed. Unfortunately, the rest of the world ignored them.

I leaned back on the couch and rubbed my eyes. What I'd give for a margarita right now, sugar-rimmed with a wedge of lime. My phone buzzed in my bag. I reached inside, and my hand closed around the small flip phone. Cell service, like many modern conveniences, was hit-and-miss here. So, it was no surprise that the indicator light alerted me to two new voice-mails even though it hadn't rung in two days.

I hit the playback and listened. The first was from my mom. I closed my eyes, soaking up the sound of her voice as I began the *long* one-way conversation. She asked if I had received my sister's wedding invitation, how I was doing, and if I was eating enough. The second was from Cara. It was brief. She asked if I'd be at the wedding, and her voice was excited as she talked about bridal showers and bachelorette parties that she knew full well I wouldn't attend. There would be six bridesmaids, a three-tier red velvet cake, and a live band, and her fiancé had surprised her with tickets to France for their honeymoon.

I wanted to be happy for my sister. I *should* be. And yet, all I felt was annoyance at what a frivolous waste of money. Knowing my sister, she'd spend on the wedding what most people made in a year. My temper flared. Tens of thousands of dollars, and for what, a single day of extravagance? The good that could be done with that money. The people I could help. The children that could get clothes, housing, and food.

I clicked the screen closed on my phone and leaned over to my left, searching for the charging cord. Once plugged in to charge, I opened a new window on my laptop and looked up a 24-hour news station streaming online from America. I sat back on the couch. The chill night air fluttered across my face, drifting in from the door I'd left propped open. As I went to close it, a jackal's high-pitched, mournful cry echoed from somewhere in the dark.

They were close tonight, which sometimes meant a storm was blowing in. I shut the door and locked the deadbolt.

The news anchor announced they had new images from the ongoing insurgency along the Syrian and Iraqi border. I flopped back on the couch and tugged the blanket from the back so I could tuck my bare feet under me. The smiling anchorwoman — her skin an adjacent shade of orange from her noticeable spray tan — described the latest attacks and bombings. As she spoke, my ears picked up the names of familiar cities and locations. Then, the anchorwoman disappeared, replaced with photographs and live video of missiles being launched and buildings on fire. I bit my lip, waiting.

Two years this October, I'd been doing this, and yet my heart raced every time I saw the photographs, *my* photographs on the monitor. A series of photos, displayed in rapid succession on the screen.

First was a family, their eyes downcast as they embraced each other. U.N. soldiers stood around them, rifles in hand. Another showed a skinny dog being fed a scrap of food from a kneeling Syrian soldier. The last one was of a mother clutching a tiny infant. The right side of her face and exposed dark hair were matted with blood and dirt. She carried an infant in her arms, swaddled in a bloodstained blanket.

My chest tightened.

I'd forgotten about that one.

I closed my eyes, forcing myself to remember my purpose. I *needed* to capture these pictures. These moments in time had to be shared. And if they brought my emotional pain, perhaps others would feel it too.

The screen flashed back briefly to the anchorwoman. Her sad face shifted lightning-quick to a toothy grin as the redhead cheerily announced a reality dance competition that would be airing that night.

"*What lucky couple will go home a winner? Tune in to—*" I closed the browser tab.

Images of wind-blown dunes flowed across my screen as the memory card continued uploading. Mood dampened, I leaned back again and tried to quell the frustration.

I gritted my teeth and picked up my camera. I imagined holding it over my shoulder, contemplating how hard I'd have to throw it to make it smash into pieces on the opposite wall.

What the hell am I doing?

Hands shaking, I let out an exasperated sigh and placed the camera beside me. I rubbed the tension on my forehead and retrieved a bottle of Arak from the cabinet. I poured a glass. The alcohol soothed the rage induced by the broadcast and warmed my cheeks.

My laptop beeped, signaling the download had finished. I set the empty glass on the side table and clicked open the folder. I cycled through the hundreds of pictures I'd taken over the past week. Most were from inside the city, and they showed business owners re-opening their shops, kids grinning with handfuls of dried fruit, and a few soldiers laughing while conversing with people in the streets.

Soon I found the ones from earlier that day. I zoomed in,

examining them. I'd got a clear shot of the two men in the garage.

Typically, terrorists don't wear name tags. Instead, they appear like the average citizen, dressing, behaving, and looking like everyone else. To an extent, they are until they decide—or are brainwashed or coerced —into strapping on an explosive vest and entering a coffee shop.

I'd need to spend several hours tomorrow editing the photos, but seeing them again piqued my curiosity. I clicked ahead to the final picture. On the truck's tailgate, the three men leaned over the crate with its lid cracked open. I highlighted the crate, enlarging the image. On the side of the box, I saw the same Russian writing and then stamped in smaller bold red, read:

PROPERTY OF THE U.S. GOVERNMENT.

A shiver ran down my spine. Since it was smaller and positioned to the side, I'd missed seeing it when I'd been there.

Instinctively, I leaned closer to the screen and used my laptop's keypad to bring the details of the men's faces into focus. I expected to see the men's faces illuminated. But instead, they remained as they were, cast in shadow from the dull light above. No light glowed from the crate.

How odd. Doubt clawed at the back of my mind. I'd been so sure I'd seen the light from the inside. My hand went to the top of my bag and took out the statue. Cradling it in both hands, I examined it in the lamplight and glow from my laptop screen.

In the center of the eight-pointed star embraced in the woman's arms was an amber-colored stone about the size of a quarter. An overpowering urge to touch it consumed me. My thumb reached up, caressing the surface. Smooth and warm. A tingle rippled up my arm as if I'd experienced a static shock, and reflexively my hands tightened on it, the muscles in my arms contracting.

The statue's surface began to emit a pulsing yellow glow as if it were translucent.

I held it up to my face, my eyes seeking the source of the luminescence. I leaned closer, looking deeper into it, and felt the room spiral around me. My eyes focused on the details, sifting through the complex crystallized shapes housed inside. Too uniform to be organic, yet the intricacies had to be manufactured.

The lamp beside me flickered out. My laptop's screen went black, plunging the room into abrupt darkness. My pulse thrummed in my ears. The golden statue's luminescence intensified, and a low drone filled my ears, vibrating my chest—a single bright sun in an abyss of black.

The brilliant light pulsed heat waves, warming my face as if too close to a campfire. Carefully, I rose to my feet. The statue had grown too bright to look at it, and I averted my eyes. Something burned my hands, and I yelped.

Startled by the pain, I released the statue, which fell with a thud to the rug at my feet. At once, the light from it dimmed. My chest heaved; my eyes fixed on the metal idol lying on the ground. I knelt to pick it back up, but before I could, it erupted in a dazzling display of blinding white-hot light. I squeezed my eyes shut and felt my head sway. I fought against my drooping eyelids and staggered a step forward as the floor rose to meet me.

FOUR

A musty, damp odor tickled my nose.

Drip, drip, drip. Water trickled from somewhere unseen.

I wasn't in my apartment anymore. Next to me, fissured rock walls ascended into a domed ceiling high above where I stood. I looked down at the black glittering sand at my feet. Thin ivory fabric fluttered around my bare legs and feet.

My head swiveled, taking in the strange place. *Where am I?*

Off to my left, an arched entrance, twice as wide as my front door, let in a cool breeze. It brushed across my face as I gazed through it into a boundless night full of stars. I could see the silhouetted outline of jagged mountains and cliffs hundreds of feet below.

I estimated the cave to be twenty feet across and the ceiling secured by carved stone pillars. Wooden torches flickered on the walls, reminding me of a virtual reality dungeon game my sister had talked me into playing last Christmas. All of this could've been taken straight from some sort of dungeon crawler or historical survival game. The torches flickering light could not reach the cave's depths, so the corners remained hidden in shadow. In the center sat an enormous round stone, dark brown and bigger than Taamir's car.

A noise caught my attention. A group of people in hooded robes of deep midnight blue gathered around the circular stone table. Their faces were mostly obscured, but I could tell they were all women of varying ages.

My head spun like I was drunk, and I rested a hand on the carved stone wall beside me to steady myself.

The stone felt like mud as I pressed my fingers into it. I recoiled, staring at the light gray substance that now coated the tips of my fingers. I rubbed them together, feeling the grit of the material. On the side of the wall was a perfectly shaped mark of a hand, reminding me of the handprints my uncle had Cara and I do when he'd poured a new driveway.

Slowly, I placed my hand back on the wall, and as if reacting to my touch, the stone liquified — and like water washing away a sandcastle on a beach, it flowed into the indentation, filling it in, leaving the wall smooth and unblemished.

What the hell was going on? Tempted to try it again, I reached out but was interrupted as the group began to chant. Although I was fluent in five languages, this low-cadenced rhyme was one I couldn't piece any phrases from.

I inched closer to the group, but my right toe kicked a rock loose, and it shot forward with a loud, obnoxious clattering over the ground. The air froze in my lungs as I stared at the people, not daring to move. Waiting on bated breath, that group would turn on me, pissed off that I'd disrupted whatever they were doing. The irony was not lost on me that I'd spent most of my adult life in some of the most violent, war-torn countries, and *this* was how I was destined to die. The middle of fucking nowhere, inside a foul-smelling cave and wearing a flimsy dress.

But nothing happened. The people continued chanting,

seemingly oblivious to the sound and my presence. I took another tentative step forward, still unconvinced they wouldn't realize I was there, and squeezed myself against the wall, hiding behind the pillars. Closer now, I saw that the enormous rock table was an altar, and I'd been right to guess they were performing some ritual.

On the altar's surface was an engraving of an eight-pointed star like the one I'd seen on the golden statue. Their voices grew louder, their chanting intensifying.

In choreographed unison, the people revealed a hand from under their robes. In the palms of their hand, they each held a small stone. Together, they positioned their stone at the points of the star. The glass-like stones portrayed a rainbow of colors, from the deepest violets to the most crimson reds. The instant the last stone was in place, the chanting ceased. Spiraling black sand twisted up from the floor like smoky tornadoes, and the torches sputtered out. The cave descended into darkness.

Unable to not see a hand in front of my face, I counted my breaths.

One. Two. Three.

Maybe this was it.

Four. Five. Six.

Maybe now would be a good time to wake up from this dream.

Seven. Eight. Nine.

A blaze of color illuminated the room. I shielded my eyes, momentarily blinded, but lowered my hands once I was sure my retinas weren't permanently damaged. One by one, the stones glowed in sequence and outlined a point on the engraved star. A bright beam entered from the doorway, projecting like a spotlight toward the stone altar.

I squinted as my eyes followed the shaft of light. It continued, far off, and out into the night sky. A woman walked along the shimmering beam. A shapely figure of soft curves and angles, a veil-like, nearly see-through dress draped her body. Her skin glistened and glittered as if she'd applied an opalescent shimmer spray over her entire body. Holding her held high, she acted as if descending from the stars on a pathway made of iridescent light was no different feat than strolling the bike trail at Central Park. The woman's presence stole the breath from my lungs.

She stared intently, as if focused on something in the distance. Her radiance showered the cave in light. A humming reverberated in my ears, causing my teeth to chatter. The same strange smell from the parking garage filled my nostrils.

Then, the woman tilted her head and looked directly at me.

Shit.

FIVE

The woman's gaze locked with mine, and I twisted my fingers together to avoid fidgeting. Her eyes were large and striking on her delicately featured face. The color of her pupils shifted from the palest of turquoise to a deep, nearly black midnight blue, reminding me of the auroras I'd seen once on a trip to Alaska.

Raven-black hair cascaded thick waves down her back, and atop her head, she wore a golden crown studded with different colors of sparkling gemstones and eight points fanning out from the band.

The woman's intelligent eyes fixed upon mine like she was waiting for me to say something.

I cleared my throat. "Uh, hi there. I'm Eleanora. Ella for short."

The woman gave me a knowing smile, and while her mouth didn't move, I heard her. "*I know.*"

"Who are you?" I said aloud.

"*I am Enheduanna. High Priestess of the Temple of Ur, Daughter of King Sargon of Akkad.*"

Awesome. That really cleared things up.

"Okay, Enheduanna," I said, proud I didn't stumble over the mouthful of a name. "Do you think maybe you could tell me where I am? Or what I'm doing here?"

"*You're where I need you to be,*" Enheduanna said. "*In five days, the Bridge of Vela will appear. You, Eleanora, are its only guardian. You must guard the bridge to save the world.*" She smiled, and it was a dizzying display of breathtaking beauty; it took every ounce of willpower for me not to close the space between us and kiss this creature on her seductively perfect mouth.

I'd always preferred men, but damn if this woman wasn't doing things to me, making me reconsider my choices.

"*You possess the gift of Inanna now,*" Enheduanna continued. "*The fate of Ur is in your hands.*"

The robed people continued to hunch over the altar, with their foreheads pressed into the stone. Then, going unnoticed, Enheduanna moved between them and raised an exquisitely long-fingered hand to her breast. She withdrew a shimmering golden ball of dazzling light as if a miniature sun were buried where her heart would be.

The woman held the swirling sphere of light and set it on the altar, precisely at the center of the stone engraving. The instant the star touched the stone, a sharp, mind-shattering pain pierced my skull. I squeezed my eyes shut, slamming my hands against my temples in a desperate attempt to stop the pain. The cave floor vibrated, and the sounds of cascading rocks and crashing stones came from all around me.

Just when I thought the agony would draw me entirely under, drown me, it stopped.

Silence saturated my ears, yet the echoes of the painful throbbing lingered. Not trusting the pounding in my skull not to return, I stayed crouched and sucked in slow breaths in my nose. When another moment had passed, and nothing happened, I compelled one eye to open. I blinked, bringing my vision back into focus.

I was back in my living room.

My pulse steadied at the sight of my familiar things. I stood slowly and searched for any indication of what had happened. Morning light filtered in through the one tiny window in the back, magnifying the spinning particles of dust. A light breeze disrupted them, causing the particles to dance and twirl. My head snapped to the front door, and I saw it was wide open, its deadbolt lock dangling limply from the splintered wood.

I let out an exasperated sigh and strode over to the doorway. What the hell had happened last night? All the memories were so foggy and nebulous. When I tried to grasp onto one, hold it tight enough to examine it, it disappeared like a snowflake evaporating when it landed on exposed skin. So, the memories left to me were a feverish amalgamation of stars, naked women, and people in robes. A frat boy's wet dream, if I'd heard of one.

I scanned the outside, half-hoping a person in a bear costume would be waiting with a bunch of balloons that would prove I'd wholly and undoubtedly lost my mind. Unfortunately, there was only the back wall of Taamir's house and the trilling call of a Serin finch in the juniper bushes. I released a groan while shutting the door.

I filled a glass from the sink, gulped down the water, refilled it, and returned to the living room carrying it. I sank onto the threadbare sofa and glared at the laptop before me, willing it to spark some revelation about what had occurred.

One by one, I mentally cataloged all that I could remember clearly.

First had been dinner with Taamir, then I'd come back here, downloaded my photos, and thought about Jason, which, as it often did, led to the bottle of Arak being drunk and then...nothing.

Maybe the isolation was getting to me more than I realized, as my mother had warned. Perhaps I should head home for the wedding and take a mental health break.

I massaged the sides of my head and hissed, and a jolt of pain bloomed on my left hand. My scalp tingled as I narrowed my eyes to examine the eight-pointed star — the seared outline a bright, angry red—burned in the palm of my hand.

I stroked the edges. It was sore to the touch but bearable as if the wound had occurred weeks ago, not hours.

I leaned back, studying the mark on my hand, and my pinky toe snagged on something hard. I peered down from where I sat reclined on the couch. The bronze figure was next to my foot, on the corner of the rug. My mouth twitched in annoyance. *That* was it. It had to be.

Whatever had happened to me last night had to be connected to the statue. So, wanting to avoid a repeat of my acid-trip dream, I spied a discarded sock under the end table and carefully draped it over the figure as one would an oven mitt.

With the sock a barrier between me and the statue, I gazed down at it, curious to see if some residue or toxin was coating it. I'd heard of drugs so potent that their absorption into your bloodstream would send you on a wild trip or to the morgue, depending on how much exposure you had.

The figure appeared dull, tarnished in the dim morning light. The amber-colored gem in the center was a muted yellow. No glow. Nothing.

I flipped it over and wrapped it entirely.

Holding the sock-wrapped figure, I went to the kitchen and stashed it in the tiny frosted-over freezer compartment. My body tensed at the thought of what I'd do next. An idea I'd struggled to ignore, but the event, vision, dream, whatever the fuck it was, had frayed my nerves, weakening my resolve.

I stood, holding the phone in one hand. I pressed my tongue on the roof of my mouth.

The pictures.

The statue.

The spontaneous appearance of a star-shaped scar on my right hand. Yeah, that was just fucking peachy. Guess I better invest in a new glove collection unless I wanted funny looks and uninvited questions.

This crap show had grown beyond what I felt comfortable telling my contacts.

There was only one person I could trust with all this.

The man I'd fallen head over heels for, who'd captured my heart, captivated my mind and made me smile until my cheeks hurt.

But life, as it so unapologetically did, had ruined it.

I frowned and scrolled down the list of contacts, hoping he hadn't changed his number and that he had his phone on him.

"Good morning, Elly," he said, calling me by his favorite nickname. "What do I owe the pleasure of this call?"

My hand tightened on the phone. "Hey, Jason. I need your help."

CHAPTER

SIX

"Elly, I..." Jason stammered, his tone edged with worry. "Is everything alright?"

"Um, no. Not really," I said. "I have something I think you need to see. But it needs to be in person." God, this was even harder than I'd imagined. I sat down and closed my eyes, gripping the phone tighter.

You can do this. I told myself and took a deep breath. I needed to do this. The new, weird mark on my hand would have to wait. For one thing, even if I told Jason about it, it's not like he knew anything more than I did. While Division 12 agents were stealthy, disciplined, and discreet, I was pretty sure spontaneous changes to one's anatomy was definitely not on the list of rookie agent training course. So, until then, I'd have to live with what I did know. One minute it hadn't been there, then I'd touched the statue, had a vision, and bam: star-scar.

The more urgent reality, was that I *did* know those men had other crates. Crates that very likely were full of stolen explosives. Jason was a secret agent for Division 12. As a privately funded security firm, Division 12 worked alongside all military branches. Often behind the scenes, lurking in the shadows, they pulled strings or moving pieces the governments of the world felt was "too hot to handle."

They would be the surest way I'd know the right people with the right resources could track down these guys.

"Okay," he said. "I'll come to you. Where are you?"

I gripped the phone tighter. "I'm in Deir ez-Zur." Deir ez-Zur was a hotbed of social unrest and violence. The exact place a combat photojournalist should be.

"Oh, Elly," he said, his voice heavy with disapproval.

"Please, Jason, don't start."

"You and your damn death wish, I swear."

"Can you help me or not?" I snapped, wondering if this had been a mistake.

He sighed. "Yeah, we've got an off-the-books safe house an hour out of town. Our base of operations is in Baghdad, but I will if someone will loan me a truck. How can I find you?"

"I'll text you my address," I said.

"Alright," he said. "Hang tight, Elly. I'll be there soon."

The phone clicked, and he was gone. I dropped the phone on the couch beside me and rubbed the back of my eyelids with my hands.

You did the right thing a voice chimed in my head.

I forced down the lump that had lodged in my throat.

As I knew they would, memories of our time together last Summer flashed before me. The feel of his callused hand in mine as we'd strolled Central Park, sipping wine on a hotel balcony, screaming our lungs out at a dodger's game smelling of beer and popcorn. It'd all seemed...*perfect.* Too perfect to last. Our last few weeks together, I'd found it hard to believe I could be that happy.

I glanced at the sparse and worn furnishings of my apartment. The brutal shock of reality rushed over me with icy claws.

Even with time, the wound's edges remained tender, as if I pressed them too much, I knew they'd bleed fresh crimson.

I sniffed, forbidding myself from crying. This was work. Business.

Get your head together.

I sat at the table, opening my laptop. Taamir had the next two days off. He'd promised his wife and daughters they'd travel up North to visit his parent's house.

When I wasn't scouting the city streets, I'd spend my free time editing photos or reaching out to my other journalist contacts for updates or information.

In this region of the world, a satellite Wi-Fi connection was my lifeline. A computer whiz friend back home had installed the latest virus, encryption, and security software. All my emails were encrypted to protect against the risk of photos, videos, or any correspondences relating to my precious contacts in the region leaking out or tracing back to me.

That didn't mean I didn't occasionally enjoy the fruits of my labors. For example, just last month, when I'd seen a larger than usual payment from CNN dropped in my account, I'd paid for a ride to the larger cities of Damascus or Aleppo. I'd holed up in a nice hotel room for a night, splurged on a bottle of champagne and room service, and made video chat calls with my friends and family back home. However, with the recent liberation of Deir ez-Zur, it'd been over a month since I'd done so.

Glancing at the fridge with the statue tucked inside, a bitter ache pinched my ribcage. It'd be even longer now before I'd get another break.

I shoved away the sting of resentment and stood. I walked the small distance to the bathroom and flipped the lever on the pitiful excuse for a shower. There was no hot water tank, and the shower consisted of a plastic sheet hung from the ceiling around a small open drain on the floor. The cold water streamed down from the holding tank above me. Most days, a cold shower was welcome after being in the scorching desert heat. Today, however, I shivered under the torrents of icy water. My body felt sore, achy, like I'd run a marathon the day before and forgot to stretch. Sleeping on the floor would do that to a person, though, I supposed.

I made a mental note that I'd be lying on my comfortable bed the next time I touched the statue.

If I touched it again. The jury was still out.

Afterward, I dressed in denim jeans and a red t-shirt with the Columbia University lion. Go Roar-ee.

I slipped on my leather hiking boots and ran a brush through my damp hair. When Cara had been in Kindergarten, she'd wandered into my room, saw me brushing my hair, and giggled as she told me my hair was the color of chocolate.

When we were kids, Cara had been fascinated that her own hair was blonde while mine was brown. I didn't have the heart to tell her that it was because we had different dads, and instead lied and said hers might change color someday too.

After my rough breakup with Jason, I chopped my hair off to rest above my shoulders.

Fresh starts and all that.

Since I'd been in Syria, it'd grown enough to braid again. I re-entered the living room and stood before the glass mirror on the wall behind the couch. Taamir's wife had found it at a street fair and insisted Taamir give it to me.

"A lady must always make herself presentable should she seek a husband," Larissa had told me. I recalled how Taamir had blushed as his wife held out the paper-wrapped gift. Crafted from pieces of an antique picture frame, bits of chipped paint and globs of glue spotted the edges where the frame had been attached to the mirror.

Oh, my mother would be happy if I found a husband like

Cara. But if anything good had come out of my summer with Jason, it was the realization that I wasn't ready to trade in my passport for a sedentary life in the suburbs. Sure, it was lonely at times, but the drive inside me still pressed me to seek out the most violent places on earth and document them.

I was damn good at what I did. And my pictures *had* made a difference. Drawn attention to foreign aid groups and high-lighted unknown regions so politicians had been cornered into acting. I'd tasted the power my camera's lens held and was addicted.

Gazing into the mirror, I noted the bronzed tan of my skin and the scattering of freckles on my nose. From a small makeup bag, I dabbed on concealer, blush, and mascara.

Feeling refreshed and pretty, a smile curved up at the corners of my mouth.

A diesel engine rumbled outside, and a car door slammed. I swiped on a dab of lip gloss. I'd choked down scrambled eggs and toast before he'd arrived, hoping it would be enough to settle the unease souring my stomach from seeing Jason again. My breathing quickened as his intensely blue eyes met me from the doorway.

Suddenly, I felt naked, exposed, as if all my thoughts and emotions were laid before him, and I was glad I'd put on makeup. Armor.

"Ever hear of knocking?" I said, resting a hand on my hip.

Jason shrugged. "You should lock your door."

"It broke, and I haven't had a chance to fix it."

With his broad shoulders and six-foot-three frame in my apartment, my cozy space seemed even more cramped. He wore black jeans and a T-shirt with an unbuttoned plaid flannel over it. He shook his head. "That's not smart. You know, even out here—"

"I know," I snapped, interrupting him. God dammit. We were arguing less than a minute back in each other's company.

Jason idly scratched the side of his arm. A dark blue dragon encircled his bicep, and two black, intricate daggers peeked out from under his left shoulder and up the sides of his neck muscles. The dragon he'd had before, but those were new.

He sighed, his eyes softening as he tried to defuse the tense conversation. "You look good, Elly. How have you been?"

I plastered a tight-lipped smile on my face. "Fine. I've been fine."

Feeling his eyes on my face, I stuffed my camera, phone, and charger into a shoulder bag. Then, when there was nothing else to distract me, my gaze returned to his.

Reflected in the blue eyes I'd spent hours staring into, I glimpsed a thousand emotions: Hurt. Regret. Resentment.

I huffed out a breath. "Thank you, really. You look good, too." That was the problem, though. Jason *always* looked good. Naturally athletic, he had muscle in all the right places. His golden-blonde hair and sky-blue eyes could have made him plucked straight out of a surfing magazine. His self-assured and confident air, gleaned from his four years in marine spec ops, drew the attention of everyone in the room, women and men alike.

"Someone let you borrow their truck?"

Jason chuckled and held up a pair of keys with a pink Eiffel Tower key chain. "Not exactly. But Jameson is on leave until next week, so he won't miss it."

I scoffed.

"I assume I only need it for a day or two?"

I nodded though I wasn't entirely sure.

He handed me the paper bag, smelling of honey and cinnamon. "Donuts fresh from Damascus."

"Damascus is six hours away."

Jason shrugged. "Fresh-*ish*, then."

I sighed, selected one of the round sugary dough rings, and handed it back. They weren't warm, but still, they were delicious.

While we ate, his eyes swept my apartment's interior. "I like it, very minimalist. Decided you were done with the bohemian vibe?"

"It was *one* wicker armchair," I said defensively. "And it *was* comfortable."

A mischievous grin appeared on his face, recalling a particular memory I was sharing. One involving that specific chair and not a lot of clothing.

"Anyway," I said, trying to redirect the conversation from past us, to the very much *not*-together present us. "I like this place. It's secluded out here and cheap."

I put on my darkest-tinted sunglasses, hoping to signal an end to the awkward small talk before it drifted into —'You seeing anyone?' or 'How is your family?' — land.

I slung on my shoulder bag, weighed down with several changes of clothes, essential toiletries, my camera, and laptop, and glanced around to decide if there was anything else I bring with me.

The fridge caught my attention. The idol would be safe until I got back, and until I knew who wanted the statue and why, I thought it best to keep it hidden, even from Jason.

I chewed the inside of my cheek. "Alright, let's go." Jason opened the door, and we stepped out into the blinding sunlight.

SEVEN

I stared out the window as we drove along the busy stretch of highway heading East from Deir ez-Zur. I picked at a frayed thread on the thigh of my jeans. Across the endless desert, hazy heat waves blurred the dark and jagged mountains miles off in the distance.

"So," Jason said. "You ready to tell me what's going on?"

I pressed my lips together, unsure of how much to tell him or how to begin.

"I think I saw a handoff yesterday."

"A handoff of what?"

I sat up straight and cleared my throat. "I'm not sure. There was this group of guys I followed—"

"Followed?" Jason interrupted. "What do you mean *followed?*"

"There was some shady shit going on. One of my contacts was acting dodgier than usual. I saw him get paid to transport something."

Jason's hands tightened on the steering wheel, but didn't say anything.

"Look, before you get your panties in a twist, I was careful."

I tossed my hands up, emphasizing the point. "Taamir stayed back a safe distance. We drove behind them, and then he dropped me off."

Sand and scrubby bushes swept by us as we drove. Jason detoured around the city, avoiding the heavier trafficked areas, and continued South past Deir ez-Zur's defunct airport toward Al Mayadin.

"And then what happened?" Jason pressed. "Or do I even want to know?"

"And then I trailed behind where they went into an underground garage. That's where I saw another guy get out of a nice car. He paid Jamil and the truck driver an envelope of cash." I paused, hesitating to tell him about the bronze statue, but decided against it. So, instead, I closed my right hand, feeling the familiar ridges of the mark.

One problem at a time.

"There was a stack of crates. They had Russian writing on them and spoke English, but I couldn't catch much of the conversations."

The muscle in Jason's jaw twitched. He sported a five-o'clock shadow, and I wondered if they'd just pulled him from undercover.

"This hardly seems enough to warrant Division 12's investigation, but I'm assuming you have proof? Pictures of this alleged deal happening?"

I nodded, patting the bag with my camera.

"Very well," he said. "We'll get to the safe house and can look them over now. See if what you have is worth looking into."

The truck followed the base of a hill, and the glistening surface of the Euphrates River reflected the mid-morning sun. Its banks were thick with olive trees and palms. A sacred space of green among the rocks and sand. I rolled down my window, letting the loose strands of my hair whip me in the face, and closed my eyes. The smell of the river summoned the fragmented images from my dream.

"You remember Agent Jackson?" he asked, breaking the silence.

I opened my eyes from the edges of sleep. "Hmm, yeah."

He adjusted his hands on the steering wheel and looked sideways toward me. Our eyes met, and a flicker of heat grew low in my abdomen.

He tore his gaze from me and focused on the road. My heart resumed its normal rhythm, blindsided by how much he still affected me.

I could handle this. He *needed* to see the pictures. There was a chance someone at Division 12 would recognize the men. Perhaps, if I were careful enough, I'd also uncover more about the bronze statue.

Like why it gave me crazy hallucinations of half-naked women in caves.

I wrinkled my nose, remembering the smell of the musty earth and the eerie chanting of the women gathered around the altar. I opened my phone, running an internet search for "Enheduanna." It took several attempts to guess the spelling of the name. I skimmed through websites saying she was a Sumerian princess who was believed to be the first named poet. She'd told me the truth. She was the daughter of King Sargon, who lived—my heart skipped a beat, double checking I was reading the print on my screen right — over four thousand years ago.

"You remember then he was the lead commander for this region," Jason continued. "He offered me a position at Division while still in spec ops. He's the one who encouraged me to pursue private security work and had my back when all that Project Scorpion shit went down."

I kept my eyes outside, pretending only half to listen as we flew past the cargo trucks and buses. I knew Agent Gary Jackson very well, having met him while with Jason. A father figure to Jason, he'd hand-selected him from the army when he'd just turned twenty. Already a skilled fighter, Jackson refined his combat abilities.

He'd crafted him into a not only formidable soldier but one who could also plan and initiate systematic attacks. When Jason had found himself in front of a court-martial two years ago, Jackson stepped forward, placing his personal reputation and esteemed career on the line. Attired in a nicely pressed suit, he'd accompanied us to dinner with his girlfriend. In his mid-sixties, he was balding, and his trimmed beard and mustache were peppered with gray. He and Jason had laughed, exchanging stories that had occurred the previous year in Iraq. Catching glimpses of Jason's sparkling eyes and seeing him for once truly at ease still burned in my memory.

"He, uh," Jason forced a nervous half-laugh. His tone changed, darkening when he spoke again. I'd heard Jason begin similar stories this way. Often ending with Division 12 notifying a next of kin. My gut twisted.

"Well, he, uh, he retired last month," he continued. "Bought a condo in Palm Beach and found himself a new wife. She's Cuban, I think?"

I let out a relieved sigh.

"Retirement. Well, that's good to hear. I'm glad he's doing well," I said.

"Yeah," Jason chuckled. The truck slowed as he turned down a side road toward the river. The desert landscape had given way to more buildings. As we bumped along, I spotted a group of young boys running behind them. We turned again, and Jason parked the truck in front of a grocery store.

"Here we are," he said and, catching my confused face,

added, "The safe house is the hotel upstairs." Jason reached behind him, grabbed his black duffel bag, and stepped out of the truck. I followed, slamming the heavy door. I gazed up. Above the store was a series of balconies, and I counted it three stories high. A few older men sat in chairs out front, and the smoke from their cigarettes hung in the air by the front door.

Inside the store, I was both surprised and pleased to see the boxes and cans of food on the shelves of the store. A woman with an armful of shopping bags passed by me, smiling warmly. Her two young boys — munching on bags of dried fruit— bounced playfully behind me as we exited the store.

Everywhere I looked, it felt like the city was healing.

As we approached the rear of the store, two men in bullet-proof vests carrying assault rifles stood in front of a wooden door.

They saw Jason, and the one on the left said. "Agent Price, this is a surprise."

"I need to use room eight for a bit," Jason said. He used his flat, the one that commanded respect and no questions.

"Sure, of course, but who's—?" the man said, eyeing me.

"A friend," Jason supplied.

Satisfied, the man said nothing more and stepped aside. A keypad had been set up near the door, hidden behind a wooden placard indicating it was 'Employees Only.' Jason placed his thumb on the pad, and a second later, it beeped.

I stood a few feet behind him, and the suspicious gaze of the two men lingered on me. Heat rose to my cheeks as I could only guess their thoughts. Maybe I wasn't the first woman Jason had brought here? It wasn't any of my business what Jason did in his spare time like it wasn't any of his what I didn't with mine. But what if the assignment required him to get *cozy* with an informant? Division 12 was founded on efficiency and results. Success equaled everything to them.

The door opened, and I straightened my back, taking self-assured steps as I passed the agents. Jason led, and I followed as we trudged up a stairwell.

"Friend, huh?" I asked, stopping to catch my breath on the third-floor landing.

Jason arched a brow. "Yeah, why not. Worked, didn't it?"

"Is it a common thing, then," I said, gesturing to him. "For Division agents to bring 'friends' to safe houses?"

Jason scoffed, starting up the next flight of stairs. "C'mon, you know I'm not at liberty to say. It'd violate my confidentiality agreement."

I rolled my eyes and continued climbing past him, and I didn't miss the impish grin lingering on his lips. Okay, fine, so maybe I was a little curious *and* a little jealous. I hadn't dated anyone since we'd broken up, but I'd made my peace with that. A full bed to spread out in, no sharing a bathroom, and watching all my favorite shows without having to sit through tediously dry nature documentaries. Single life had grown on me.

On the fifth floor, Jason led me eight doors down a hallway. The number eight had been painted on the chipped laminate of the wooden door.

Jason slipped a key in the lock and opened it.

The room smelled of mildew and stale air. Heavy curtains blocked the sunlight from outside, and Jason flipped the lamp inside the door. A sickly muted orange hue illuminated the double bed to the left, a small writing desk, and a plastic chair.

I resisted the urge to run toward the bed, springing onto the mattress and wrapping myself like a burrito in the sheets.

Jason sat down a black duffel bag on the desk and opened it. The sound of a zipper being pulled reverberated comically around the room.

Jason chuckled and puffed his chest. "Thirty seconds from

door to touchdown. Remind me to ask the front desk if the hotel has a trophy for breaking a record."

"Don't flatter yourself," I said, crossing my arms even as a smile tugged at the corners of my mouth.

Jason shook his head, still laughing at his dirty joke, and retrieved a military-grade laptop from his bag. After setting it on the desk, he pulled his pistol from the holster at his hip and sat it next to the computer.

A custom-made 9mm TTI Sand Viper. His favorite.

An army buddy had told Jason about this start-up gun manufacturer with a reputation for making pistols that were as durable as they were accurate, and so we'd taken a little detour through Oregon wine country when we'd headed to the west coast for the fourth of July to meet my parents.

I'd scoffed at the price tag, but he'd teased me, asking if I could put a price on his life since it's what he'd take with him on missions.

After he'd made his purchase, we'd found a bed-and-breakfast for the night. We'd been booked for the honeymoon suite, so we had taken full advantage of the in-room jacuzzi tub and California King.

Desire sent heat to my core, remembering the very vivid details of that night.

Jason pivoted in the chair and waved his arms as if presenting me with a new car. "Well," he asked. "Make yourself at home."

"Charming," I said, laughing. But I couldn't deny the full-sized bed, access to hot water, and flush toilet were alluring.

"Alright," he said, powering up the laptop. He straddled the chair in front of the desk. "Let's see what you've got."

I took the memory card from the side pocket of my bag and held it out to him. Our fingers lightly brushed as he took it, causing me to become keenly aware of all the things that had occurred the last time the two of us were alone in a hotel room. I withdrew my hand, wiping the sweat from my palms on my jeans.

"I'm technically not supposed to be here," he said. "So, everything that happens after I look at this just between us, okay?"

I nod, my teeth raking my bottom lip, and his dipped to my mouth. Shadows streaming from the gaps in the curtains obscure the side of his face, highlighting his well-defined jaw and vivid blue eyes.

Ten months. Nearly a year had passed for me to recover and mend the shattered pieces of my heart into something that didn't make me want to stay in bed all day and cut myself off from the world. And, yet, the hurt lingered. Surprising me with how readily it seeped back into me, squeezing my chest, threatening to pull me back under.

Jason clicked the memory card into the computer, and I positioned myself behind him, looking over his shoulder.

I swallowed the surge of emotions, glad to have something else to focus on than our failed past.

Jason opened the drive through some strange encryption software before hundreds of photos appeared on the screen.

"There, that one," I said, pointing at a thumbnail image.

Jason clicked it open. He zoomed in on the crate first, and I caught sight of his face. His jaw shifted, and he furrowed his brow to look closer. He zoomed out again and moved in, this time on the side of the man in the black suit's face.

"This guy, do you have any better angles of his face?" he said.

I nodded and pointed to another small image on the screen two lines down.

"There, try that one."

Jason clicked the next one, and it did indeed show the side

profile of the man. Although the resolution was good, it still only showed half of his face. Jason nodded and opened his email, attaching it to an outgoing message. As he moved to enter the email address, his fingers hesitated above the keyboard. He tilted his head to the side, giving me a side-eyed look.

Classified, got it. I stood and turned my back to him, considering moving to the window before thinking better of it. Many agents at Division 12 knew of our history, and if he wasn't supposed to be here, the fewer people that saw me in one of the agency's safe houses, the better.

Behind me, Jason tapped away at the keys. My hands fidgeted with the strap of my shoulder bag.

Sharing this room with him had left me feeling restless, *trapped.* I just needed to keep my cool until he'd downloaded the pictures, then I could convince him to take me to another hotel, just until no one was onto me.

The truth was, when I was around Jason, everything became muffled — like a fog formed in my mind, blurring the good decisions from the bad. My wants and needs becoming one and the same, which I'd so painfully learned, was a bad idea.

Jason's voice cut through my tumultuous thoughts.

"Elly, I..." his voice faltered.

I turned to face him. "Did they identify that guy?"

Raw emotions swirled in his eyes, and I prayed my knees would support me.

"Not yet," he said, standing. "Listen. I'm actually glad you called. I've been so busy but wanted a way to make things right with what happened last Summer..." he paused. "Look, I'm sorry for the way things went. I wish I—"

"Stop!" I snapped, shaking my head. "Please, Jason, I can't." A vice clamped around my throat, and I choked on the words.

Hurt darkened his eyes.

"Not right now," I said, my words softer. "This isn't a good time, okay?"

The dagger-like edge of repressed pain twisted deeper. Frustration and the reopened wound caused tears to sting the backs of my eyes.

"Please, Jason," I whispered, holding his eyes.

"Alright, Elly," he said. "I understand."

Jason returned to sit at the desk as I slumped on the side of the bed.

The minutes dragged. Jason switched on the TV, and immediately, raucous cheers from a stadium full of people filled the room. Jason swiveled in the chair to face the TV, his attention on the soccer game.

I pulled out my phone. Two emails had come through, including a registry for Cara's wedding. I scrolled through bed sheets, dish sets, and wine glasses.

An hour had passed when Jason's phone on the desk finally vibrated. He picked it up and read a message. When he looked up from the screen, his expression was grim. "That's from my guy at Central. He got a hit from those photos. They can't tell me anything, though. I'll have to run across the street to reply. They've set up a secure line there."

He was at the door a second later, not waiting for me to respond. He stopped, his hand pausing on the knob.

"Stay here," he said. "I'll be right back." Worry flickered across his face, and for a second, I thought he would say something else, but the moment passed. He stepped into the hallway, shutting the door behind him.

I walked to the window. From below, Jason exited the store and jogged across the busy street. He moved effortlessly, weaving through the traffic. Broad-shouldered, his arms were composed of taut muscle. He'd been a natural athlete. He excelled at sports in high school and even had a college try to pick him up for their sports program. The fourth in a generation of a military family, he'd regretfully declined their offers; his path had already been chosen.

After Jason had disappeared around the side of the neighboring building, I'd moved to the edge of the bed and sat. Alone in the dreary hotel room, the silence dragged, broken by angry horns of cars outside or an occasional barking dog. My mind and body yearned to move. 'Restless,' my mother had called me. But in truth, most of my childhood I'd spent confined to a single-wide trailer.

The experience had left me weary of languishing in cramped spaces. However, I could manage the sedentary hours spent editing my photos provided it was interlaced with hot yoga or kickboxing sessions.

In New York, I'd lace up tennis shoes and go for a brisk run nearly every day. But here, that wasn't a possibility. Besides the scorching desert heat, it was uncustomary for a woman to be caught alone without a male escort. Hence, my need for Taamir. He provided more than just chauffeur services; he was my male companion.

I paced the floor. How long had it been since Jason had left? No more than twenty minutes, perhaps thirty? What was taking him so long? I shoved down the worry that bubbled up and went to the tiny bathroom. The light switch was broken, and a thin coating of sticky grime coated the floors.

For shit's sake.

Cautiously, I went to it and peered in the peephole. Two men in t-shirts and jeans stood outside.

My voice wavered, unsure if I should say something. Maybe if I ignored them, they'd go away. But when I looked again a second later, they were still there.

"Uh, hi, yeah. Can I help you?" I said through the door.

"Agent Price sent us. It's important we talk to you face to face."

Shit. Something had happened to Jason.

I unlocked the door and opened it. "Is Jason alright?"

"Do you mind if we come in?" the first agent said. Older than me, he looked to be in his mid-forties, his hair already receding. The second was younger. His fingers fidgeted with the snaps on his jacket. Both were overdue for a shower and a shave.

"Uh, sure," I said and stood aside, holding open the door.

They stepped inside, and I closed the door behind them.

They made their way to the center of the room, their eyes lingering on the untouched beds.

"What's this about?" I said, keeping my voice flat.

The first guard turned. "We need you to come with us."

In a blur, he lunged, his hands reaching out for me. His fingers encircled my forearms and held fast. I bucked and kicked, my foot connecting with his groin. I heard a satisfying crunch, and he groaned, doubling over. His grip loosened, and I staggered forward. The second one darted toward me. With adrenaline, I pivoted fast, but my foot caught on the edge of the crumpled rug. I fell backward, my shoulders slamming into the concrete. My ears rang as a shooting pain shot from my tailbone to my neck.

Blindingly fast, the other guy seized my vulnerable position, launching himself on top of me. He tried to grasp at my flailing arms, but I managed to keep one free. I thrust a hand in his face, pressing my palm against his cheek, and pushed up against him. The muscles in my arm burned with the strain of his massive weight. A pulse of electricity vibrated up my arm, and the expression of rage on the man's face turned to one of terror. He grimaced and reared back, releasing me. I scurried backward on the ground. He clutched at his face, spewing a string of curse words as he bellowed in pain.

"You fucking bitch!" he screamed. Tendrils of smoke wafted from between his fingers, and disbelief clouded his face. He dropped his hand, revealing giant blisters and red pustules on his left cheek. His left eye was nearly swollen shut. The smell of charred skin filled my nostrils, and I slowly rose to my feet, feeling like a zookeeper confronted with a lion no longer interested in a beef-only diet.

The man's eyes were wild. "What the hell did you do to my face? You burned my fucking face!"

The first guard, now recovered from my assault to his sensitive bits, ignored his partner's spitting insults and affixed me with a menacing stare.

"I was *told* to bring you alive, but now I think I'll make a different call."

In five steps, he'd be on me. My heart jackhammered against my ribs as the memory of Jason's voice echoed in my ears, telling me how to defend myself when overpowered or outnumbered. *'The element of surprise is the only advantage you'll get.'* I gritted my teeth.

It was now or never.

I launched myself forward, bolting for the door. As my hand had just gripped the metal handle, something grabbed my hair, yanking my head backward. Intense pain ignited where the hair was attached to my skull as he jerked me back into the room.

Another hand clamped vice-like around my throat. I struggled to breathe, black dots appearing in my vision. My survival instincts kicked in, and I struggled, grasping wildly to break his grip.

He sneered at me, unaffected by the claw marks I left on his arm. "Got you now, bitch. I don't know what Mr. Kane wants you for, but he better pay double to fix Garrett's face."

His grip tightened, and suddenly, my feet were no longer on the floor. My lungs burned, desperately trying to suck in ragged breaths.

Tick, tick, tick.

The black dots coalesced, rimming my sight. Every swing of my arm was weaker than the one before it.

The room spun as I neared the fringes of passing out.

You are the guardian. The gentle voice of Enheduanna spoke. *There is no one else.*

She was right. Jason was MIA, and there wasn't a knight in shining armor that would miraculously appear. If I wanted to survive this, I'd have to do it myself.

Tapping into my fading strength, I willed the muscles in my left arm to work. My fingers clasped the man's bicep, feeling the hard knot of muscles under his shirt as he strained to cut off the oxygen from my brain.

The same familiar tingle of fluttering energy shot up my arm, growing in intensity like an ignited chain reaction. A sizzle filled the room like bacon on a skillet as my fingers seared black marks into his flesh. The man wailed, releasing his hold.

I crumpled onto the floor, coughing, and sucked in great gasps of air. The man's skin on his arm bubbled, the skin peeled, the edges charred black, the effect radiating up his neck.

I climbed to my knees, watching the man's expression shift from surprise to horror.

Our eyes met, and his expression shifted to one of pure horror. A heartbeat later, flames erupted from the man's body licking and engulfing him in the fire. No matter what I did, I couldn't look away.

Shrieks of agony filled the room as he collapsed on the floor. The flames snuffed out as quickly as they'd appeared.

The dead guy's clothes were still smoldering as the other agent ran past me, shouting how the money wasn't worth it, and fled out of the room.

I sat, unable and unwilling to move, watching the lingering smoke stream from the tattered remnants of the man's clothes and charred skin. I fell forward on my hands, gagging down the bile in my throat. The scent of scorched flesh and singed hair enveloped me, lingering in the air.

CHAPTER

EIGHT

Wisps of smoke hovered over the dead body of the guard on the floor. My eyeballs stung from the smoke, and I maneuvered myself to the farthest part of the room. I stared at my hand in dazed bewilderment.

He'd just *burned*. Both. I'd burned them.

As I hadn't slept for days, fatigue plagued me, gnawing at my skull as weariness seeped into my limbs.

When no other guards came, I went to the door and locked it. A multitude of scrambled thoughts bombarded me as I strained to make sense of what had happened. I was no stranger to death, but those times, I'd had time to prepare mentally. The knowing that I was arriving at a scene where a bomb had gone off or an incursion was set to occur, that I'd witness the aftermath.

But nothing could've prepared me for this.

The realization that *I* had caused a death left a hollow pang in my gut. How would I move on from this? This new reality that I had taken someone else's life.

Sure, he was seconds away from killing me, and if I hadn't

acted, drawing on whatever hellish magic I now possessed, I would be in his place right now.

Guardian? Protector? How was this protecting? I'd burned a man *alive.* He was a bastard but also someone's father, brother, or son. A person with hopes, dreams, and goals. A person with a life that I had ended.

I laced my fingers through my hair, wincing at the sore spot where roots had been torn from my head.

I should call Jason and tell him what happened, but now that feels like an insurmountable task. One which I'm just not up to doing right now. I shivered, hugging myself at the waning effects of the adrenaline. Finally, exhaustion made me slump onto the bed.

Adrift in a void, Jason's frantic voice beckoned me back to reality.

"Elly," he said, "Elly?"

I opened my eyes. Jason stood silhouetted against the doorway, his eyes darting around the room. "Holy shit!" he said, spotting the charcoal corpse on the floor. "Are you hurt? What the hell happened?"

The light through the window had faded, and the sun dipped behind the neighboring buildings. I tried to speak, but my tongue felt thick, and my throat was sore from where the jerk had nearly crushed my windpipe. The room spun as I sat up.

"I—" I stammered, the vivid memories rushing back. "I don't know."

"You don't know? Jesus," he said, walking over to me. He set the white paper bag he'd been carrying on the desk, and tantalizing aromas of herbs and grease drifted from it.

My stomach heaved, and I covered my mouth, recoiling at the thought of food.

Jason crouched, inspecting the body burned beyond recognition.

"Tell me, Elly. Exactly what happened?" There was a finality to his voice as he looked at me.

I pressed my lips together, trying to find the right words so Jason would understand and not think I was crazy.

Jason's jaw twitched. He was losing his patience.

Shame forced me to stare at my balled fists resting on my lap. I couldn't look at him, not after what I'd done.

"Those guards," I started. "The ones from downstairs. They came here and attacked me," my voice shook, but I trudged on. "I didn't have a choice—"

Jason placed his hands on his hips and stared at the body.

"Okay," he said, scratching the back of his neck before settling his eyes on my face. "I'm at a loss for why they'd attack you, but go on."

My vision blurred, and I fought back the threatening tears. Tears for the life I'd taken. But also tears for whatever monstrous power I harbored.

"Jason, I don't know. They came after me, and I just *reacted.*"

Jason didn't reply, his face like a statue.

"I felt this energy. This *power.* I knew they would kill me, and my only choice was to stop them."

He pinned me with a scrutinizing gaze.

"It's the truth, Jason. I swear."

He moved to the desk, resting a hip on the edge, and folded his arms, his eyes searching my face. I clenched my jaw, unwavering in my conviction He needed to believe me. Trust that what I said wasn't crazy, if only to prove it to myself.

Finally, he sighed and waved to the dead body. "So, this power you have, it did this?"

I nodded.

"Did you have this when we were…?" he didn't finish the sentence, but I knew what he was asking.

I shook my head. "When we were together? Seriously? No. I just—" I paused. "It's new. I can't explain it."

Relief smoothed the wrinkles on his forehead. He was quiet for a while as if absorbing everything I'd said. I couldn't blame him. I doubted if I'd believe him had the roles been reversed.

When he spoke again, his voice was low, as if he was talking to himself. "I've done several missions with these guys. Stevens was only a year in the agency, and McKinley has a baby on the way, for Christ's sake."

Guilt coated my tongue. "Did they at least say what they wanted?"

I couldn't bear to look at him anymore, so I rubbed the backs of my eyes. "They said they'd received orders to take me *alive.*"

"Orders from whom?"

"I don't know."

"Think, Elly."

I squinted, dropping my hands and struggling to sift through the details. It had all happened so damn fast. "They mentioned a name," I finally said. "Someone named Mr. Kane."

"Well, a name, at least, is a start." Jason moved from the desk. He ran his hands under the rug to roll the body into it like a horrifying burrito. Then, he dragged it into the bathroom and shut the door.

That'll be quite a scare for housekeeping.

Next, he moved to the window and pulled open the curtain an inch.

I watched, motionless, from the bed as he peered outside.

A minute passed. His eyes still scanning the street outside, he withdrew the phone from his back pocket. This one was different from the one I'd seen before.

"It's Price," he said, holding it up to his ear. "I need a cleanup team at number eight." He hesitated, sliding me a sideways glance. "McKinley and Stevens, yeah."

Anguish swept over me, wondering which one I had killed.

Maybe it would have been best if I didn't know. Muffled words played from the other end of the line before he ended the call. He turned to face me, his lips tightly pressed with a grim expression.

"They'll be here in twenty. We have to go."

I tilted my head, searching his gaze for any indication of his feelings, but found a mask. If he was angry or frightened, he didn't show it.

He turned his back to me and repacked his laptop into the duffel bag. He took out his pistol. Holding it up, he flicked the slide back and squinted down the sight before snapping it securely back into its holster.

"Let's go," he said, and without waiting for me, he was by the door.

I sat upright, scrambling to tie the laces on my boots. Snagging my shoulder bag from where it hung on the back of the chair, I followed him out. I closed the hotel room door behind me. Jason led me down the stairs, and I had to quicken my pace to match his stride. He pushed through the now unguarded door downstairs, and we continued through the store and out onto the sidewalk.

Shoppers and vendors crowded the streets. I half-jogged behind him as we made our way to the right. Like a wedge, Jason cleared a path for us.

Jason hurried us down three blocks until, upon reading a street sign, he pivoted on his heel and turned left. Then we went down a narrower street that twisted through rows of apartment buildings until ending at a graveled playground. An empty fountain — the base cracked and pitted from age and bullet holes — sat amongst a swing set and a slide.

Jason continued to where the road curved around. An older model red jeep sat parked on the corner of the opposite street, with fresh paint and decent tires.

He scanned both sides of the street and then reached for the driver's side door. I scurried around the front of the Jeep and climbed in. Jason threw his duffel bag in the back before settling behind the steering wheel.

Here was a fully gassed-up vehicle with keys still in it only a couple blocks from the hotel.

The devil works hard, but Division 12 works harder.

I buckled the lap belt as Jason gunned the engine. Out on the road, he weaved among the dense flow of traffic.

Chaos.

That's what driving in Syria was. People sold goods from every corner, and women and children carried bags of clothing and food. And to top it all off, the traffic laws were not only not enforced, they were non-existent. No one halted at stop signs or waited at crosswalks. And to date, I'd failed to see a single speed limit sign.

By the time Jason reached the highway, the sun hovered low over the distant mountains. Only the dash lights illuminated Jason's face as we headed South. I hoped my face, too, was concealed in shadows. The silence was excruciating. I longed for him to say something. Anything.

How could he ever see me the same?

We passed a sign on the side of the road: Baghdad 510 km.

Jason had moved his eyes forward. Gripping the wheel, he watched the road. A dented cargo truck and a bus spewed clouds of inky black smoke in the oncoming lane beside us. The truck whooshed by, causing Jason to correct the jeep as the gust of wind bullied it on the road.

I couldn't stand the quiet any longer. "Any chance you could tell me where we are going?"

Jason adjusted his grip on the wheel. "We're going to Baghdad. There's someone there that can help."

"But what about Division 12? Why aren't we going there?"

The muscles in his neck tensed. "There's been a security breach at Division 12."

"What? Are you sure?"

"Yes," he slid a glance my way. The solemn look told me it was true. He returned his eyes to the road before continuing. "We were subcontracted out as security for an archaeological site near Deir ez-Zur. My contact at Central informed me that some classified information regarding the site had been compromised. They're still investigating how much got out, but as of now, they're assuming there's at least one mole."

"An archeological site? What would be so valuable to know about some broken pottery and bronze shovels?" I said.

Jason shrugged. "I don't know. All I know is they wanted extra security for the site. We weren't told what they'd discovered, but apparently, it was important enough to require extensive protection."

"The U.S. government. Is that the crate from my pictures in the parking garage?" I said, turning to him.

"Your pictures, they were part of the breach." He sighed. "Someone is monitoring our email. We keep our IP addresses hidden, but somehow, they traced us to that hotel room."

His face looked strained as he wrestled with what to say next. "No more bull shit. You need to come clean and tell me what is going on."

I squirmed in my seat under his intense glare.

"The crate in the picture. It fell off the truck when they were ambushed," I paused. I needed to choose my next words with care.

"I went over and opened it," the words rushed out.

Jason frowned. "Dammit, Elly."

"I had to!" I said. "It said property of U.S. Government. I couldn't just leave it there."

"You absolutely fucking *could* have," Jason said. "You should've contacted the Syrian police or tracked down one of the NATO patrols. Shit, the goddamn U.S. Embassy would've been better. Somebody would've sent a military team to come pick it up."

A lump settled in the back of my throat. "There were people everywhere, Jason. That crate was minutes away from being in the wrong hands, or a shit, a kid finding it."

Jason stretched his fingers on the wheel, his nostrils flaring. "Fine. And what was it?"

"Was it *what*?" I asked.

"What was in the crate? Bombs, drugs, guns?"

My chest constricted, debating on whether to tell him or not. I'd wanted to keep the statue a secret, but it was obvious that it would put us all in more danger. It was time to tell him the truth. At least, the parts I knew.

"Neither," I said. "It had an old bronze statue."

Immediately, Jason's white-knuckled hold on the wheel relaxed.

"A statue? Like an artifact?" he asked.

I shrugged. "Yeah. It's of a woman," I held up my hands to demonstrate. "About a foot tall, and there is writing on the base. She's holding the symbol of a star."

With the thought, my left hand curled into a ball, feeling the dull pang of the burn. I'd told him about the statue. The mark could wait.

"A statue, huh? Why in the world would terrorists be smuggling statues?"

I had no answer for him. Not yet, anyway.

CHAPTER

NINE

Jason and I drove in silence for the next two hours. I must have nodded off because when my eyes fluttered open, we were passing the sign for the border crossing into Iraq.

I still couldn't believe it. I'd put five thousand miles between New York and me, trying to leave behind the pain and heartache from last summer, and yet it'd followed me here. Or I guess, more specifically, he'd followed me here. No, that wasn't fair. I'd been the one who called him; he'd simply picked up the phone.

A pair of passports and IDs lay on the console. The woman portrayed in the photo was definitely not me. Her eyes were brown instead of hazel, but she was a brunette like me and was about my age, so I supposed if it was dark or the person checking it didn't look close enough, it *could* work.

"Bill Orzo and Wanda Cavatelli?" I said, flipping through the passports. "We're pasta, Jason."

He chuckled. "Yeah, I saw that. Meg likes to use names of people that probably don't exist. Less chance of innocent people getting detained trying to get on cruise ships or flying into Cancun."

"How considerate," I said, smiling and shaking my head.

At the border crossing, Jason showed the guard Bill and Wanda's passports. "Evening," he said, speaking Arabic.

The uniformed patrol agent eyed the passports, compared them to our faces, and then scanned them in the booth. "Bill and Wanda," he said. "What brings you to Iraq?"

"Visiting family," Jason said without missing a beat. "I have an aunt who lives near Baghdad."

The man peered down to look at me in the passenger's seat. The first hints of suspicion pinched at the corners of his eyes.

"We're engaged," I blurted. "And we wanted to tell her in person."

Jason gave me an adoring look, and his hand went to mine.

"She's right," he said, bringing my hand to his lips to kiss it, sending a thousand tiny shivers down my wrist. "My aunt is like a mother to me, and I can't wait for Wanda to meet her."

God, he was good at this. No tremor in his words, no hesitation. It was like he'd slipped into this Bill persona seamlessly.

The guard nodded, the tension leaving his face, and passed us back our passports. "Very well. Congratulations on the engagement. Enjoy your stay."

Jason thanked him and drove forward, merging us through the four lanes of border traffic back onto the freeway.

Soon after, he rolled down the window, letting in the pleasant night air and the sounds of croaking frogs and nocturnal birds.

My uncomfortable nap, compounded with being cooped in a car for three hours, had made me restless. I still couldn't wrap my head around the fact the entire foundation of my reality had changed. Magic, for lack of a better term, existed. A powerful, unseen force had come from me. And I'd used it to take a life. How was I supposed to move on from this? I should be a mess, right? Isn't that how normal people reacted to traumatic events? Rocking back and forth and muttering to themselves. So why wasn't I? More so, why was Jason acting so cool with this?

Then again, maybe he wasn't. "Jason?"

"Mmm," he said.

"I'm sorry for dragging you into this."

"It's fine."

I laughed. "It is totally *not* fine. Two Division agents attacked me, and now I have these strange superpowers. I don't know what I'm going to do."

Jason's glance passed over me. "If you're trying to scare me off, it's not going to work. This friend of mine has resources and connections. If anyone has the answers to fix all of this, she will. I promise we'll figure this out together.

Fix this? Did he mean fix me? I didn't think I was broken. I felt fine, better than fine, surprisingly enough, given the circumstances. But maybe I was too close to it. Maybe he saw more of a change in me than I did.

"We're almost there," he said, and the sound from the tires changed, shifting from the bouncing rocks to a smooth, powdery, quiet surface as he turned the Jeep onto a private road. Bright lights caught my attention soon after, casting a golden hue on a cobblestone driveway. I stared out the window at the expansive estate of smooth stone and stucco, as if a mansion had been plucked from England and dropped here in the middle of dry grass and rocky hills.

The walls extended a hundred feet in each direction, where it met the embracing arms of a U-shaped courtyard. Perched above it, a high stone balcony set with intricate colored tiles. Statues of prancing horses six feet high flanked on either side of the arched entrance.

Jason put the Jeep into park and turned to face me. He perched his elbow on the seat between us.

His blue eyes caught the slanted light from the house.

"Until we figure out whatever the hell is going on. I need you to trust me, okay?"

I forced down the lump in my throat and nodded.

"Good," he said, his tone cold. He turned from me, but not before I'd seen the fleeting glimpse of the true Jason. The man I'd fallen in love with. The man — who, when our bodies were intertwined among a pile of rumpled sheets—had promised me a future together. But he'd inevitably chosen a different path, a different life.

One that didn't have me in it.

We exited the Jeep, and Jason led, his boots crunching through the gravel driveway. The surrounding landscape was shrouded in black, but I could make out the subtle outlines of olive trees planted in perfect symmetry along the length of the U-shaped estate. As we walked to the front, I caught the smell of horses and heard a whinny, sharp and shrill, somewhere nearby.

I'd thought we would be here alone, but as we drew closer, a pair of armed security guards clad in black masks approached us, seeming to materialize from the shadows under the archway. Both appeared to be in their mid-thirties and had assault rifles strapped to their chest.

Jason marched on, unfazed by the men's defensive stances, and they held up their hands, signaling for us to halt.

"I'm Jason Price," Jason said. "Tell Katherine Mayberry I'd like to speak with her."

Their faces placid, the older one pressed a finger to his ear as if listening to an earbud under his hood. I examined the archway fifteen feet above them, trying to ignore the suddenly awkward and tense situation. As my eyes took in the details, I spotted — disguised in a notch beside a crimson ceramic tile— a security camera lens no larger than a quarter. Whoever this Katherine was, she didn't skimp on security measures.

A minute later, the man nodded and stepped aside, letting Jason and me pass through.

The archway hadn't been the actual front door but instead led us through a solarium. The air became dense and humid, smelling of moist earth, and enormous tropical plants spilled out of brightly colored vases. Like a commercial greenhouse, the balcony above was set with clear glass windows so whoever was on the second floor could enjoy the view.

At the end of the indoor greenhouse was a set of stone stairs, and at the top was an entryway consisting of a massive pair of double doors. The heavy wood was a stained deep mahogany and intricately carved with horses with their necks arched and their tails held high as they galloped across the polished wood.

Once inside, a black man greeted us. He was dressed in a pressed shirt and black tailored pants and loomed over Jason at nearly seven feet tall.

"Good evening, Jason," he said, an African accent tracing the edges of his voice. He directed a solemn gaze on me.

"Hi, I'm Ella," I said, my voice hovering on the overly cheery, Southern California tone, sounding like my sister Cara, who had actually been a cheerleader in high school, had it mastered.

"It is nice to meet you. Welcome to the Mayberry Estate," his face remained somber. "I'm Ms. Mayberry's assistant, Assem. Please follow me."

Jason and I exchanged glances, and he gave me a reassuring nod.

A red terracotta tile covered the floor of the foyer with twenty-foot-high vaulted ceilings and could have fit my entire apartment. A grand staircase spiraled up from the center, splitting into two encircling balconies. Various paintings of all sizes and styles hung neatly on the plastered walls. Antique vases and sculptures, some waist high with decorations of dancing horses or fern leaves carved into them, dotted the corners of the room and hallway. An emerald and ivory striped carpet ran the entire length of the hallway, muffled our footsteps as Assem led us into a sitting room.

A fireplace, with only embers and a tiled chimney, sat against the far wall flanked by two couches with leather close to the color of melted caramel, and I imagined equally as soft to the touch. Assem walked to the corner of the room and stood, holding his hands in front of him. His lips formed a thin line, and he seemed almost annoyed that we were here. Maybe he didn't like unexpected company. Or maybe he just didn't like me, a stranger, appearing at this house at such a late hour.

An older woman with silver hair laced into a thick braid sat on the far end of the couch. She peered over her teacup, sipping from it as we entered. "Ah, Jason, dear," she said, her voice a lilting British accent. "I'm so glad you called."

Long, flowing curtains billowed from a floor-to-ceiling window behind her, and the setting sun had cooled the air that drifted into the room. She pushed herself to her feet, and her cotton robe shifted off one of her shoulders, revealing a long plaid nightgown similar to one I'd worn in the Christmas Carol musical in eighth grade when I'd played one of Bob Cratchit's children. Although stiff, her steps were light as she walked over and kissed Jason on both cheeks.

Still gripping his duffel bag, Jason bent down so she could reach his cheek, nearly a foot above her.

The woman stepped back, her eyes appraising Jason, then turned her attention on me. "And who might you be?"

"This is El—," Jason supplied before I could answer.

"Shush!" she hissed, waving a dismissive hand. "Unless her tongue doesn't work, I assume she can speak for herself."

Jason frowned.

"I'm Eleanora Dawson," I said. "But I prefer Ella for short."

"Ella," she said as if tasting the words. "I'm Katherine Mayberry, but you can call me Kat. I have to admit I was surprised by Jason's call so late at night. He was vague on the details, but it seems you may have gotten yourself in a spot of trouble and need somewhere to retreat to for a while?"

"Seems that way," I said. "I appreciate you letting us stay here on such short notice. I promise it won't be longer than necessary, and just until I can sort some stuff out."

"Whatever you need, dear," she said, her voice reassuring. "Any friend of Jason's is welcome here." The woman stepped closer, and deep-set wrinkles creased around her eyes as she looked up at me. She took my hands in hers, and something shifted in her eyes, and she looked down.

I tried to pull my hand back, but it was too late. She'd seen the mark.

"That is an awful burn, dear," she said, frowning. "We have a well-stocked first aid kit here, and Assem has medical training. Do you mind if we take a look at it?"

I balled my hand into a fist as I pressed my lips together, the rush of fear coiling low in my belly.

Jason cleared his throat. "It's okay, Elly," he said, apparently sensing my worry. "I've known Kat for a long time. We can trust her."

The tension slowly left me, and I extended it for her, revealing the shape of the eight-pointed star burned into my hand. The skin was puckered and pinkish-red, and I resisted the urge to look away. I hated living with a mark on my body like this forever, and in a way, it felt like I'd gotten a stupid tattoo on spring break that I regretted.

Kat pursed her lips and gently took my hand, her fingers careful not to touch it. "Fascinating," she said, almost reverently. "I don't suppose you'll tell me how you came about to have this?"

I bit my lip. Jason had said I could trust her, which was saying something considering he was the most suspicious person I knew. The guy didn't trust a pizza to be delivered without them having a tracking app he could watch their progress on.

"It's a funny story, actually—"

"And one I'm dying to hear," she said, interrupting me. Her eyes darted to Assem, then back to us. "I'm sure you must both be exhausted from your trip." She patted my hand. "I'll have some bandages and ointment sent up, and we can finish this discussion in the morning. Assem will take your things."

Before I knew it, we were being ushered out of the room and up the curving stairwell I'd seen when we'd first entered.

To our right were a dozen sets of doors, each stained dark cherry, and to the left was a waist-high wrought-iron railing. We strode by several doors before Assem abruptly halted, unlocked one, and swung the door open. His face blank, he motioned us inside.

Jason and mine's gazes met, and a small bubble of panic arose inside me. It hadn't occurred to me what the sleeping arrangements would be. While we'd dated for six months, we'd never moved in together, always staying for a few nights at my apartment or his and then returning home. And up until approximately eight hours ago, we hadn't even laid eyes on each other in almost a year.

Jason's face paled, and it was clear he was picking up on the moment's awkwardness.

That made two of us.

It was silly. We were adults and *should* be able to share a room, but just thinking about being alone with him made my stomach tumble. I had been anticipating having a night to myself to decompress and sort through all my thoughts.

"Uh," I said to Assem. "I don't suppose you have another one for me?"

Assem lifted his eyebrows, understanding spread across his face, and he nodded, motioning to an adjacent door.

"Please let me know if there is anything you need to be more comfortable," Assem said. He half-bowed, then returned to the stairs.

"Will do," I said, entering the other room.

Jason hurried into the first room. His blue gaze, overcast with a storm of emotions, briefly met mine before we both shut our doors.

TEN

The guest room at Kat's estate was nicer than most five-star hotels I'd stayed in. The spacious room had a four-poster bed sat against the wall, and its banisters were of carved cherry wood and engraved with flowers and vines. Snug against the footboard sat a leather steamer trunk with a set of plush blankets neatly piled atop it. A low wooden dresser sat beside an open, aired window. A pair of long white curtains fluttered in the cool breeze. The bathroom was off to my left. The floor was of the same terracotta tile, and the walls were again the smooth stone finish. A sink made from pounded copper was recessed in a mahogany pedestal. An enormous framed Renaissance painting of two dogs splashing in a lake hung on the wall, and beneath it was a clawfoot bathtub. I suppressed a squeal of joy.

It'd been weeks, no, *months*, since I'd had a hot bath. My hands caressed the brass knobs. Hot water cascaded from the faucet, and I cupped my hand under the down rush of water, letting it slip through my fingers and splash my arm. Steam filled the room.

I couldn't wait any longer.

I stood. A porcelain tray sat next to the sink with fluffy hand towels, paper-wrapped soaps, and tiny bottles of lotions. I held them up, inhaling their scents one by one. Overwhelmed by the luscious vanilla, lavender, and citrus aromas, I settled on a Jasmine-scented one.

I lowered myself into the tub and lathered my skin with the bar of creamy soap. Making my way to my hands, I found the scar still sensitive but not as tender. I studied it, still confused about how an inanimate object had marked my skin like that.

There must be some scientific explanation. Perhaps a chemical reaction or electric current had reacted with the salt on my skin? But no matter how many ideas I came across, none seemed to fit. So how could I explain what *I* still didn't believe?

I closed my eyes, relaxing as I sank into the heavenly water. Eventually, when the water cooled and my fingers and toes were wrinkled, begrudgingly, I climbed out. A fluffy robe hung from a hook nearby, and I slipped it over my shoulders. I returned to the bedroom after wrapping my hair in a cotton towel. A pair of silk pajamas had been laid out for me, and a plate of food. Wearing the pajamas, I munched on a chicken sandwich, grapes, and cheese. I sipped from one of the water bottles and then collapsed, arms splayed on the blissfully soft bed. The day's events bombarded my thoughts, forcing me to sift through everything that had transpired. When I'd awoken that morning, I never would've guessed I'd be sleeping somewhere as unimaginable as this place. Although my mind simmered with excitement, the bath had relaxed my muscles. So much had happened in so little time.

Within seconds, I was asleep.

THE TRUMPETING NEIGH of a horse awoke me from my deep, dreamless sleep. Sunbeams shone through the slit in the veil-thin curtains, and I sat up and stretched. Like a bear emerging from its Winter den, my limbs were stiff, and I had to force them to cooperate.

I rubbed my eyes and swung my legs off the bed. In the bathroom, a set of personal hygiene products had been placed by the sink. Although I wouldn't say I liked the idea of someone coming into my room while I slept, I was grateful for a tooth-brush and deodorant. After re-dressing in my jeans and button-up shirt from the day before, I laced up my boots. Following the scent of fresh bread and maple, I headed downstairs.

The dining room looked lit with the morning sun. Floor-to-ceiling windows streamed morning light into the dining room. The table was long, a light oak color, with a tapestry runner on it. Embroidered on the red velvet were two peacocks, their tails a flourish of reds, golds, and blues. Moroccan. No, perhaps Turkish.

When I entered, Assem was refilling Kat's tea.

Jason was already seated in the center of the table. His hands fidgeted with the cloth napkin beside him. The muscles worked under his clean-shaven jaw.

At the left end of the table sat Kat. A pretty, olive-skinned woman I didn't recognize sat on the far right. Assem stood, statuesque and intimidating, in the far corner.

"Good morning, dear," Kat said to me, beaming. "Please join us?"

I couldn't help but mimic a pleasant smile to the woman as I moved to pull a chair from the table.

Jason didn't look up. His attention focused on the plate before him of scrambled eggs, fruit, and toast. If Kat sensed the tension between us, she didn't show it.

"This is Zhalika, my partner," she said, motioning to the woman across from her.

From her rich brown eyes and rows of black, braided hair, she was stunning. No wonder Kat liked her.

"Zhalika," Kat continued. "This is Ella. She's a friend of Jason."

Jason lifted a glass of the champagne mimosa and drained it in a smooth gulp. I reached my hand out, ready to do the same.

"Jason filled me in on the details regarding your attack at the hotel yesterday," Kat said. "After breakfast, I'll show you to my office. There is much we need to discuss."

"So, Ella," Zhalika said, her English weighted with a Nigerian accent. "You are American, no?"

I swallowed my bite of the cinnamon bun, nodding. "Yes. I grew up in Southern Oregon, on the Western side of the U.S. But when my mom remarried, my step-father moved us to his place in Sacramento, California."

"Us?" Zhalika asked.

"Yeah, a few years after they married, they had my sister, Cara."

"Ah, and what made you come all the way here?" Zhalika said and waved toward Assem, who brought a pitcher of water to refill her glass.

"I graduated from Columbia with a major in Political science and a minor in history, intending to work as a diplomat or state department. However, when I took a summer off to join the Peace Corps, helping with a natural disaster, I brought my camera to document the trip. After seeing the response from my friends and family back home, I knew that was what I wanted to do."

It was Kat who spoke next. "I admire your courage, but I bet your family wasn't too happy about that career choice."

I shook my head, laughing. "Whoa, no. My mom nags me all

the time to come home, and although I visit, I still feel like I'm not done, you know?"

"Oh, I do know," Kat said, nodding, keeping her gaze steady on mine.

Another man my age entered with tanned skin, dark eyes, and dirt-covered jeans and boots. He wiped his hands on his shirt and whispered something into Zhalika's ear.

She pushed her chair back and stood. "I'm very sorry, but I must see to a matter at the barn," she said, addressing the table. Then, directing her gaze to Kat, she continued. "It's Kharamina. She's off her feed this morning."

"Oh dear, go ahead then," she said, shooing her. "I'll come if you need me."

Zhalika left the room, the stable hand behind her jogging to keep pace.

"Well then, if you're ready. Let's head to my office, shall we?" Kat said, standing.

I tipped back my glass, draining the last mimosa, and stood to follow her.

Jason trailed behind us as we entered the high-ceilinged room.

The office—as Kat had referred to it—did have a desk and a computer. However, what captivated me most were the shelves upon shelves of books. Varying in size and color, they lined the walls ten feet high. A large table sat in the center. Kat strode to it and scooped up the papers and books that were stacked on it. A few rolls tumbled off the side, and I rushed over to help her gather them. Maps of North Africa and Mongolia, the names of the places, seemed off, though.

"I've never heard of these places before?"

"That's because they don't exist. Not anymore, anyway. Those pre-date most French and Italian invasions." Kat stuffed the pile of papers and books on the desk, and a few stray pages floated to the ground. She motioned to a chair beside her desk. "You can put them over here with the rest."

I did as she requested before moving to the shelves. "You've quite a collection here." My fingers slid along the spines of the hardback books as I read the titles. *"Ancient Civilizations on the Tigris and Euphrates"* and *"Sumerian Mythology"*

"What exactly do you do again?" I asked.

"Isn't that the question of the century?" Kat laughed. "I've spent the better part of my career as a professor at Cambridge. Soon, I was the head of the History and Anthropology department as well as a curator and exhibit coordinator for the Smithsonian and London Historical Society. I've studied numerous cultures, but I'm most fascinated by the Middle East, specifically Mesopotamia."

Kat strode to the far end of the room. A tall stack of thick books sat on her desk, and she started loading them into her arms. The pile soon overwhelmed her short frame, and Jason stepped over to help her.

"When I retired," she said, her breathing labored as we returned to the table with the books. "I maintain a freelance contract for the Smithsonian Museum. I provide insight and knowledge on any artifacts unearthed in exchange for an opportunity to be first in line to see the discoveries. Most recently, I've been working with archaeologists at a site located in Eastern Syria. Just South of Deir ez-Zur."

I raised my eyebrow at the mention of the city.

"They believe it to be an ancient temple and have found various artifacts," she said, opening the book to a bookmarked page. The dense cover slammed on the desk as it fell open, revealing the dog-eared pages. Her eyes scanned the text and then spun the book to face me. Her finger pointed at a sketched drawing.

It was an eight-pointed star.

I lifted my hand, comparing the two.

"Exactly," Kat said, putting a voice to my thoughts. "This is the Sumerian symbol of the goddess Inanna. Often referred to as Ishtar, she is the goddess of both love and war. This symbol is over 5000 years old."

I ran my tongue against the edges of my molars. "Then why—"

"Why is a 5000-year-old symbol burned on your hand?" she chimed. "That is an excellent question. I think it's time you and I talk. Best start from the beginning, dear," Kat said.

The air in the room grew hot, and goosebumps pricked my arms. How much could I say? Kat seemed nice enough, but what if I said too much? She'd think I'd gone crazy. She'd implied her connections with the U.S. government. Would she be forced to contact them? Perhaps, even accuse *me* of stealing the statue. Until I knew more, I needed to be cautious about how much I revealed.

I recounted all that had occurred the day before, from the guys with the stolen crate to the attack in the hotel room. I left out the more gruesome details, implying that I'd been lucky to have some limited self-defense skills. I also neglected the part about the awkward car ride down.

When I'd finished, Kat's eyes were distant. "The men in the hotel room," she finally said, looking at Jason. "Were they agents with Division 12?"

"Yes," Jason said, his eyes darkening.

"And the attack, you believe someone intercepted the email containing the photographs of the stolen crate?"

"I do."

"Then there can only be two reasons for this. Either someone at Division 12 is relaying information to the person wanting that statute or—"

"The person has a contract with Division 12 to find the statue and find Ella," Jason finished for her.

Kat nodded stiffly. "So, no matter the answer, Division 12 can no longer be trusted."

She pinned a concerned gaze on Jason.

"Don't you dare think I knew about any of this," he said, slicing the air with his hand. "At any given time, dozens of agents are all working secret assignments, and it is not like we meet up at the water cooler to chat about which senator we're protecting or terrorist cell leader we're trying to locate."

He swung his eyes to me. "For shit's sake, you have to believe me, Elly."

I found myself searching his blue eyes for the truth. Every ounce of me wanted to believe him. I needed him to be on my side. And the truth was if they had contracted him to take me *and* the statue back to the agency, wouldn't he have done so already? However, there was always the possibility that he was working a long game, getting me to trust him again so I'd reveal where I'd hidden the statue. My stomach clenched at the thought. I refused to believe it. Sure, he was an asshole who'd walked out on me, but he wasn't that big of an asshole. He had come when I'd called him, with no questions, no hesitations. I had to believe he was on my side.

"I do believe you," I said, and his face visibly relaxed.

"Good. Division 12 rates ain't cheap, so whoever wants that statue wants it bad."

"Indeed," Kat said. "Which means there must be more to it we don't know."

Kat flipped the book's pages and showed us the drawing of the goddess Inanna. A figure of a nude woman that carried a rope and rod in both hands. "This symbol was all over the dig site and is a common theme in excavations in this region. What was unusual about this site was that they'd found a bronze statue of the goddess herself. While she is often depicted with the eight-pointed star near her, *this* is the first time we found Inanna holding the star."

My eyes studied the drawings, recognizing the shape and style of the Inanna to be very similar to the statue I'd found.

"This statue," I said tentatively. "It was stolen, wasn't it?"

Kat's face lit up with eagerness, and I exhaled the breath I'd been holding. "As a matter of fact, it was. Do you know anything about it? Who might have it?"

"I know," I said before I lost the nerve. The time for keeping secrets had passed. I was bobbing alone in the ocean and had nothing to cling to. If I wanted to keep from drowning, I needed to let go of the life preserver I was clinging to and climb into a boat.

Kat's eyes brightened with excitement. "That's wonderful to hear! I'd very much like to return it to the research team. And if I could examine it, I believe it would provide the answers you're seeking." She held out her hand, an expectant look on her face.

I pressed my lips together. "The thing is... I don't have it with me."

Kat dropped her hand to her lap. "Bah, I'd figured as much. I presume it is somewhere safe, then?"

"Yes," I said, recalling an image of it tucked snuggly into the frosted space in my fridge.

"Alright, we'll have to make do with what we have."

Assem appeared as if materializing from a side door to the room. He carried a tray with tea and cups and sat it on a side table before departing as quickly as he'd come. Kat took a cup and filled it with the steaming green liquid, then placed a sugar cube in it and swirled it with the spoon.

"What I'm about to tell you," she said, sipping. "Very few people know."

My heartbeat intensified and grew so loud I swore everyone in the room could hear it. Jason leaned over the desk, having attracted his attention as well.

"Last month, the Cairo Museum was subject to a break-in. An artifact in their archives was stolen. It had yet to be cataloged, but I had the opportunity to speak with an archaeologist who'd seen it. A stone cylinder, only a foot tall, it was covered in engravings from an ancient script. He believed it to be a prehistoric form of Cuneiform writing."

"Cunei—?" Jason stammered.

"Cuneiform," Kat supplied. "The oldest form of writing. It was created thousands of years ago by the Mesopotamians."

"So, it can be interpreted?" I asked. While taking a semester of ancient languages, the wedge-shaped characters fascinated me. Someone had painstakingly stamped them into soft clay tablets using a reed stylus.

"To a degree, yes," Kat said, pursing her lips. "There's a Rosetta stone of sorts that allows archaeologists to translate much of what has been discovered."

"Were they able to read it?" I said.

"The archaeologist I spoke with did manage a partial translation. Although vague, it appeared to be the directions to a location."

"Did he find out where?" Jason asked this time.

"It was unclear," Kat said, shaking her head. "It seems to point to certain constellations aligning with a specific star."

I licked my lips, leaning closer. "And this star, could this star be called Vela?"

"Yes, as a matter of fact, it is," Kat said, eyes widening with surprise.

I dug my nails into my palms. No turning back now.

Kat steepled her fingers. "The Vela star is in the constellation Vela. Well, I should say it was. It went supernova many years ago and is now only a remnant. Records stated it was brighter than the moon even during the day."

The vision of the woman ascending from the glowing bridge appeared in my mind, urging me on. "What if I told you," I said, tapping a finger on my bottom lip. "I don't think it was just a star they saw."

"Ah," she said. "Then I think we'll need Assem to bring us more tea."

CHAPTER

ELEVEN

As I relayed all I could about my vision, I stole furtive glances at Jason, hoping for any insight into his thoughts. No luck. His face remained somber, any emotion was locked firmly behind a wall.

"And this ability you say you have?" Kat asked when I'd finished. "How do you activate it? Where does it come from?"

I scratched the side of my head, running my fingers through my hair. "I'm not sure. There's this tingling feeling, and it's like a switch is flipped in here." I tapped on my chest. "As if it had been inside me all along but needed a catalyst to ignite it."

Pressing her finger against her lips, Kat didn't immediately respond as if determining which question to ask next. "Can you use it now?"

"Now? Here?" I said, scoffing. I'd done all I could to avoid thinking about the terrifying experience in the hotel room. I could still feel the hands of those men on my neck, see the look of anger in their eyes that had turned to fear when I'd defended myself. I'd reacted on instinct, possessed by a will to survive. I had no way of knowing I had the power to stop them, but still, the dark thoughts of guilt plagued me like a thousand tiny knives piercing my skull every time I thought about it.

"Yes, why not?" Kat said, motioning her arms to the space around us.

The sound of a book thumping on a table to my side caught my attention. Jason had sent one down and had his attention focused on another lying open before him.

A mixture of emotions rolled through me, doubt and fear sinking their talons into the base of my skull. How could I show her when I didn't even know what *it* was?

Kat's attentive face convinced me to try. I inhaled, recalling the feeling when the agent had grabbed me, feeling the memory of energy radiating up my arm and gathering in my palm. The vicious snarl on the men's faces. The rage.

I'd been scared. Terrified. And then had come the *anger*. The heat boiled low in my belly, simmering. I'd been so angry.

Angry both with myself and at them.

I'd been wrong to assume they could've been trusted.

Kat watched me intently as I lifted my hand, and Jason's chair creaked as he shifted uncomfortably. I scrunched my nose, remembering how I'd foolishly let them into the room.

Betrayed.

The word left a bitter taste on my tongue as the air above my hand shimmered.

The skin on my throat ached, echoing the memory of his iron fist gripping my neck.

Suffering.

Waves of heat rose from my palm, twisting as I super-heated the particulates in the air. Sweat beaded my temples, and I could feel them, the tiny molecules of pollen and dander in the air speeding up, bumping violently against each other, further energizing the reactions.

Deceived.

The air boiled. My palm burned with the intensifying heat as the air began to ignite. A spark flashed. Followed by another. Again and again, until a ball of static electricity hissed and crackled. A giggle bubbled up and out of my throat. A miniature electric storm was swirling inches above my hand.

Jason moved closer, and the spinning sphere of electricity cast a sapphire glow on our faces. "Well, would you look at that?" Kat whispered almost fervently. "In my seventy-odd years, I never could have imagined I'd see something like this."

The storm raged. The continuous tiny lighting sparks tickled my hand at the points where they contacted my skin. I willed the storm to grow, wanting to see how big I could make it. The sparks intensified until I could hear the audible pops of baby thunder. The power inside me surged as if eager to do my bidding.

A hand rested on my shoulder, snapping my attention away from my hand. Jason stared down at me, jaw set and a furrow worried the space between his eyebrows. "Elly. That's enough. It's alright."

I felt the electric sparks cease, leaving behind the ozone haze hovering in the air. I blinked and shook my head.

"That was *amazing,*" Kat said and sat back. She laced her fingers together on her stomach. "Truly amazing."

I sucked my lower lip between my teeth, unsure how I should feel. Surprised? Yes. Proud? I suppose. Or maybe relieved that with time, there was a chance I could control it.

Jason removed his hand from my shoulder, but I could sense he lingered behind me. I'd never seen that look on his face before, even in our time together. Whatever he'd seen, or thought he'd seen, had spooked him. I'd expected surprise, shock, or even excitement, but that tiny sphere of energy I'd conjured in my hand had scared him.

I didn't understand it. Jason faced danger all the time and

never turned away. So how was this different? Sure, it was a lot to take in, this new ability of mine, and it *was* strange as hell, but I'd had it under control when he'd stopped me. And how could I expect to learn to control it more if I didn't practice with it?

"No doubt now, is there?" Kat said, slapping her leg. "We've got our work cut out for us. That power of yours must have come from somewhere, and the sooner we find out what, the better." Kat stood and shuffled to the far end of the room, her eyes on a particular volume of cream-colored books.

The residual energy shivered through me.

I'd felt it. Glimpsed what the *ancient* power could do.

And I wanted to feel it again.

CHAPTER

TWELVE

Kat, Jason, and I spent the remainder of the morning pouring through Kat's library of historical references. Hoping any of them will give us clues about the burn on my hand and the statue.

The spacious room allowed Jason and me to maintain a generous distance from each other. If he'd been aloof before, now he looked at me like I was a stranger.

He'd positioned himself in a leather-winged back chair, looking entirely out of place in the academic setting. He scrolled through his phone or flipped through one of the magazines from a bin, occasionally looking up when Assem brought them sandwiches or drinks.

I reached for a thickly bound book. I cradled its faded blue linen cover and dog-eared edges, worrying it would crumble to dust from my touch. I tried tilting it, hoping the lettering of the title would reflect in the lamplight. No luck. I sat down and opened it. Inside the title page was dated 1937. Shorthand notes cursive writing briskly wriggled along the sides of the pages. I narrowed my eyes to read the small handwriting. It was French, and I could translate a few of the words.

"*'Akkad's reign in Sumeria'*" "And *'the dates of his rule are inconsistent,'*" followed by "*2334 BC.*'"

When I had skimmed through most of the book, I glanced up. Kat had seated herself at her desk. A cup of tea sat steaming next to her. Her forehead knotted as she studied a small journal in her hands.

"The Akkadian empire?" I asked. "Was that around the time of the Vela star's appearance?"

Kat absently turned a page but continued reading. "Yeah, that would be about the same time, I suppose."

Kat slammed the book closed, startling me and provoking a "What the fuck," from Jason as he spilled a glass of lemonade.

Kat raised her eyes to me, ignoring Jason's mishap. "Of course!" she shouted and leaped to her feet. Her chair wrenched across the wooden floor with a terrible squeak. She shuffled toward the shelf to her left and climbed on a small stool. She scanned the rows of books, her fingers tracing the spines until they stopped. Finally, she pulled a book with a faded linen cover free. She stepped down from the stool and was already flipping through the pages by the time she'd reached me.

She muttered to herself before exclaiming. "Hah! Here it is."

Jason made his way over, curiosity piqued, and Kat laid the book before me.

"...King Sargon," she read. "Attributed his success to the patronage of the goddess Inanna also known as Ishtar. His conquests were far-reaching. His reign is speculated to have begun in 2334 and lasted over 150 years."

"I don't know," Jason said. "That seems like bull shit."

Kat tapped a pencil eraser against her teeth in thought. "Most scholars believed the scribes meant 'seasons' back then," she said. "But maybe they were wrong."

"All the Kings back then boasted about the length of their reign and width of their kingdoms." She winked at me. "Men were the same back then as now. Claiming to be chosen by the Gods, they tended to encourage the embellishment of their records. Thus, creating legends instead of accurate records."

"This King Akkad, do you think he knew Inanna the Goddess? Is he somehow connected to the statue and my dream?" I said.

"I don't know what to believe. The timing is right, as is the location. Housed in archives worldwide are clay tablets depicting the details of his reign. Mostly written by his daughter, Enheduanna."

I sat up a little straighter at the mention of her name.

Kat grinned. "Yes, quite the name, isn't it?"

I nodded, pretending that was why I'd reacted as I had.

"Would any of these relate to," Jason said, pausing as if chewing the word. "Her abilities?" He kept his focus on Kat, avoiding my gaze.

I snorted a dismissive laugh. "Yo, I have a name."

His jaw clenched, but he avoided my gaze, focusing on Kat.

"She's right, Jason," Kat said. "Don't be an arse. But to answer your question, I don't rightfully know. I have a few more around her we could have a look through?" Kat motioned to the lowest row of books to her left, where oversized reference books had been stacked horizontally to fit.

With uncanny speed, Jason was beside the stacks as Kat shuffled over. Although petite, she positioned herself in front of the books, edging Jason out of the way.

Kat freed one, sat it on the arm of one of the chairs, and thumbed the pages. After a moment, she pursed her lips. "Bollocks," she said, shaking her head.

My heart sank. "You said there were more? Can we look at them?"

Kat wrinkled her face and scowled. "As I said, they've been

distributed globally at the major museums. I could reach out to them to see if they'd email me copies from their archives?"

I murmured in agreement. "Worth a shot?"

Kat raised a finger. "It'll take a few days for them to respond since it's the weekend."

"Are we sure that's a good idea?" Jason cautioned. "What if they get suspicious about what we're looking into? The missing statue has to have people looking for it, and keywords might trigger the authorities."

"You think I'm a batty?" Kat said, glaring at him. "Well, that may be true, but I know a thing or *two* about discretion. I'll sandwich them in with other requests that confuse anyone watching too closely and at least buy us some time."

I resisted the urge to laugh as Jason's face hardened.

"Thank you," he said through gritted teeth. "Our one strategic advantage we have right now is that no one knows where we are or what we know so far. I'd like to keep it that."

A toothy grin formed on her face. "Strategic advantage. Absolutely. Couldn't agree more." She gave him a mocking salute before returning her gaze to the book.

Jason grumbled and reclaimed his position in the chair.

A minute later, the sound of a knock and footsteps drew our attention.

In the doorway stood the young attendant from breakfast.

"Ms. Mayberry, Zhalika needs you at the barn," he said in broken English.

Kat rose from her chair and nodded toward the young man. "Thank you, Hamid. I'll be right there."

She excused herself and hurried out of the room, leaving Jason and me alone.

The stark silence grew from a hum to a roar. No matter how hard I struggled to read the books Kat had left for me, the words blurred, my mind wandering elsewhere.

"Dammit, Elly," Jason muttered. "Why couldn't you have just stayed in New York and taken photos of couples and families like a normal person?"

"You're one to talk," I quipped. "One call from Division, and you're interrogating extremists at black sites, or confiscating WMDs, or going deep undercover wherever they want for as long as they want."

"It's different," he said.

"Explain to me how it is," I said, chest heaving from emotion. "Because you have a gun? Because you take out the bad guys? Who comes after your drone strike?"

I jabbed a thumb at my chest. "Surprise, it's me. And other journalists like me. We see the aftermath that Division and the other agencies have left behind. Sometimes it's better, but sometimes..." My voice cracked, recalling the images of torn-apart bodies, wondering if one might be his. "Sometimes, it's so much worse."

Jason's jaw shifted as he got up from his chair. "I need a drink," he said, rummaging through the cabinets, flanking the bookshelves. Upon discovering a bottle of scotch, he asked if I wanted one.

"Sure. Why not," I said, pursing my lips.

After filling two glasses, he slid a book over on the table, making space to set the glass before me.

"Thanks," I said, not moving. I needed to keep a clear head. If I didn't say something I'd regret and the alcohol was tempting, I'd need to pace myself. I needed Jason on my side right now, as much as it pained me to admit it. I was rapidly losing people I could trust who could help me find answers.

He swirled the glass of amber liquid and tossed it back. He peeled his lip over his teeth, sucking in a breath. "This'll do."

He poured himself another and sipped, eyeing my untouched glass.

"I never should have left you last September."

I shook my head, surprised by the admission. "Then why did you?" And just like that, I asked the question that had eaten me alive for months.

He stared at his glass. "Because I *had* to."

"Because Division 12 called."

He shook his head and looked at me. The sky blue of his eyes was haunted. "Yes, but that's not the only reason. I had to because the more time I was with you, the more I could feel it growing harder and harder to leave. I'm a top agent, and I do good things with Division. I get the wrong people off the chessboard and the right people on it." He ran a hand over the side of his face. "You, of all people, should understand."

It was my turn to drink, and I welcomed the delicious burn as the whiskey coated my tongue and throat.

"It was one of the most difficult decisions I ever made." Jason frowned. "And now..."

"Now what?" I pried.

"Now I know I chose wrong." The empty teacups left from earlier rattled as he forcefully sat the glass on the table. His eyes gripped mine, and there was no way I could look away if I wanted to. "If I'd turned down that mission, none of this would've happened. You wouldn't have come to Syria. You never would've found the crate or got that mark on your hand, and you damn well wouldn't have this new...*gift* or ability or whatever the hell is."

I shrank at the angry tone in his words, feeling like a student being scolded by a teacher but not entirely sure why I was in trouble.

I clenched my teeth, feeling my hackles lift. "But you *did* leave. And I *do* have this gift. So, the sooner you get over it, the faster we can move on and deal with the real problem."

Before I had time to react, he closed the space between us.

My traitorous heart flitted like a maniac against my rib cage as I could smell the smoky, sweet scent of the whiskey on his breath.

I pressed a hand against his chest, feeling his heartbeat under his shirt. Jason's eyes bore into mine. "No," I warned. "Don't you fucking dare do this."

I clung to my waning reserves of self-preservation. Thanks to him, I'd worked too damn hard to build these walls, and it was taking every atom of my body to keep them from crumbling.

"From the second I wake up to when I fall asleep, I think about you, Elly." He peered down at me, our faces so close I could see the pale lashes that hooded his eyes and the faint silver scar above his left eyebrow. "I wonder where you are," he continued, his voice low. "Wonder if you're alone at night, wonder if you are okay."

My skin tingled. I couldn't think, couldn't breathe. The world had evaporated, leaving nothing but me, him, and my frantic heartbeat.

"As soon as you took that statue, you put a target on your back. Whoever wants it has powerful connections, and they have already got to Division 12. I can't stop thinking how at the hotel if I had only—"

"Stop," I said breathlessly. "Just stop, okay?"

The color had drained from his face, and guilt tightened his forehead.

"Look," I said, steadying my voice even though I was still reeling from everything he'd said. "I didn't ask for this." I gestured to my hand. "You think I wanted to go on the run? Wanted to burn people alive? Wanted to worry that the people I care about are going to face the fallout from this? No, of course not. But I *have* to deal with it, and so do you."

Jason blinked, and a crooked smile appeared on his face.

"Dammit, I hate it when you're right." His brows drew together, and he leveled me with his gaze. "Fine. But just so we're clear, I don't like any of this."

I gave him a toothy grin. "Fine. You don't have to like it. You only have to help me until I stop whoever is after me and the statue, or I die."

Jason scoffed. "I'd prefer the former option."

Glad we can agree on that, at least.

He reached for my arm and slid a hand down, leaving a trail of goosebumps as he made his way down to the marking on my palm. His fingers traced the outlines of the star.

"Jason," I whispered. His eyes danced from each of mine, and I didn't back down, letting him search for whatever he needed, see everything.

"Elly," he said, and before I could react, his mouth slammed into mine. Blood whooshed in my ears, and my insides liquified. His lips were firm but soft. His gentle hand cupped the side of my face. Startled by the press of his body against mine, I placed my head on the table to keep from falling. My head swam with the rise of emotion, and my rapid heartbeat galloped in my ears.

Somebody unlocked the door handle, and the sound of metal jiggling made us both break the kiss. In one lightning-fast motion, Jason returned to his chair in the corner. My lips tingling from the kiss, I pressed them together and picked up a book, pretending I'd been reading it. Kat entered, her feet shuffling in the muck boots she'd put on.

I smiled to myself, overwhelmed by what had just occurred. Jason stared at his phone, swiping the screen as though he were attending to an important email.

I stifled a laugh, feeling like I was in middle school again.

Kat resumed her position in the chair next to me. "So, you two have fun without me? Find anything interesting?"

I shrugged and shook my head. "Nothing we didn't already know."

Kat picked up one of the empty teacups and sat it back on the saucer. She began to hum a soft melody. I squirmed in my seat when I recognized it as 'My Heart Will Go On' by Celine Dion.

Nice. Real subtle.

~

It was past noon when Kat suggested we should all take a break.

"These eyes of mine are beginning to cross," she said and exhaled. "Let's rest a bit, hmm? We can pick up this tomorrow. I can send those emails to my museum colleagues this evening, but I'm sure they won't respond until Monday."

Jason's eyes seemed distant, distracted. A shade darker than their usual ocean blue, he stared intently at a passage from an open book on the desk.

"I think I'll head to my room for a bit," I said.

"Very good," Kat said. "Let Assem know if you need anything. Dinner will be at six."

The kiss had been unexpected — and although not unwelcome — I needed some space to process all that had transpired. So, scooping up my laptop bag, I caught the door before it closed behind Kat.

~

A bottle of water and a bowl of dried fruits and nuts sat on a tray on the nightstand in my room. I sat cross-legged back on the bed with the laptop perched on my lap. The screen flickered awake, and its internal fan hummed against her knee.

I scrolled through my friend's social feeds and news and replied to emails. My favorite current playlist, classic rock circa the '70s and '80s, blared into my earbuds, transporting me to memories of my father. He'd left when I was five, and although mom had thrown away all his pictures, I could recall his face. Or at least I thought I could. I pictured his green eyes and brown hair looking like mine, sitting at a park while classic rock played on a portable radio.

The one clear memory I had: he had loved classic rock.

Steve Miller crooned while I scrolled through the mountains of mostly junk emails. Ads for camera equipment and travel insurance cluttered my inbox, and I deleted them all in a fell swoop. Several more were from U.S. presses, including the Times and USA Today, which had contract renewal statements attached, and I'd have to read those later.

Cara had forwarded a group message from her wedding Pinterest boards.

I munched on the nuts and fruit and sat back, settling on a "Looks great!" and "Pretty" as a reply to flower arrangements and centerpiece ideas.

I needed to remember to book a plane ticket home. But it'd have to wait since I had more pressing matters to attend to. Like the group of people tracking me down and trying to kill me.

The sun wavered low on the horizon when I finally powered it down. I was peering out the window when a knock came on my door.

"Yes?" I called out.

An unfamiliar man's voice spoke through the door. Tinged with an Arabic accent, he said, "Ms. Mayberry wants you to be informed it is time for dinner."

"Alright, I'll be right down."

I dabbed on some makeup and tossed my hair into a ponytail. After lacing up my boots, my thoughts lingered on Cara's wedding and the extent of fallout I'd face if I didn't go. My mom was the "queen" of guilt trips, and I suspected I'd never get the chance to live it down.

As I descended the stairs, the last of the setting sun disappeared, and the automatically timed sconces illuminated, casting a warm glow on the solarium outside and the foyer below.

In the dining room, trays of roast beef, grapes, and assorted cheeses had been spread out. My stomach growled. If I stayed here much longer, I might lose my appetite for Cup O' Noodles and be forced to learn how to actually cook a meal.

"Ah, Ella," Zhalika said, seated next to Kat. "So glad you decided to join us."

Kat flashed me a pleasant smile and resumed reading a newspaper.

I took the chair opposite them and noticed the empty one. "Where's Jason?" I asked.

Kat glanced up from her reading. "Hmm," she said. "Why, he left, dear."

CHAPTER

THIRTEEN

"He left?" I asked. "Where did he go?"

Kat frowned. "Not sure. He asked Assem to drive him but insisted he couldn't say where, only that he was looking into something that could help us."

"Did he say when he'd be back?" I pressed.

"All he told me was that he'd be back as soon as he could."

All at once, the air in the room was both too hot and too cold. A sinking sensation filled my stomach at the realization that he'd left... *again.*

"I'm sure he had his reasons," Kat said, trying to console me. "Jason isn't one to run from a problem. He'll face it head-on to find a solution, no matter how dangerous."

But she was wrong. So wrong. Jason had admitted as much in the library that his feelings for me were making him question his dedication to Division 12.

And so he *had* run from a problem. He'd run from us. From me.

Zhalika set her cloth napkin on the table and cleared her throat. "Perhaps I can find us a bottle of '72 Chateau Leoville in the kitchen."

"That sounds lovely," Kat said.

Zhalika stood. Her long black dress hugged her curves, and iridescent beads traced the outline of the low-cut neckline as she glided out of the room.

Kat handed me a bowl of pita bread, clearly looking for ways to distract me. "Eat something. I'll not have you starving over a man on my watch."

I grumbled in protest but took a piece.

"Don't be so hard on yourself," she said, sensing my thoughts. "No one is immune to love's cheeky ways. Heartbreak is a part of what it means to be human."

I spooned a few pieces of hummus onto my plate, dipped the bread, and tore off a bite.

The last night Jason and I had been together in New York, he'd ordered a bottle of champagne from room service that had cost half as much as my rent. I'd been so sure he was going to propose.

Instead, the champagne had been intended to smooth things over when he broke the news that Division 12 required him back in the field. He'd flown out the next day, leaving me alone in New York with a cold bed and a terrible hangover.

And here I was again, experiencing the worst kind of déjà vu. I'd barely had time to process what had happened in the library. No goodbye, nothing. Did he not trust me enough to tell me why he was going? It had felt like we'd finally had our first real, honest conversation. Had it all been a lie?

Zhalika re-entered, carrying a bottle of wine with a browning label and a corkscrew.

"Do the honors, Kat, love?" she cooed.

Kat pushed her chair back, opened the bottle, and handed the cork to Zhalika. Zhalika giggled and inhaled as Kat held the cork for her to smell. Then, satisfied, Kat held the cork for me.

"Whatever it is, I'll drink it," I said. The food had only made the pit in my stomach worse, and perhaps a drink wasn't the worst idea.

Kat poured three glasses to the rim, no less, with the deep violet liquid.

"Fe Sahatek!" Kat said, and Zhalika echoed the Arabic phrase for good luck but was often used for toasting.

In many Middle Eastern countries, alcohol was illegal, including in Iraq. However, since we were so near the Syrian border, it must've allowed them to acquire the liquor undetected.

As if reading my thoughts, Kat said, "It's because of the horses. We ship crates of wine back with them when we import new breeding stock from Europe."

"It's worked well so far," Zhalika said, laughing. Her cheeks were flushed, clearly already feeling the effects of the wine. "Remember when Ghazida kicked the crate in her stall?" she said, "And Amin thought she'd started to foal on the plane?"

Kat clapped her hands and grinned. "Yes! And poor Amin, he'd been terrified to fly in the first place!"

Zhalika and Kat howled with laughter as they continued their story. Each time, their voices grew louder until they were both wiping tears away with the corners of their napkins. I should've enjoyed the company of their bond—one of years of friendship and love—. But, instead, it had made my mood grow even more sour.

Taking my glass with me, I pushed my chair back quietly, attempting to slip away undetected.

"Won't you stay for dessert?" Zhalika said, seeing me try to escape. "There is a cheesecake in the fridge."

"I'm tired," I said. "I think I'll call it a night."

"Very well," Kat said. "I have a few contacts at the museums I can send word to, see if they have anything that may help us in their archives."

As I made my way to the bottom of the landing, I overheard Zhalika saying, "She's something special. Jason is a fool for not seeing that."

I heard a muffled reply from Kat but was already too far up the stairs to hear more. I opened the door to my room and threw myself onto the bed. Zhalika was right. Jason was a fool, but then didn't that make me a fool too? I hated the idea that the kiss in the library had been nothing more than a heat-of-the-moment impulse—a momentary lapse of judgment on *both* our parts.

But it had *felt* so real. So right.

His actions, however, spoke louder than his words or, in this case, kisses, no matter how good.

I kicked off my boots, flipped off the lamp, and buried myself in the covers. The air flowing off of the river was cool, and I closed my eyes, drifting off to the chorus of frogs singing outside my window.

FROM THE MOUTH of the cave, a boundless horizon lay before me. The dark-silhouetted mountain tops arched into a night sky full of shimmering stars.

Here we go again. I thought to myself, feeling the ethereal sensation of being transported to another place. Another time.

Ursa Major and Minor, Cassiopeia, Pegasus. I recalled the names of the constellations. But a single star, I didn't know, outshone all the others, ablaze with a blinding light.

I shielded my eyes as the light dimmed, and an iridescent bridge emerged from the star. It flowed down to me, ending in front of my feet like a carpet being rolled out. I looked down. My feet were bare, covered in the strange, otherworldly black sand. The overwhelming urge to cross it seized my body, and I gave in.

I placed my feet upon the translucent light beam, unconvincing it could hold me. It rippled with the press of my feet, lightly tracing my soles and between my toes. Softer than silk, my feet seemed to melt into it as I stepped out of the cave and into the night air. Through the translucent walkway, I could see the landscape of crumbled rock and sand hundreds of feet below me. The sounds of the night birds carried up to me, mixed with the plaintive howl of a jackal.

The stars twinkled in the painted smear of the Milky Way in the pitch-blackness of the sky overhead.

I continued to step along the iridescent path. My breathing was rapid and shallow at the awareness that one misstep would cause me to plunge to certain death. I titled my chin up, refusing to let the fear overtake me, and ascended. The air cooled as I gained altitude, and I knew I was nearing my destination.

A sudden tremor shook the bridge, and my arms shot out instinctively, looking for something to grab onto. But there was no handrail, nothing but open air. I fell to all fours as the bridge continued to shake. A man's voice called out from behind me, and I glanced over my shoulder.

He stood at the cave's opening by the foot of the glowing bridge, his body obscured by swirling shadows. I remained in place, frozen, as he rested his hands on the beam of light.

The bridge swayed. My fingers grasped, digging into the slippery tendrils of light. The sounds of men screaming, war drums beating, and the thud of pounding hoofbeats carried up from below. I peered through the glassy surface of the bridge. A battle had erupted. Stampeding warriors in armor brandished their spears and swords. The ground blackened as if charred by fire. Waterfalls of red erupted from the sides of the mountains, cascading into pools of blood far below.

He's causing this.

The celestial bridge lurched again as the man pulled the light toward him, as a fisherman brought in their nets.

If I only could get closer, I could make out the details of his face, find out who he was. My fingers clawed at the bridge, dragging myself along the slippery surface as if scaling a cliff wall made of gelatin. The beam of light flickered, and spider-web-like fissures materialized with each burst of discharged energy.

I willed myself onward over the dying bridge.

Every atom inside of me chanted the same phrase: *Stop him.*

Twenty feet.

I willed myself onward, my arm muscles screaming in protest.

Ten.

I saw the curve of his chin and the tip of his nose.

Five.

He tugged again at the light, drawing it to his face like a shimmering rubber band. A white-hot light burst forth from it, illuminating everything in its path.

A wave of shimmering light pulsed through the bridge one final time before it winked out. I hurled my body off it, attempting to jump the remaining distance to the cave; instead, my fingertips brushed the rocky ledge, and I fell.

I SAT UP IN BED. My heart beat frantically against my breastbone, where my shirt clung to my sweaty skin. The images scattered, flitting away into nothingness.

I knew it had been another dream, another vision, but this

one had seemed *so* real. The fall too. I'd felt the air whoosh over my face, the weightlessness as the bridge had disintegrated. I stared at my hands.

I'd touched starlight.

Just thinking it sounded insane, but I knew it to be true. Deep down in the marrow of my bones, I had felt it. I rubbed my fingertips together, remembering the silkiness, the way the light had playfully danced around my hands like little shimmering tadpoles. The feeling of the numbing coldness, though not unpleasant, had seeped into my knees, hands, and everywhere it'd touched my skin.

All of it *had* been real. And while I couldn't explain it, it had been the most important vision I'd seen yet. I'd seen the bridge. The bridge that I'd been chosen to protect.

I threw the covers off and strode to the bathroom. After splashing water on my face, I stared into the mirror as if my eyes would tell me something.

What was I missing? The others had shown me an event that had occurred long ago. This one had been *different*. The person in the shadows had modern clothing underneath, and the air seemed different, newer.

I pressed a towel to my face and breathed in the fresh scent of the cotton from its time drying in the sun.

I tossed the towel on the counter and scowled at myself in the mirror. It was useless. Not yet morning, I returned to the bedroom, deciding to catch a couple more hours of sleep.

However, the crunch of tires on gravel drew me to the open window. I held the fluttering curtains to the side and gazed at the driveway below.

A black Jeep pulled in, and the headlights blinked off. Assem exited the driver's side door and moved to the passenger's side. Two of Kat's security guards emerged from somewhere near the front of the house, and a man was pulled from the side of the jeep into their awaiting arms. His head slumped forward as they hoisted him up. With slowly mounting terror, my hands began to shake as the lights from the jeep illuminated the familiar cargo pants and tan t-shirt.

Jason.

Panic rising up to choke me, I flung myself out of the room and down the stairs, catching myself on the handrail as my knees threatened to give out. My mind lurched ahead at the multitude of reasons why he was hurt. Where had he gone? What had happened?

Was he even alive?

With the last thought, I leaped down the last three stairs, landing on the tile floor with a thud. A crowd had gathered around the doorway as Assem carried an unconscious Jason inside.

Kat, Zhalika, and two other attendants I didn't recognize, all in various styles of pajamas, were helping to guide him inside.

"Take him into my office," Kat said, holding the door for them.

Assem's big arms held Jason firm, but beads of sweat stains had formed under his arms, and his forehead knotted with effort.

Upon reaching the couch, Assem laid him down. Too many people hovered around him and blocked my view. I struggled to get closer, to lay my eyes on him.

I forcefully shoved myself between Zhalika and Assem, and if they protested, I didn't hear.

Jason's clothes were filthy. His face was the color of ash, and his lips and forehead had bloody gashes. Two purple bruises stained the skin around his jaw.

I scanned him for any other external signs of injury and breathed a sigh of relief as his chest rose and fell.

"Esam, go get the med kit from the bathroom," Kat ordered.

Esam scurried off out of the room.

Zhalika, wearing her black laced nightgown, stood near Kat, her face pinched with concern. I stepped closer, my shoulder pressed against Zhalika's in the ring of bodies that had formed around the couch.

"Thank you, Assem, for bringing him here," Kat said, her eyes meeting the towering black man. His lips were pressed firmly together, his face grim. He nodded, and his eyes darted from Kat to Jason.

Esam returned with a metal case. Zhalika took it from him and moved to Jason's side. Pulling her long nightgown up, she knelt, setting the case to her side.

"A damp rag, please?" she said without looking up.

Assem disappeared. My eyes focused on Jason's face, waiting for any signs of him stirring to consciousness. Assem returned and handed the wet washcloth to Zhalika. She took it and gently wiped Jason's forehead, moving to his neck and arms. It reminded me of the ritual baths they would give kings and Pharaohs. Methodically, painstakingly wiping a person clean of all Earthly contaminants before burial.

Fear knotted my stomach. He'll be fine. This is Jason we're talking about.

He moaned as if he'd read my mind, and his eyes flitted open. His slate blue eyes squinted in the lamplight.

"Jason," I whispered. "We're here. Are you okay?"

His eyes wandered the room, disoriented as if searching for the origin of the sound.

"Do you know where you are?" Kat asked.

Jason struggled to sit up.

"No," Zhalika said firmly and placed a hand on his arm. "You've been hurt. You need to lie down until we know you haven't suffered a brain injury."

He surrendered and relaxed his body, laying his head on the pillow.

Zhalika took a bandage from the box and dabbed a cut on his arm with alcohol. He hissed in protest.

"Since you're insisting on bleeding all over my furniture, I think an explanation is in order?" Kat demanded.

His eyes met mine, indecision flickering briefly.

"I met with my contact at Division 12," he said, his voice hoarse.

"What the actual fuck?" I said. My stomach hardened. "Why would you do that?"

Kat rested a hand on my shoulder, my body shaking with rage.

"They can't be trusted, remember? Or did you forget how they tried to kill me?"

Jason grimaced, and Zhalika patted more alcohol on the cuts on his hands.

"I didn't have a choice. I thought there was one I could still trust," he said, then added, "I did trust him."

My palm tingled; my power was aroused by my emotions. I flexed my fingers, feeling them bloom and grow. I needed to get out of here before I said anything I regretted or did anything I regretted, like accidentally making *this* the time to freak Zhalika and Assem out with my magical abilities.

"You've put my entire household in danger," Kat said, ignoring me as I stood and retreated to the doorway. "I hope you gained something useable out of this little excursion?"

"My contact, Brian," Jason said, refusing to look at me. "He found out the person who hacked into my email is the same one that hacked into the museums and research departments for the past year. They've set their search perimeters to pick up when keywords are used in an email."

"What words?" Kat pressed.

Jason shifted his body and squeezed his eyes. "I don't know. I'm assuming ones related to archaeological sites and Sumerian statues."

I chewed my lip. Like an obedient but steadily growing more impatient dog, my power awaited me to command it. And I wanted to, oh, how I wanted to unleash it, dig into the anger and hurt from the fallout of Jason's reckless actions pour from me in powerful gusts, igniting the furniture and the curtains, watching as the pipes burst and flooded the house.

The hair on my arms and the back of my neck lifted.

This was so not good. The magic was making me think things, *bad* things.

I fled to the front door, sidestepping around a hovering Assem and down the front steps into the night air. The mark on my hand burned, and I stuffed it under my armpit. The power coursed through me, writhing as it heated my blood.

I ignored where I was going, driven only by the need to distance myself from everyone, and ended up in a secluded garden of citrus trees and rose bushes. The delicate scent of lemon and orange touched my nose as I worked to steady my breathing. I sat on a bench seat made of ceramic tiles and wrought iron legs and armrests. I needed to stay calm. I still didn't know my limitations and was working off of pure instinct, a fact that was becoming increasingly alarming. I had no guide, no teacher.

If I wanted to figure out how to wield this power safely, I needed to figure it out on my own.

I released my hand from where I'd wedged it under my armpit and stared at the mark on my hand. The exterior lights from the house filtered through the leaves of the trees, and a faint shimmer passed over the surface of the mark as if acknowledging my attention.

The little knowledge I had discovered was that my magic

was tied to my emotions. When I'd summoned it before, it had been when I was frightened or angry.

But that couldn't be the only way I triggered it, could it? If I was a protector, a guardian, as Enheduanna had so assuredly told me, I had to have full control of it, regardless of where I was pissed off or fighting for my life.

I plucked an unripe lemon from a tree branch that dangled over my left shoulder. Its skin was still green with a light dusting of yellow.

I centered it on my palm directly over my mark. I stared at it, clearing my mind from any intrusive thoughts. No fear. No anger. No...nothing.

The magic gathered, trickling down my arm until a warmth grew in my hand. Nothing happened. I twisted my mouth in thought. Perhaps I needed to give it direction. But what? Explode? Liquify? Catch fire?

The magic reacted at once, leaching from my hand into the fruit. Tiny flames flickered over the rind as if I'd doused it in alcohol and lit it. The little fire danced, leaving sooty smears over the surface, rapidly blackening it. The smell of caramelized sugar and charcoal permeated the air.

Okay. That was a start.

I tugged the magic back, and to my surprise, it came willingly.

A laugh burst from my lips, delighted at my small victory.

"Are you alright, dear?" Kat asked.

My spine stiffened, startled by her voice.

Shit, how much had she seen? I gave myself a second to compose myself, subtly tossing the charred lemon into the rose bushes, and stood.

Kat stepped into the small clearing wearing a cotton robe. "Assem said you left in a hurry. I just wanted to check that everything was okay."

I forced a smile and wiped the remaining sticky residue on the side of my shirt.

"Yeah, I'm all good," I said, although my voice sounded strained. Then added, "It was getting crowded in there and needed some air."

Kat slowly tilted her chin to the side. "It was a shock to us all to see him like that. And it is understandable." She gestured toward herself. "Why don't you come back inside? I think there's something you need to hear."

I wrapped my arms around myself and followed. With every step back to the house, the flood of emotions followed, seeping into my aching neck muscles and forming knots in my stomach.

Back in Kat's office, Jason was sitting upright. Some of the color had returned to his cheeks. His eyes located me and darkened with concern. Kat moved a chair and motioned for me to sit.

"I'll stand, thanks," I said, and Kat waved a dismissive hand, muttering something about being surrounded by stubborn people.

Zhalika gathered a pile of bloody gauze and bandages from the table and left the room. Her eyes passed over me, and a smile crept onto her face, and I couldn't help but smile back.

Kat clapped her hands. "As you were saying..."

Jason coughed and winced, his hand clutching his shoulder.

"Brian managed to trace the hacker to an IP address in Dubai. After I'd told him I needed more information, he'd hired a Blackhat to trace it since the hacker had pinged it worldwide, trying to hide its origin."

"Dubai?" Kat asked.

Jason nodded. "The branch office of Kane United, to be exact."

My ears perked at the name. Kane United was a US-based corporation that had made millions in cell phone technology, then billions in alternative energy. You couldn't drive two blocks in New York without seeing their name on a billboard or TV commercials.

"Kane United sponsors many archaeological projects here and is a large donor for museums," Kat said. "Why on earth would they need to steal the information when they could so easily ask for it?"

Jason shrugged. "I don't know, and we were ambushed before he could tell me more. Someone had followed him. We got separated. I told him to run, but he didn't listen…" his words faded. The tendons in his neck tensed.

"They shot him," he continued. "There must've been twenty at least, and I shot my way out of there. I took out a dozen of the bastards before my clip was dry, and then I got the hell out."

For a while, the room was silent. Finally, Kat stood and exchanged words with Assem about increasing shifts in security.

I didn't move, keeping my arms crossed firmly in front of me.

Zhalika returned and helped him remove his shirt so she could place a gauze bandage on a four-inch-long gash bleeding on his right shoulder—a graze from a bullet, from the looks of it. My chest tightened at how close he'd been to dying. Was this the norm for him, though? Just a part of his daily job?

I clenched my jaw so tight I swear I would crack my molars at the flat line of his stomach and defined shoulder and arm muscles.

No. I refused to allow my anger at him to waiver just because he looked a-freaking-mazing.

I inhaled sharply as the tease of light hair on his chest called forth memories of when I'd traced my finger down the length of his body in an effort to commit each freckle, each scar, to memory. Jason raised his left hand to hold the gauze while

Zhalika taped it, exposing his forearm and black Delta Force squad tattoo.

Tattoo.

The word jolted me from my increasingly growing impure thoughts. The man from my dream who'd broken the bridge had been hidden in shadows, except for the split second he'd cupped his hands and drank, for lack of a better term, the starlight. My pulse raced as the image materialized in my mind's eye. On the back of his hand, between his thumb and forefinger, there had been a tattoo of a black bird with its wing spread as if taking flight.

A phoenix.

A phoenix was *the* logo of Kane United.

FOURTEEN

The pain meds Zhalika gave Jason caused him to nod off soon after, and a yawning Kat shooed everyone to bed, including myself.

But running on fumes herself, Kat had no patience for my protests and threatened to have Assem carry me to my bedroom if I didn't obey.

She watched me from the hallway as I closed the door feeling fifteen again when Mom had caught me sneaking in late from a party.

My mind buzzed as I lay back on the bed. The ramifications of the connections between Jason's discovery and my dream haunted me. There was no way I was going to sleep. However, the next thing I heard was a knock at the door and Assem's voice.

"Ms. Mayberry has requested your presence."

I wiped the sleep from my eyes as the daylight beam shone through the gaps in the curtains.

"Alright," I grumbled. "Be right there."

My head pounded like I was nursing a hangover, and even

after brushing my teeth and washing my face, I barely felt human. Mysterious creatures with gaping mouths that swallowed everything in their path had plagued my sleep, leaving me restless and exhausted.

I yawned, meeting Kat in the foyer. She appeared to have showered, applied makeup and styled her gray hair into a half-ponytail. For a woman in her seventies, I was in awe of her energy levels. "How's Jason?" I asked.

"He's alright, dear, just resting. Besides the cut to his shoulder and some nasty bruises, I think he'll be right as rain in a few days."

That was good, at least. However, I was still angry that he'd gone off on that mission without telling me. But I had to admit, *it* had proved useful. And while we now knew more of who was after the statue, we still didn't know why or how long we had before they did find me or it.

"In the meantime," Kat said. "I think it'd be good if you got out and got a spot of fresh air," then added when she'd noticed my hesitation. "I'll leave Assem with him. He'll come to fetch us if he wakes up."

I dragged my teeth over my lower lip and nodded. Maybe fresh air would clear the fog from my brain.

Kat led me out of the back of the house and through a side door that exited onto a courtyard. "Zhalika is down at the broodmare barn," she said as Assem handed her a basket, giving me a slight nod.

"We've had three foals born this week," she said. "Care to accompany me while I bring her lunch?"

"Sure," I said.

"Excellent," Kat said and grinned.

I followed Kat through the courtyard under a pergola with bright flowers in reds and oranges in full bloom. The lightly sweet scent tickled my nose, and I breathed it in.

Kat flipped her sunglasses off her head and continued along a stone path. The sounds of horses and the smell of hay drifted up to greet us. And soon after, two large barns with clay-tiled roofs came into view.

The house perched on a high knoll while the stables sprawled in a valley below. Round arenas and paddocks with yellow-painted wooden fences bordered the barns to the left. Further in the distance, the browns and blacks of horses grazed in the pastures along the banks of the Euphrates. The green grass edge gradually faded to parched yellow the further it grew from the river.

We paused at the top of the path, gazing at the view.

"Lovely, isn't it?" Kat said.

"It is," I said, as my eyes took in the details of lush trees and young horses kicking and bucking as they played in the fields.

We made our way down the path, soon catching up to Kat's lilting gait. For a woman in her seventies, she was in remarkable shape. At the bottom, the foot trail passed by a stack of hay to the right and the arenas and pasture to the left. I counted at least a dozen people, mostly young men but a few women attending to the various chores at the barn, filling troughs, mucking stalls, or feeding. The stalls had both an interior window and an exterior. Kat chose the interior one. The shade provided a pleasant relief from the blaring sun as they entered. Within seconds, horses' heads popped out of their stalls. A chestnut with a narrow stripe down his handsome face nickered to Kat.

She grinned and pulled a broken carrot from her pocket. The brass nameplate on the front of the stall said: "Abu Zazari."

"This is Zaz," she said, feeding him the carrot. "He's one of the original stallions we purchased ten years ago. A lightning-fast racer in his youth, he's since retired to the breeding shed for the remainder of his days."

Zaz crunched the carrot happily and immediately craned his long neck to me. I stroked the stallion's face and laughed as he greedily nudged me for more treats.

Moving further into the barn, Kat introduced me to more of the horses. An old gray gelding who was nearly white. A bay mare that was entered to run at a racetrack the following week. A yearling colt they hoped would replace Zaz as their top stallion.

We passed under a covered walkway, shielding us from the mid-day sun, and entered the adjacent barn. The stalls in here were spaced wider apart, and in several, I saw mares either heavily pregnant or with foals by their sides.

Zhalika emerged from a middle stall, wearing knee-high riding boots and jeans. Her pink polo shirt was dirty and stained.

She slid the stall door closed, spotting Kat and me.

"Oh, lunch," Zhalika said, wiping sweat from her brow.

"Yes, it's something normal people do around noon," Kat said.

Zhalika rolled her eyes. "It's foaling season. There is no normal schedule." She said, using air quotes around the word 'normal.'

She kissed Kat on the cheek and took the basket from her. She motioned us to a circle of chairs at the end of the barn under a covered porch. "Some of the mares give us early signs," she said, sitting. "The others," she let out a light laugh. "They like to surprise us unexpectedly with no signs until we peek into their stall and find a perfectly healthy foal frolicking around its mama."

We sat in the chairs under a collection of fans that hung from the rafters, and the air instantly cooled by twenty degrees. Zhalika opened the basket after setting it on her lap. She withdrew a water bottle and rummaged again inside, finding a sandwich.

"How's Jason doing?" she asked after taking a bite.

Kat and I exchanged a look. I was grateful when Kat took the lead and answered. "Better, I suppose. I have Assem watching him, and we'll go up in a bit and check to see if he's awake."

Zhalika merely nodded since her mouth was full.

A young woman, late teens perhaps, appeared from behind them. Under her headscarf, her dark hair had been cut shoulder length. She wore dirty jeans, a T-shirt, and boots. A horrendous burn dimpled the flesh on the right side of her pretty face. She wore an eye patch over her right eye.

She spoke Arabic and glanced at Kat and me first before talking to Zhalika. "I did as you asked for Amira, but she still seems restless."

Zhalika forced down the last bite of her sandwich and stuffed the wrapper in the basket. She picked up the water bottle and nodded to the girl before standing.

"Thanks again for lunch," she said, leaning down to kiss Kat.

Kat whispered something in Zhalika's ear and picked up the basket.

From where we sat, we had a direct view of the arena and could see horses being led back and forth along the corridor between the barns and the arena. Barrels overflowed with flowers and bushes along the edges of the barn and corners of the arena. Horses' coats gleamed, and their hooves were polished and neatly trimmed.

When we were in high school, my stepfather had taken Cara and me to the racetrack in Santa Anita. These horses were nothing like the leggy, tall thoroughbreds I'd seen there. These were smaller, with large nostrils and dished faces, and held their long tails up high, waving like flags behind them.

"Arabians, am I right?" I asked.

Kat's cheeks wrinkled around her eyes. "Indeed, they are," her eyes looked wistful. "'Created by the gods from the desert sand and wind,' or at least that's how the legend goes."

"But how—"

"How do I keep them all?" she answered. "I can't take all the credit; that's where my Zhalika comes in. While I do admire the gorgeous animals, Zhalika is the true horsewoman. Her father bred and raised Arabians for wealthy sheiks. However, with the economic downturn, many horses were stolen or slaughtered. So, she's procured them at various horse markets, including Baghdad. I won't lie; some cost a pretty penny, but we can sell them easily for double what we paid for them in Europe or the United States."

The thought of such frivolous use of money among such squalor made me cringe. "I don't understand," she said. "The price of one of these horses could pay for a month's food supply at a refugee camp."

Kat raised an eyebrow, looking taken aback by the harsh tone of my words. "Of course, you're right, dear, but—"

"How can you sit here among all this?" I said, getting to my feet. I'd heard enough and wanted this conversation to be over with. "When families are torn apart, and more children are orphaned daily?"

Kat pursed her lips as if waiting for me to finish.

Blood boiling, I got to my feet. "Here you are, drinking your fancy wine and wearing fine clothes, and not ten miles West, people are starving!"

My chest heaved as Kat sat, unmoving, her face twisted in thought.

"I want to show you something. Would you follow me?" Kat said and immediately stood, not waiting for me to answer.

The short woman tottered out from under the porch and toward the arena. I shook my head, confused by the lack of reaction to what I'd just accused her of, but then had to choose to follow.

In the arena, three horses were being worked, two ridden and one being long-lined. They trotted in the shade along a grove of trees, their hides slick with sweat.

Kat paused at the fence and rested an elbow over the top rail. I came up beside her and stood to the left of her shoulder.

"You see that young man over there," Kat said, pointing to the man on the ground lunging a young gray mare. "That is Qadir. He's been with us for two years this Summer. He's seventeen. His entire family was killed in a military strike." Kat's eyes grew distant as she gazed out toward the boy. "They'd sat down for dinner when Qadir's mother had asked him to retrieve a birthday present for his father. A missile struck the side of their house, and Qadir watched his home burn, clutching his father's wrapped gift in his hands."

I swallowed, unsure what to say.

Shit, now *I* feel like an ass.

Kat rested her back against the fence rails and motioned to a woman and older man attending to a pair of water buckets. "Sayyid and Jasmin came a few months ago. Jasmin lost both her husband and son to suicide bombers. Sayyid is her father. His brother joined a cell and was responsible for the attack at an apartment complex."

"Okay," I said, a little tentative. "What are you trying to say?"

Kat flicked an annoyed look toward me. "This." She motioned around her. "Is more than meets the eye. Violence has affected all these people you see in one way or another. We welcome them here, providing a decent wage and housing, and transport out of the country if needed."

My eyes widened. Had I heard what I thought I heard? They were smuggling immigrants out of Iraq. And to think I'd raised a judgmental eyebrow at their contraband wine last night.

I narrowed my eyes, meeting Kat's solemn gaze. "You can't be serious."

Kat knocked on the wood rail behind her. "Serious as a heart attack."

"But how?"

"The same as the wine." Kat shrugged. "When we export horses out of the country, we have to send a few hired hands to go along as well to tend to the horses en route, make sure they're cared for, fed, and are looked after. And once they're safely delivered to their new owners, wherever that may be, there are times we get only the empty shipping containers back."

I chuffed a laugh. I couldn't believe it. It was almost *too* clever to work, yet it clearly did.

"And you've never been—" I trailed off.

"Been caught?" Kat supplied and shook her head. "Not yet, and we hope to keep it that way." She shot me a stern don't-tell-a-soul-or-I'll-kill-you-myself look, and I shrank quickly, nodding my head. I felt honored that Kat had disclosed such a secret to her. I'd never betray it. However, someday, they'd get caught. The authorities would get tipped off eventually and shut them down. But until that day, I hoped I could help many more lives.

"Does Jason know about this?" I asked.

Kat laughed. "Of course. Every time he's been stationed nearby, he'll request a few days' leave and come visit. You know how a keen observer he is. It was only a matter of time before he noticed the high turnover rate among the staff."

I pursed my lips and asked the question that had been bothering me for some time. "So, remind me again. How do you know Jason?"

"Don't you know, dear?" Kat said, tilting her head.

"When we were together." I inhaled a deep breath. "He kept the conversation light. Division 12 forced him to keep secrets, and this barrier felt like it was always between us."

Kat shook her head in agreement. "Yes, unfortunately, that does happen in people like Jason's situation." She scrunched her face in thought. "Jason's mother, Susan, was an assistant professor at Cambridge when I was heading the Archeology department. After Jason was born, Susan worked part-time at the community college, and with no real family of her own, she'd fly over to London to visit me in the Summer. She couldn't come every year, of course, but she came enough that I got to see Jason grow into the man he is today."

I knew his mom had worked at the community college, but he'd never told me about her being at Cambridge. I wonder if something had happened for her to lose the position that Jason was ashamed of. "So, you were close to Jason?"

"As close as I suppose anyone can be with him."

Glad I wasn't the only one that felt that way.

"He sends me email updates, holiday cards."

I licked my lips and watched the horse being led back to the stables. "Then you know about us and how it ended."

Kat's face went grave. "I must admit, he didn't look the same in the photos he sent after you broke up. He was not as happy, and I missed seeing his smiling face in those pictures. So handsome, you know?"

I knew. The rare site would snatch the breath right from my lungs. I'd desperately tried to capture a mental image of it as much as I did with my camera.

"If you want any love advice from an old gal, which I'm

quite certain you don't, don't close your heart yet. 'Like desert storms, rain doesn't choose where it falls. It merely does."

This was the most I'd spoken about Jason to anyone. Even my mother, who'd only met him once, knew very little of my time with him or the reasons behind what had happened at the end. Something about this funny old woman made her easy to talk to. Whatever it was, I had to admit, it had felt good.

Kat showed me the yearling barn, introducing me to horses and people alike as we snacked on the chips and sliced veggies Zhalika hadn't eaten. From the sounds of it, they were expecting a good foal crop this year. Zhalika had arranged breedings with her top mares to select stallions in Syria, Lebanon, and Iraq.

Once flourishing in the Middle East, the horse industry took a heavy hit after horse racing was outlawed in the 70s. Since the ease in tensions, breeders had begun to see the market improve, and horse racing was thriving. However, Kat's previous years had not been so. The farm was self-sufficient, but it'd been years since she'd seen a profit.

"How do you survive then without making anything from the horses?" I had asked as we strolled past the rows of stalls.

"My pension from Cambridge helps, but mostly from my dear husband, Reginald. Bless his soul. He served for 38 years as a Navy captain before his heart finally gave out. To my surprise, I was left with a hefty life insurance policy he hadn't told me about and the remainder of his pension."

Kat had been married to a man. I fathomed I could spend weeks talking to her and still not know her whole life story.

We paused at an oval track as the bay mare from earlier galloped by in a rush of thundering hoofbeats, and Kat cupped her hands and shouted, "She's looking brilliant, Hakim," at the rider.

"Ms. Katherine, Ms. Dawson," Assem said, having appeared next to us. I swore, if I didn't see the guy walk, I'd think he apparated like the ghostly forms of people moving in long-exposure panoramic shots.

"Has there been an update on Jason?" Kat said, turning to address him.

Assem's eyes flitted to my face before settling back on Kat's. "Yes. He is awake."

***

By the time Kat and I entered the study, Jason was standing. His bare chest was exposed, displaying the full extent of his beating in the light of day.

I sucked in a breath through clenched teeth. Although the bruises were several shades of blue and green, his face seemed less swollen. He slung his shirt over one arm, pulling the sleeve over his bicep. He repeated the same on the other side and cussed as the fabric snagged on his right shoulder.

Before I knew what I was doing, I was by his side, grabbing at the neck of his shirt so it could more easily slide over the bandage.

Jason's body stilled at the touch of my fingers, but I didn't stop. I could be mad at him, but that didn't mean I was cold-hearted.

"Assem told us you were up," Kat said. "How are you feeling?"

I re-joined Kat in the center of the room.

"I've been worse," he said. "I know one thing; I can't stay

here when a mole is chewing its fucking way through Division 12."

My body tensed at the anger contained in his voice. Of course, he was angry. Division 12 was everything to him. More than a job, it was his purpose. He'd given up everything, including me, to dedicate himself to it completely.

And now... now it was tarnished, the shine worn off as the impossibly high pedestal he'd placed it on had collapsed.

He sat on the couch, found his boots from where Assem had taken them off the night before, and began pulling them on.

"What are you doing?" I asked, but I already knew the answer.

"Like I said," he said, not looking up from where he laced his boot. "Someone inside Division 12 is aiding a potential terrorist group. I've got to find out who."

"Do you even hear what you're saying?" I said, my voice raising an octave higher than I would've liked. "You can't go back out there. If they see you, they will kill you."

I grappled with the fear enveloping my body, seizing the breath from my lungs.

His shoulders slumped as he hung his arms off his knees, looking defeated. "I know. But the longer I stay here, the more danger I'm putting all of you in. All because of that goddamn statue. And we won't find anything more sitting around here."

He was right. I had to agree. Kane United was a big freaking company with thousands of employees, any of whom could've had a fanboy tattoo. We'd moved from searching for a needle in a haystack to searching for a needle in a pile of needles.

"Stubborn as a mule," Kat muttered, moving over to him. Fresh blood had soaked through the gauze and Jason's shirt. "You're in no shape to do anything except get yourself killed," Kat called for Assem to bring the first aid kit.

Jason cursed at the sight of the blood and sank back onto the loveseat.

"Kat's right, you know," I said, resting a hand on my hip. "Unless you plan to go to Division 12 headquarters and interrogate each agent one by one, it's better if you stay here."

Jason lifted an eyebrow as if he were actually considering it.

I scoffed and shook my head. He had balls, that was for sure. But if he went out there injured and half-cocked, he could get captured or killed. Both of which were *not* scenarios I was ready for.

"Look," I said, sitting on an armchair across from him. "Kat has security personnel that the agency won't recognize. They can drive by where you and Brian were ambushed and see if anything was left behind."

The muscle in Jason's jaw ticked. What I was asking him to do went against everything he believed in. He was a soldier, a warrior. He took the lead, pistol in hand, and led the charge.

"Screw it. Okay," he said, leaning back. Then he added, narrowing his gaze on me, "One day. I'll give them one day to find anything, and then we're out of here. I can find another place for us to lie low, and the agency can't track us too."

One day wasn't remotely close enough for his shoulder to heal, but I knew it was all I could convince him of. "Okay," I said. "One day."

Kat re-entered with a washcloth, first aid kit, and fresh bandages.

Jason had changed into a button-up shirt, and with Kat's assistance, he had it undone and his shoulder exposed. He rested his elbow on a throw pillow, allowing Kat to examine it. She grimaced and gently pried off the ends of the athletic tape. Six butterfly bandages cinched together the edges of the wound, and blood oozed from it as Kat dabbed it with alcohol.

It didn't look infected, which was good.

I told her the suggestion about sending some of her security while Jason stayed here while she worked to apply a new bandage. She'd agreed and mentioned that Assem would oversee it.

"I'll speak to him as soon he returns from errands with Zhalika." She gathered the discarded bandages and alcohol. "I suggest you make use of your decision and get some rest." She turned from Jason, raised her eyebrows at me, and left.

I stood and wiped my hands on my pants. Jason peered up at me, the front of his shirt still open, exposing his chest and firm abs. "I.." I stuttered, feeling suddenly nervous. "I'll see you later."

"Elly," he said, stopping me as I made my way to the door.

Our eyes met. "I know you're pissed, and I'm sorry for not telling you where I went." He swallowed, his throat bobbing. "I didn't want you to be liable if my guy turned on me and Division 12 somehow found their way back to you. I did it to protect you."

My heart fluttered at the earnestness in his eyes. I'd caught a guy on fire, and he thought I needed protecting. I worried my lip and glanced at the mark on my hand as an idea occurred to me.

My eyes returned to his. "What if you didn't have to?"

"What do you mean?" he asked.

"I'm saying you have a gun and like training on fighting and stuff, and I have." I showed him my palm. "This."

Jason lifted his chin, studying my face and trying to decipher what I was getting to.

I sighed. "Remember when you got your new pistol?"

Jason nodded.

"What was the first thing you did with it?"

"I inspected it," he said flatly. "Then took it to the range and sighted it in." Recognition dawned on his face, and he lifted his eyebrows.

I tapped my hand. "I've used this gift once, and it had been pure instinct. I'm terrified to use it because I don't know how. But if I did..."

He stared at me as if I'd suddenly sprouted a third eye. "You want me to help you, 'sight in your magic'?" He shook his head and laughed at the ridiculous way it sounded.

"Yeah, exactly," I said, grinning.

"Alright," he said, surprising me with how quickly he'd agreed.

"These meds are kicking my ass, so give me a power nap so Kat doesn't bust my balls, and we'll do it."

I thanked him and left, smiling like an idiot all the way up to my bedroom. It finally felt like I was taking control. I'd been wrong last night. I did have a mentor. Jason was a soldier, a protector just like me. While I used magic, he used guns and knives, but fundamentally, we were the same. Enheduanna had assigned me as a guardian but had said nothing about me having to do it alone.

While Jason rested, I found Kat in the library scribbling notes from a giant reference book that Jack and Rose could've shared—yes, this is the hill I'd die on — and told her about the plans we'd discussed.

She'd hesitated at first for fear of the staff witnessing my magic but quickly agreed when I consented to her suggestion of having Assem accompany us to make sure everyone else on the estate, and we were safe.

The downside to the deal was that Assem would now be a third person who knew of my abilities. However, Kat assured me he wasn't a superstitious man and would be fine so long as we didn't directly involve him in the tests.

No worries there. I didn't even want Jason involved but

needed someone there in case I, you know, caught myself on fire or something.

Maybe this was a bad idea.

Before I could back out, Kat had summoned Assem and told him to take Jason and me to an abandoned rock quarry on the north side of the property.

She was vague on the details but assured him I'd explain why when we were all here. Assem's face had remained blank, and I almost believed that Kat was right about him not being freaked out by my gifts, and it would make more sense to show him than explain.

A few hours later, I met Jason and Assem in the study. Jason had showered and dressed in dark-washed jeans, a black t-shirt, and aviator sunglasses. His shoulders and back were straight, revealing no obvious signs that he had been injured.

Assem gestured for the door, and we followed.

Jason patted the sidearm on his hip. "Kat told him and the other household staff we would do some target shooting."

That wasn't all that far from the truth.

Assem led us in the opposite direction of the stables, crossing by the familiar grove of fruit trees and down a dirt road used for access to the perimeter fence enclosing the property.

The river glittered far off to our left as the landscape shifted to a series of small rolling hills.

One hill had been dug into, and below it were piles of sand-stone rocks and gravel. We maneuvered by a rusted excavator overlooking a murky, shallow pool of water.

In the hill's shade, Assem halted.

"Ms. Mayberry wanted my discretion, and I will never betray her trust." He cleared his throat. "However, my duty is to protect the property and those that live and work here. Should I discover any threats to it, I will need to intervene."

When it was obvious he was waiting for me to say

something, I said, "Okay, so the target shooting was all bull-shit." I explained about finding the statue and somehow gaining its magical ability. I omitted the part about Kane United somehow being connected and the visions of a four-thousand-year-old dead priestess talking to me in my dreams.

Better to give it in small doses.

Assem had reacted just like Kat had said he would. With a curt nod, he'd told us he'd remain nearby in case we needed any assistance and made his way to stand, hands clasped behind his back in the shade of a copse of olive trees.

Jason turned to me and rested his hands on his hips. "Alright, so we're here. What now?"

"Uh," I said, searching the piles of rocks. "Start with what I know, I guess?"

He scratched the back of his neck. "Fine. Tell me what you know."

"I know. It's tied to my emotions." I stared at the ground, realizing several times the emotions that had set it off had been triggered by my feelings for him. I drifted my eyes up again. "Like when I'm scared or pissed. And it seems like I have to use this hand to touch whatever I want to affect."

Jason nodded, considering my words. "And it works on...everything?"

I twisted my mouth in thought, recalling the smell of the burning clothes and screams of the dying man. If I survived all of this, I was going to need so much therapy when I returned home. "I honestly don't know," I said in response to his question.

Jason clapped his hands together. "Then that's where we need to start."

Over the next thirty minutes, Jason found different things around the quarry for me to test my magic on. One by one, he'd place it on a table-sized hunk of sandstone, and I'd do my best to summon my magic.

I easily set fire to a dry twig that had fallen from the olive tree, smoldered a piece of cotton torn from Jason's shirt, and caused the water on the pond's surface to boil and steam.

However, when Jason handed me a wrench from the excavator's toolbox, I could do nothing. My magic was there, eagerly reacting as if my using it so much had excited it, but the metal handle remained cold, hard, and unaffected.

"So, that's a no on metal," I said, tilting my head.

Jason pursed his lips. "I was beginning to think you didn't have a limit. At least now we know."

I set the wrench on the stone, wondering what it meant I couldn't alter it.

"It is the chemistry," Assem said flatly as if ordering a cup of coffee.

Jason and I jumped, having both forgotten he'd been there.

"It is not organic like wood, water, stone like marble or limestone, and petroleum products like plastic.

"Metal doesn't have carbon, and neither does sand."

Understanding flickered across Jason's face.

"I think he's right," he said. "Try this." He bent and scooped up a handful of sand.

He poured it into my hand, the grains smooth and warm from the sun. I cupped it in my palm, willing the magic to alter it. But same as the wrench, nothing. It was as though I couldn't sense it, like the molecules that made it up were invisible.

"Hmm," Jason said, pulling out his phone. He showed me a quick internet search for what materials have carbon in them, and I scanned the website meant for fifth graders. All animals, plants, some stones, air, of course, and surprisingly enough, diamonds were pure carbon.

"Carbon materials only.," he said. "Check." He smiled,

looking a little more than excited. "Now we know *what* you can effect; let's see how *long* you can do it."

Acting as normal, as if he were coaching me for a marathon and not having me manipulate matter, Jason timed me on his phone for the next few hours to see how long I could keep the twig ablaze or a snowball made from carbon dioxide from melting. At first, it'd been easy, but as the afternoon waned, my neck and shoulders ached, and sweat dripped from my brows.

Also, I was hungry. Like, I could eat five hamburgers and ask for a milkshake hungry.

Proving once again that Assem was some level of psychic who knew our needs before we did, he had left briefly to return with a golf cart carrying chairs, a table, and food. Without waiting for Jason's permission, I wiped the residue of soot clinging to my hands on my jeans and went to join Assem.

The broad-shouldered man had seated himself in a folding chair next to a table next to what could've been a scene from a Regency romance movie. A white cloth fluttered on top of a round table with square-cut tea sandwiches, a two-tiered silver platter, a pitcher of water, and crystal glasses placed upon it.

The three of us sat, eating the sandwiches, quenching our thirst with the ice-cold water, and discussing the theories of my power's limitations. Assem mostly listened, although occasionally, he'd add a bit of science beyond mine and Jason's scope. I was a history major, and my knowledge of chemistry had ended the second I didn't need to take it anymore for my degree.

It was dark by the time we returned to the estate. Jason and I were walking while Assem ferried the supplies back from lunch.

I could tell Jason was more relaxed now that we'd gained some insight into my abilities. And, although I was tired, I, too, felt a peace I hadn't felt in a while, a hope that maybe Enheduanna hadn't been wrong about choosing me.

Assem waited for us at the door.

"Ms. Mayberry would like you to attend her dinner."

Jason and I both laughed at the formal tone he'd assumed the second he'd been back in the house. He'd literally witnessed my magical ability, which was as near to seeing anything intimate on a person, and yet acted like we were no more significant than any other guest.

I tried not to be offended since his cold demeanor would keep the other staff members from becoming suspicious.

Jason and I went to our separate rooms, and I stripped off my boots and dirty jeans and took a quick shower to rinse off the dust and sand.

Kat had left a flower-printed sundress on the bed with a note: *Embrace the rain.*

I slipped it on and combed my hair, left it down to air dry.

Everyone had assumed their usual positions at the table, and three sets of eyes watched as I entered.

Most of all, I had Jason's rapt attention; the intensity of his blue eyes fixed upon me stole the air from my lungs. Jason cleared his throat. "Whoa, Elly."

Kat and Zhalika exchanged a knowing look and shared the same smug expressions.

"The dress is one of my favorites," Zhalika said. "It is lovely on you."

"Thank you," I murmured, suddenly self-conscious at the heat of Jason's stare.

We were served a delicious lamb soup with fresh herbed cheese, pita, and roasted eggplant. It felt nice to play pretend and eat a nice meal in fancy clothes. One could almost forget that we were days away from a celestial gate opening and unleashing whatever the hell had destroyed the Akkadian empire.

Protect the bridge, save the world.

That was what I planned to do. But first, I had to locate the bridge, all while trying not to get captured or killed before then. And then, somehow, when I found it, I used the magic I hardly understood to seal it and stop a person with powerful connections from crossing it.

Sure. No problem. It's just the fate of the world in my hands.

We were so screwed.

Jason's laugh crossed the table as Kat, and he conversed. I sighed. Then there was him, and all the confusing feelings of being around him again were dredging up.

I refilled my wine glass, making it my mission to drain it.

As we ate, the discussions were mostly about the horses, but they eventually leaned more toward politics and Iraq's economy. Throughout it, however, I felt Jason's attention. He kept stealing glances at me as he sipped wine or only half-listened to the conversations while keeping track of me through the corner of his eye. Whether he knew I was aware of his staring or not, it didn't stop him.

The longer I stayed, the more I questioned my feelings toward his rapt attention. Past, Ella would've eaten it up and asked for seconds, but Ella hadn't woken up with Jason in sharing her bed and then been blindsided when he'd walked out the door and hadn't come back.

And the truth was, until yesterday, the lines defining who Jason was to me had been firmly set. My feelings toward him are defined by rigid boundaries. We hadn't spoken in months, and I still couldn't get over the fact he'd even answered when I'd called, but now...*things*, preconceptions were changing by the second as if I were straddling the side of a sand dune.

Eventually, when the plates were clean, I made a break for it and stood. "Thank you again for hosting us and for the delicious food," I said, setting my napkin on the table.

Jason watched me as I said goodnight to everyone and

escaped to my room. I'd made significant progress today with my magic, thanks to Jason. But I'd also realized what he planned next for us was wrong. His idea that we could keep running from safe house to safe house was unrealistic. I couldn't deny the truth just because I wanted to. This very second, people were searching for me and *now* for him. Corrupted Division agents that had years of professional training in torture, tracking, and killing.

I couldn't hide forever. It was time I left; everyone would be safer if I were on my own.

This would be my last night here. Tomorrow, I'd leave in the morning for Baghdad.

SIXTEEN

I lay on my bed, my thoughts swirling with my plan to leave tomorrow.

Assem would drive me. At least, I thought, if I could convince him too, which might give me enough time to disappear in Baghdad before Assem returned and Jason discovered what had happened.

A knock on the door interrupted my thoughts, and I sat up.

"Yes?" I called out.

"Hey, it's me," Jason said.

I hesitated. I'd been holding out hope that I could slip out undetected tomorrow and not have to face him. My poker face was good, but Jason was a freaking walking lie detector.

He knocked again. "I come bearing a gift," he said. His voice was soft and enticing.

What was I going to do? Tell him to fuck off? Yeah, like *that* would work. If anything, it'd make him *even* more suspicious.

I sighed and swung my legs over the side of the bed. "Yeah, okay, come in."

The door opened, and he stepped inside wearing the same button-up over a t-shirt and black jeans from dinner.

He held a bottle of wine in his right hand, and on his left, he had two glasses.

"Compliments of Ms. Mayberry herself," he said, holding the bottle proudly.

"You stole from her wine cellar?"

"Borrowed," he said, looking mildly offended. "Besides, they're two bottles deep already. I'm sure they won't remember a third disappearing."

He set the bottle and glasses on the trunk to my right and returned to the door to close it. The audible 'click' caused my heart to skip a beat. My thoughts clouded with the building storm of emotions. I steadied my breathing.

A few drinks wouldn't hurt, and I could lie about being tired or something, and he'd leave.

The plan for tomorrow was still on.

He popped off the cork and poured the crimson liquid into the glasses. He held one out to me and stood facing where I sat on the bed.

Jason took a drink and smacked his lips. "Maybe I should've taken the rest of that scotch." He hesitated only briefly, however, and took another sip.

I stared at the glass in my hand. The blood-colored liquid swirled as I peered into it and raised it to my lips. The liquid touched my tongue, and I anticipated the sweet cherry, fig, or chocolate notes, but instead, it burned sour and bitter.

I spit it back into the glass. "Son of a bitch!"

I glared at the wine glass. "It's fucking vinegar."

"Come on, Elly," Jason said. "It ain't *that* bad."

My tongue begged to differ, and I curled a lip in agitation. "No, it really *is* vinegar," I insisted.

"What? Are you sure?"

"Yes," I said, turning my annoyed glare to him. "I think I know vinegar when I taste it."

Immediately, Jason was beside me, a look of concern on his face. I didn't need to look at my hand to know what I'd see. My mark fluttered with the magic that had activated *without* me wanting it to do so. My stomach knotted, feeling betrayed by it. "The sugars in it are carbon, and I must've shifted the ratio altering the composition." I groaned and ran a hand through my hair. "I can't even enjoy a glass of wine anymore." It took every ounce of willpower not to throw the wine glass into the fireplace, watching it shatter.

Jason set his hand on mine and gently took the glass from me.

I clasped them on my lap, keeping them from shaking with anger. "I never wanted this," I whispered. "Sometimes I wish I'd never found that statue and could return to how things were. Back to normal me."

"I know," Jason replied after setting the wine glasses down.

"I never wanted to be a protector of a bridge. Or be a guardian. I just wanted to take pictures, help people, and maybe make enough to buy a house on the beach someday." I paused, biting my lip, and Jason's hand touched my chin, turning it to face him.

"You can do this, Elly," he said. The resolve in his voice made her shiver. His fingers touched my chin and turned it toward him. "I know you, and you're the most marvelously fierce woman I've ever met. I fucking know you can." His eyes danced between mine, letting the words sink in.

My throat tightened at the seriousness of his words.

He twisted on the bed to retrieve his wine glass and then held it out to me. A mischievous spark danced in the blue of his eyes.

I reached out to take the glass, but he shook his head and held it out of reach.

"No. Let me," he whispered. He pressed the glass to my lips

and lifted it. The wine caressed my tongue, and I tasted the delectable flavors—Grapey, a little sweet, and *strong*.

After a moment, he pulled it back. "Better?"

I smiled and wiped a drip from my mouth, and his eyes blazed a bright blue with desire. "Much," I said, playfully licking my lips.

In an instant, he was on me. He placed a hand behind my head, his fingers weaving into my hair. He pressed his forehead against mine, and his gaze burned into mine, waiting for me to tell him no. The wine had affected my senses, lulling me into a relaxing state, but I still was in control. I knew what was going to come next. I'd seen this look in Jason's eyes dozens of times. Until a few days ago, I never imagined seeing it again.

I would be leaving tomorrow, possibly never to see him again, so what did it matter? I could play the adults with needs cards, but I was terrified of what the daylight would bring, and this, the wine, *him* was a welcome distraction.

Tomorrow would come soon enough. Until then...

I tilted my head closer to his, giving my silent consent, and he responded immediately, crashing his lips onto mine. He tasted like the black cherry and currant from the wine, and while we kissed, I inched closer to him on the bed.

While his right hand cradled the back of my head, I felt his left hand move to her neck. Warm and a little rough, I savored the feeling of releasing control to him and allowing him to direct our movements. My heart beat faster, fluttering against my breastbone.

A moment passed, and he broke the kiss.

We breathed heavily as our faces remained inches apart. His jaw shifted, and I felt his shoulders tense under my hands.

His blue irises burned with a desire so intense my arms prickled with goosebumps. It was more than I'd ever seen from him as if he'd been thirsty for months, and an oasis with fresh glacier water had materialized in front of him.

"Elly, you…" he started, then paused. Whatever war raged inside him, a similar one had stirred in me. The feeling of his hands in my hair, his fingers tingling the back of my neck. The world faded away until only his radiant blue eyes remained.

I flashed him a reassuring smile and nodded. "I want this too."

Relief washed over his face. "You don't know how long I've wanted this." His voice was husky as the words tumbled out, and he kissed me. The last sound I heard before his body was on top of mine was the wine glass shattering as he dropped it to the floor.

CHAPTER

SEVENTEEN

Afterward, as we lay under the blankets, Jason tucked his bandaged arm over me and pulled me close. The warmth of his body cocooned me and was better than any blanket. I found myself dozing to the sound of his steady breathing.

"I applied for Commander Jackson's position," he said softly, rousing me.

"Hmm?" I said. "Oh, I didn't know you wanted to be a commander."

What an odd time to discuss his work, although Jason's pillow talk had never been his strong suit. Sex, yes, talking all mushy and romantic, not as much. But really, where was he going with this? Why did he think now was the time to tell me this? Did he honestly think he'd be able to return to working at Division 12 after everything?

"Don't you ever just relax?" I said and flipped over to face him.

Jason smirked. His cheeks were flushed from our momentary lapse in better judgment, and he caressed my face. "What do you call what I did for the twenty minutes?"

"Oh, I could call it many things, but taking a break isn't one of them."

He gave me a wry grin and moved to kiss me. Light and gentle, still, it sent a flurry of butterflies to flit about in my belly.

"What I'm trying to say," he continued. "If the mole is found out, and Division isn't totally comprised, and somehow I still have a job, a commander position would place me at commander headquarters in Manhattan."

My eyebrows narrowed, still unclear what this meant.

Jason laced his fingers into mine. "It could mean we could have a chance, Elly. You know, to make this work."

My mouth opened and closed, but no sound came out. Alarm bells rang inside my head as my defense system launched into red alert mode.

It was all happening again—the same words spoken so sincerely, the same promises readily broken.

He was waiting for me to answer.

"Wow, Jason," I said, my voice cracking. "I don't know what to say. This is..." I stammered, unable to put into words what this all could mean.

"Say you'll give this another shot. Say we'll try again when you move back to New York." His eyes searched mine, seeking answers to a question I'd been blindsided by.

My thoughts warred with each other, some pushing me to say yes, while others screamed no, drawing attention to the lingering ache in my heart and my plan to leave tomorrow.

"Jason," I said, shifting the weight on my side. "How can you possibly think about the future? We're literally hiding in the middle of nowhere from dangerous, powerful, and *very* connected people. Division 12 would just as soon shoot you on sight as make you a commander."

It wasn't the answer he was looking for. The skin pinched between his eyebrows, and he squeezed my hand.

"After what just happened—" he said, but I interrupted him by sitting up. I'd put on his shirt when I'd gone to the bathroom to bring us back a glass of water, and the smell of him permeating my nose made what I was about to say all the harder. But it needed to be done. Jason clearly needed a reality check, and regrettably, I was the one needing to give it to him.

"What just happened was," I said. "Two people looking to have some fun in a fucked-up world?"

The color drained from his face, and he released his hold on my hand, letting my fingers fall limp to the pillow.

My chest tightened, but I pressed on. "You know as well as I do we're broken. This doesn't change that."

"It doesn't if you won't let it," he said, his voice edged with anger. He got off the bed and pulled his underwear and jeans back on. Still shirtless, he moved to the door. His hand hesitated on the handle, and he cast a look over his good shoulder to where I stood, arms crossed. His jaw ticked, and pain flashed in his eyes. "Keep the shirt," he said and left.

A SINGLE SONGBIRD'S trilling melody awoke me to the early morning light. A cool breeze swept over my bare legs, and I rolled over. In my half-awake state, I anticipated finding Jason's enormous form sleeping next to me, but my hand felt nothing but empty sheets. I lay motionless for a while, listening to the birds and mulling over what I'd said to Jason. The sudden urge to use the bathroom drew me out of bed, and I padded barefoot to the bathroom. After using the toilet, I noticed my reflection in the mirror and the black shirt that belonged to me, now. I hugged myself as the stabbing pain of guilt plunged deeper into my heart. I leaned against the cabinet of the vanity and cried.

Cried for the life that I'd had and the life I could've shared with him.

It was like we'd broken up all over again, the scab torn from the wound and doused with fire.

When my tears ceased, I returned to the bed, wanting nothing more than to curl up into a ball, but it was useless. I had a plan to leave, and no matter how broken my heart was that I'd had to hurt Jason to make it happen, I needed to stick with it. For his safety and everyone else I cared about.

I dressed in the same pair of jeans as yesterday, although Kat had loaned me some shirts she kept for guests. I selected a white t-shirt with the Bangles band and a cotton button-up to tie around my waist. I stuffed Jason's t-shirt into my bag and packed the few other items I'd brought with me.

Not wanting to wake the rest of the house, I stepped into the hallway and shut the door softly behind me. The house was quiet this early, and my footsteps resounded on the wooden floor.

Stomach growling, I caught the pleasant aroma of coffee and headed to the kitchen. Hopefully, there would be some leftovers from last night's dinner, or maybe I could make myself some toast and jam before finding Assem.

However, my entire plan was incinerated when I found Kat seated at the kitchen island with her laptop.

Well, shit.

The first light of morning filtered in from the windows. She heard me enter and looked up. She wore a floral print robe, and a silk headband held back her silver-gray hair that ran down the length of her back.

She smiled broadly. "Ah, dear, good morning. I'd hoped you'd be up soon," she said, then her gaze drifted to my hair. A curious smirk curved up the corners of her mouth. "I trust you slept well?"

It took every ounce of my strength *not* to go to my hair and determine the extent of the damage the foray with Jason had done. If it was messy, so be it. Smoothing it would only reveal my guilty conscience. Which, to my sudden surprise, I didn't have. At least not the sex part. The lying to him that it had meant nothing. *That* I would probably forgive myself for.

While I didn't want to broadcast to the whole estate that we'd slept together, there was no denying that I'd enjoyed last night with Jason. It had been like coming home, only better...

A shiver ran through me, remembering all the places where his hands and mouth had been. Even though it'd been a few hours ago, it felt like a distant memory, clouded by dark smog that hung over it from what had come after.

"I did sleep well," I lied. "Thank you."

Giving me no indication of pushing the subject, she said, "Excellent to hear. Since you're up, I have some news to share."

I lifted my chin to show I was listening. Secretly, I was sifting through all the ways I could still make a break for it. I needed to find Assem.

"The museum curator at the Baghdad Museum I was telling you about," Kat continued, gesturing to the laptop screen. "He responded to my request. He's agreed to allow us an escorted visit to their archives. I was discreet in my interest, but he said they are home to one of the world's largest collections of Cuneiform tablets."

My pulse raced. Cuneiform, like the very ones Enheduanna had written on. They were my only real connection to her and my only chance at filling in the missing pieces to the puzzle she'd given me, like where the bridge was located and how I was supposed to protect it.

My elation quickly dissipated when I realized that this meant I would be staying. And so would very soon have to face

Jason again. Jason, who hated my guts right now. Which I could hardly blame him for.

However, with any luck, by tomorrow, I'd know the true reason for my sudden powers and, even more, how to stop those who wished me dead.

"Kat, that's great news," I exclaimed. "So, when do we leave?"

Kat smiled and shifted her weight in her chair, squinting at the glowing screen.

"Sounds like he has availability this afternoon," she said. "It's an hour's drive. We should leave here at noon to avoid traffic. Zhalika will be cross if I go without her, so let's keep this between us for the time being, alright?"

I nodded.

After folding the laptop screen down, Kat stood and stretched. "There's coffee and hot water for tea in the kitchen if you'd like any."

We stepped by each other as Kat stepped out of the room, and I made my way to the kitchen.

The light blinked on the electric teapot next to the coffee percolator. My hand gripped a mug, and I reached for the carafe handle.

"Don't forget, Jason," Kat's voice called, muffled from behind me.

My body froze. *So much for keeping it a secret.* I sighed and swallowed the pang of guilt, leaving with only my single cup of coffee.

CHAPTER

EIGHTEEN

Kat, Jason, and I stood in front of the house, waiting for Assem to bring the car. The midday sun crested the palm trees, and sweat clung to my hairline. Per Kat's wishes, we agreed to keep Zhalika in the dark regarding our little trip.

Jason had avoided looking at me since Kat called him for breakfast. So, I'd made myself scarce, retreating to the library or checking emails on my laptop in my bedroom.

I worried how long we had before the others caught on to our behavior, not feeling entirely optimistic about the hour car ride.

Assem was attired in his white-collared shirt, black slacks, and shoes, looking the professional driver part.

The four of us got into the immaculately clean car and gave insight into what Assem did in his free time. The dash gleamed, and I inhaled the leather-scented aroma. Jason sat in front beside Assem, Kat in back with me.

The car glided over the rough bumps on the gravel driveway and smoother still once we hit the freeway. Assem hit the throt-

153

tle, and the motor roared as we sped past cars and trucks. The landscape changed rapidly the closer we drew to the city. Squat stone buildings and houses with tarps for roofs cluttered the edge of the road. Assem swerved the car with agile grace through the throng of parked cars and pedestrians. Traffic was at a standstill on the main thoroughfare, and I peered out of the window at the looming towers reaching high into the dusty sky. The car turned right, and Assem took a side road to continue West.

During the trip, Kat filled us in on Baghdad's current economic state, and Jason added his opinions occasionally. The U.N. had flushed out many of the ISIS rebels, and the city was hard at work rebuilding. Hospitals and schools were reopening, and new restaurants and hotels were popping up daily.

"Hello?" Kat said, putting her cell phone to her ear. "Ah, yes, we're looking forward to our afternoon visit." I half-listened as I gazed out the window. The number of people on the streets was overwhelming. Men, women, and children in all manner of dress filled the sidewalks on their way to work, school, or shopping.

"We're being tailed," Jason said. The urgency in his voice caused all of us to startle, and Kat said an abrupt goodbye, ending her call.

"Are you sure?" she asked.

Jason placed his pistol on his lap, which was an answer in and of itself. "Assem, we need to get off the main road. Take the next exit and then two lefts."

Baghdad was a big city, and even though I'd visited a handful of times, all the alleyways and one-way streets could make it easy to get lost. However, Jason was either more familiar with it, or his intent was for us to get lost.

I looked out of the rear window and saw two cargo trucks and a white car directly behind us. It wasn't until Assem switched lanes to exit that I spotted the blue Toyota SUV. The front headlight was broken, and the license plate was missing. The sunlight glared off the windshield, making it impossible to see who was in it.

It switched lanes shortly after us but stayed two cars behind.

"We can't lead them to the museum," I said.

"I know," Jason said, drawing back the slider on his gun.

"You can't shoot them," Kat stammered. "There are people everywhere."

"I know," Jason repeated, then shouted at Assem to keep going through a red light. Horns hocked as we cruised through, going well above the speed limit.

"We have to split up," Jason said, peering back at me. "If this is Division 12, they're after me and Elly. We'll make sure they see us and draw them away from you. We can lose them in the crowd while you and Assem keep going in the car. Then, once we're both clear, we'll meet at the museum."

My scalp prickled. In the car, we had a chance, but on foot? Would we really be able to outrun them? More so, were these the type of people who wouldn't hesitate to fire a gun into a crowd? I hated the thought that I'd be the reason an innocent person died today.

Assem nodded. "He is right."

Kat cursed under her breath. "I don't like this idea, but I have to agree. The most important thing is we get to the museum, read the tablets, and find out the bridge's location."

Jason's eyes found mine. "When I say go, we go, okay? You stay right in front of me the whole time."

I chewed the inside of my cheek before nodding. "Okay."

The road had been barricaded for a street fair two blocks ahead of us.

"Okay. Drop us off there," he said, pointing ahead to where

people were unloading boxes of vegetables from flatbed trucks. "We'll find a car and meet up as soon as we can."

"Godspeed, and be safe," Kat said, squeezing my hand. I plastered a smile on my face — wondering if doing crazy dangerous things like *this* was becoming a new hobby for me— and leaped out of the car the instant it stopped.

The Mercedes' tires screeched a second later as Assem slammed down on the gas and sped off.

Clutching the pistol by his side, Jason's eyes searched the road behind us while urging me toward the market.

The sounds of voices, music, and grilling food engulfed us, and fluttering fabric above each vendor's stands filtered the sunlight as we speedily walked into the crowd. Dozens of people formed a sea of bodies, and we followed the current past brightly colored spices and herbs. A group of vendors joked with each other while one basted a liquid over stacks of meat. The man carved off a thin shawarma strip and held it to a waiting customer.

We continued through the alleyway, Jason constantly checking over his shoulder and keeping his pistol gripped low but in front of him.

Even without his Division tactical gear, Jason's stiff-backed posture and the way he constantly assessed his surroundings radiated military training, and while I could blend, if anyone looked hard enough at him, they'd notice he most likely wasn't there to buy figs or a copper pot.

As Ramadan had ended last week, people were busy shopping, refilling their pantries, and sampling sweets. The music grew louder as we pushed through, where a dozen people had gathered to listen. A man and a teenage boy played drums along the curb as Jason barged through. I tripped over the basket, sending coins spilling onto the sidewalk, and at least five different curse words were shouted at me. I held my hands up, apologizing in Arabic, and dove into the crowd on the opposite side.

"On our six," Jason whispered. "Two of them. A man with a brown hat, and—Don't look," he said when I started to peer behind me. "There's a woman also, a redhead with a blue jacket."

We exited the alleyway and into a wooden building containing piles of dead fish on ice-covered tables.

People strolled through, assessing the hundreds of different types of seafood and the humped ridges of live carp swimming lazily inside plastic tanks.

We half-ran to the end of one aisleway and were forced to stop as a forklift blocked our path.

A shout came from behind, and the redhead woman pointed in our direction, yelling at her partner, who had gone to the left.

Without warning, Jason fired his gun. Two shots ricocheted off the wooden pillar beside the woman, sending wood splinters into the air. The third shot hit her squarely in the chest, and she fell back, clutching her ribcage.

All around us, people screamed and ran in every direction. Vendors ducked behind tables, and a distracted forklift driver drove into a pile of cardboard boxes, sending a landslide of shrimp and ice spilling onto the floor.

The sound of the shots caused a ringing in my ear, and Jason's shouts at me sounded muffled, like we were underwater. A second later, my hearing returned.

"We have to run," he said.

I dashed forward without needing any more encouragement, and he quickly followed, keeping pace by my shoulder. Adrenaline surged through my veins, and the magic swelled inside me. We sprinted to the left, then Jason pulled me under a metal walkway and into another section of the building. Customers and vendors leaped out of our way, desperate to clear a path. A bullet whizzed past my left ear, and I veered to the right. Imagining them on my heels, I refused to slow, pushing my cramping muscles to reach a higher speed. The doorway at the end was quickly approaching. On the street, we'd be exposed. Jason pumped his arms, looking like a goddamn machine beside me. We were running out of time. I needed to do something.

The mark tingled, and the ancient magic strained to be freed.

I gave in, running my hand along the piles of ice. My fingers brushed the slimy scales of dead fish and squid, the ice crackling as the heat from the heated fish melted it. The smell of smoked and cooked fish filled my senses as hundreds of gallons of water cascaded off the tables. People yelled as the tsunami-like tide flooded the concrete aisle way, carrying with it loose boxes and sweeping people off their feet.

Stealing a glance over my shoulder, the man trudged through the water, apparently having left his partner behind, and like a wolf stalking his prey, his steely-eyed gaze was fixed on me.

A shiver raced up my spine as Jason fired off another round, and the man ducked as the bullet flew past his left shoulder.

"Agent Price," the man shouted, even as Jason shot again. "This is a job and doesn't involve you. You've still got friends at Division, you know. Give me the girl, and I promise the agency will welcome you back."

"Fuck you," Jason said and shot two more times. He fired a third, but the clip was empty. Jason reached into his jacket pocket for a fresh one, and the man seized the opportunity to dart behind a vendor table.

"Dammit, I left the clip in the car," he said as we sped to the doorway.

My lungs burning, we propelled ourselves outside, leaping over a discarded bicycle and two empty crates.

"Jason," I panted, and my legs felt like they were about to give out.

"C'mon. We can't stop," he said, tugging me to the right. "Cut through that alleyway."

Rows of vendors lined either side of the narrow street that was flanked by two concrete apartment buildings, and racks of clothing, rugs, and tapestries hung from lines draped over the center.

The agent had made it out of the building and caught sight of us as we dashed into the side street. My breathing had become labored, coming in ragged gasps, and more and more, I felt myself being dragged forward by Jason's relentless command to keep running. In the distance, police sirens wailed in response to the shootout in the warehouse.

This had been a stupid idea.

Jason could outrun him; that was obvious, but I couldn't. We needed more time to find a car.

I skidded to a stop. Jason's grip slipped as he was caught off guard, allowing me to ignite the cardboard boxes stacked next to a dumpster.

The heat from the flames warmed my face as I angrily shoved the whole pile over, forming a fiery barrier between the man and us. He slowed, a look of surprise on his face, and held up his arms against the increasing heat. The cardboard glowed as if I'd doused it with gasoline, intensifying into a ten-foot-tall inferno.

I stepped back as the flames leaped higher and watched as the nearby clothing and rugs began to smolder, and little flames spread across the fabric.

Jason's fingers gripped my wrist, pulling me, and he called out that we should go.

I spun on my heel as the sounds of people yelling, sirens wailing, and the heat of the spreading fire trailed behind me.

NINETEEN

Pain lanced through my calves and thigh muscles when Jason finally let me catch my breath. I leaned against a wooden fence as sweat dripped down my face, stinging my eyes.

Jason was breathing heavily, his face red from the heat and exertion, as he worked his way through the parking lot, trying handles.

Lots of the cars were well over thirty years old, and it took him some to find one old enough to hot wire but not so old it wouldn't reliably get us to where we needed to go. Breaking before we'd made it a few blocks with pissed-off Division agents actively hunting for us wasn't something I was keen on experiencing.

While Jason committed grand theft auto, I checked my phone and saw no messages from Kat. I could only assume that meant they'd made it safely to the museum and rationalized she would've called if something *had* happened.

An engine started nearby, and Jason popped his head up from between two cars and waved me over.

I climbed into the two-door Nissan coupe and settled in

what had once been a sports car, now home to at least four different mice families.

We drove on the road and purposely took side streets to avoid being seen should any other agents be patrolling nearby. When we'd reached the highway, Jason held out his hand. "Give me your phone."

"Why?" I said, my hand going to my bag.

"They're tracking it."

As if watching outside of my body, I passed it over.

Jason rolled down the window and tossed it out.

A pitiful sound of protest escaped me as it disappeared into a cluster of bushes in a ditch. I crossed my arms and leaned back in the seat, pouting.

I was careful about who had my number and to keep non-identifiable photos on it, but still, I wouldn't know if Cara, my mom, or Taamir tried to reach me.

"What about *your* phone?" I snapped.

Jason slipped him from an inside pocket and waggled it in front of me. "This is a burner I picked up on the way to get to you. My personal one is in my locker at the Division station in Damascus."

"That has to be how they found me, right? They went through your stuff and found your phone and saw that I'd called you?"

"Are you serious?" he said, laughing dryly. "First off, the guy I borrowed the Jeep from thinks I'm in Lebanon, and second, I have an app that deletes all my call history."

It should've made me feel better that I could check off Jason as the connection to how they'd found out I had the statue, but it meant going back to square one. We were left in the dark again about how they'd discovered who or where I was.

Speeding down the freeway with no cars nearby, my blood pressure finally returned to normal.

"What that agent said," I said after we'd driven in silence for some time. "About handing me over, and you could return to Division. Why didn't you?"

His knuckles turned white as he squeezed the steering wheel.

Wait, had he *actually* considered it? I chewed my lip, instantly regretting I'd asked it.

"He was lying," he said. "Trying to bait me into dropping my guard. He would've shot me in the back of the head the second he had you in cuffs."

"Well," I said, folding my hands on my lap as if I were waiting for a menu at a restaurant instead of a momentary freakout. "I'm glad you didn't."

He flashed me a severe look. "I never would, Elly."

My breathing quickened, and I fidgeted with my seatbelt. "Even after what happened last night?"

"Even after what happened last night?"

Jason returned his eyes to the road. "I promised to help you. And until you are safe, or one of us is dead, I'll see it through."

I could feel a tightness growing in my chest. "I'm sorry, Jason, for everything. For dragging you into this, for putting you at risk, for having Division turn against you, I—"Stop," he said firmly. "Just stop."

I pressed my tongue to the roof of my mouth. I shouldn't have said anything. Clearly, it was only making it worse.

Tension hovered in the silence between us, and combined with the coming down from the adrenaline rush, my mood darkened. But I sensed there was more to my weariness, to the drooping of my eyelids and slouch of my shoulders.

This time — after I tapped into my power — it'd been *different.*

It was strenuous but nothing beyond a good yoga session when I'd practiced at the quarry.

This time, however, it'd left my muscles achy and weak, and a hollow pang echoed in my belly like I hadn't eaten for days.

I stared at the palm of my hand, tracing the lines of the smooth pink edges of the scar, and a sharp sting of pain radiated from it, similar to how it'd felt when I'd first been marked.

Something had changed when I'd killed that man. I'd overexerted myself and was now facing the consequences. My thumb idly stroked the mark, trying to ease the pain and my worry.

Lost in my thoughts — it wasn't until Jason turned off the road that I looked up and saw the big sign marking the National Museum of Iraq.

Jason maneuvered through the parking lot and was directed by security — after giving them Kat's name — to a private VIP parking up front.

We exited the car and walked along the sidewalk, stepping in line with a group of tourists trickling out from a tour bus.

Two large square towers flanked the entrance to the massive stone building. It was designed to appear medieval; the plaque out front said it had been built in the '40s. Mature palm trees dotted the perimeter, and stone benches hugged the sides of the building under fabric awnings. Above the massive arched entryway, a carved relief replicating Sumerian art had been engraved.

Inside, we passed under metal scaffolding where masonry workers were plastering a wall.

We followed the tour group, stepping through a metal detector before being ushered into the main hallway leading to the more modern interior of the museum.

Ten-foot-tall statues of Mesopotamian-era deities and kings stood proudly along the walls. Their chipped noses and pupil-less eyes silently watched us as we passed.

A museum worker led us into a side corridor from the

central area. We spotted Kat striding down one of the eight narrow hallways. Each with a sign above it marking the Prehistoric, Sumerian, Akkadian, Babylonian, Assyrian, Achaemenid, Parthian, and Islamic exhibits. I mentally noted that I needed to visit more museums if I somehow survived all of this.

Jason's face was a mask; cold-eyed and motionless, he watched the security guards, employees, and guests. As VIPs, we were allowed to bypass the metal detectors, and I'd seen Jason hide his pistol under his jacket.

Kat approached us from under the Sumerian doorway with a warm smile. Her eyes narrowed at the scratches on my hand, and "So, how was your shopping trip?"

I eyed the lingering museum employee, a girl my age with glasses and blonde hair, who seemed curious about who Kat and we were that required VIP treatment.

"You could say that," I said, shrugging. "Jason tried to buy fish, but the prices were hard to hit."

Jason cleared his throat.

Kat arched a brow and clucked. "Interesting. Well, you're just in time. I have quite a lot to show you."

WE FOLLOWED behind Kat down the narrow-secluded corridor. Her green headscarf matched that of her emerald and gold silk vest, which billowed out behind her as she walked. Most of the museum had been repaired, but telltale scars of recent destruction remained. Varying shades of paint covered patches on the walls, and mismatched fluorescent lights buzzed from where they dangled from the ceiling.

At the end of the hallway, Kat used her hand to prop open a heavy steel door marked with a "RESTRICTED AREA" sign.

"Right this way," she said, motioning us to enter.

I stepped inside first, followed by Jason and Assem. Although I estimated the room to be over forty feet wide, the sheer enormity of books, shelving, tables, and desks filled nearly every inch of space. Stacks of papers overflowed from cardboard boxes, broken stone vases, and bowls in various states of repair sat beside Tupperware filled with brushes, pencils, and plastic baggies.

Kat rubbed her hands together. "This, my dears, is where the magic happens."

Two researchers in white lab coats looked up from their work, where they were dusting off a clay platter, and fixed Kat a questioning look. Then, with a dismissive wave of her hand, they murmured disapproving sounds to each other, set down their brushes, and exited the room. I tried to give them an apologetic look as they hurried out, clutching their iPads.

"At least once a year, the museum is placed on lockdown," Kat said. "Afterward, the collections must be inventoried, cataloged, and, if necessary, restored. In addition, archeological sites all over the Middle East are regularly burglarized. When the thieves attempt to cross the border with stolen artifacts, patrol agents confiscate them and bring them here. It is up to the museum personnel to identify them and determine where they came from."

She gestured for us to stand at a round table in the center. Clear plastic totes of varying sizes—their lids propped open — contained fragmented cubes of tan-colored clay. I moved closer, peering into one of the bins. Each piece was tucked safely inside individual foam spaces. Some were as big as a slice of bread, others smaller than a quarter. All of them were covered in strange runes and markings.

Kat picked up a magnifying glass and hunched over the table.

"Gloves are over by the sink, and I suggest a mask as well," she said without bothering to look up or give an explanation. I went and put on a face mask, followed by the gloves.

An ever-defiant Jason pulled a rolling stool from another table and sat, arms crossed, jaw set.

I could sense his sour mood from here. But didn't he realize this was how we found our answer? These broken clay pieces may hold the key to discovering who was after me, the statue, and even why.

He hated waiting.

I recalled all the nice restaurants we'd passed up because the line outside was too long. 'I know a burger place with no line and twice the size plates,' he'd say, convincing me the alder smoked salmon wasn't worth an hour-long wait.

As cliché as it sounded, Jason was a man of action. He did better when he faced his enemy head-on. I flexed my hands, feeling the tender skin pull from the mark on my hand. I feared what he might do if we didn't find something solid soon.

"Here," Kat said, waving me over. I narrowed my eyes at the triangle-shaped piece, with the same wedge-shaped runes, the size of a deck of cards, in Kat's blue gloved hand.

"*This* is cuneiform," she said. "And is a partial copy of one of Enheduanna's poems."

My eyes burned, not daring to blink. I couldn't wrap my head around how this was some of the first writing in existence. Seeing it up close solidified the irrefutable truth that Enheduanna had been a living, breathing person, not just in my dreams.

"This is one where she compares Inanna with the Vela supernova. Dozens of researchers have analyzed this passage and have all come to different theories about her interchanging the word 'star' with 'door' or 'window' or—"

"Bridge," I finished for her.

"Bridge, indeed," Kat said, setting the magnifying glass down.

"Does she say anything else about it? Perhaps what it is or where it's at?" I quickly asked.

"She does," Kat said, shaking her head. "But I'm afraid it won't help us much."

"Why is that?"

"Their navigational skills were primitive back then, and the coordinates are hazy; however, researchers have pieced together it's in Ur."

I replayed the word in my head, struggling to place it. What had Enheduanna told me? *The fate of Ur is in your hands.*

"Okay, this Ur," I said, licking my lips with cautious hope. "Is it close? How do we get there?"

Kat shook her head, placing the stone back on the table. "That's the problem, dear. The city of Ur doesn't exist anymore."

I tilted my head, feeling the glimmer of hope fading. "What do you mean?"

"I mean, it's nothing but a pile of rocks in the desert."

"But it's still a place, then?" I said. We were finally starting to get somewhere and get some real answers, and I wasn't close to giving up.

"Of course, it's a place," she said. "But, it's more like an Atlantis of sorts. For decades, archaeologists have proclaimed they'd discovered the elusive Ur, but further investigations revealed that they might have found fragments of it. No one can establish the real location."

"Myself included!" a man's voice announced.

A middle-aged man strode into the room. He could've easily been one of my college professors with his bushy black eyebrows, neatly trimmed goatee, and round bifocal glasses.

White tunic shirt and Birkenstock sandals peeked out from his blue cargo shorts.

What was the deal with archaeologists and Birkenstock's? It had to be some rite of passage, where they'd receive their first pair — affixed with a bow—when they'd secured their first dig site.

Kat grinned broadly as the man approached her. "Ah, Mr. Weber. Kind of you to take some time out of your day to join us."

"Leon, please," he said, bobbing his head. "I trust my assistant found the archive numbers you requested?"

"He did," Kat replied.

"Excellent, and have we found what we're looking for?"

He had a slight German accent, pronouncing his 'We' as 'Vee'.

Kat sighed. "I'm afraid not. I've combed through part of the tablets, but we seem to have encountered a problem."

His eyebrows pinched. "A problem?"

"Yes," Kat replied. "We're most interested in the works of Enheduanna. Particularly the pieces pertaining to the goddess Inanna and the city of Ur."

The man's eyes widened. "Ah, I understand. In my younger, naïve years, I combed through hundreds of tablets in search of the location of the lost city. But alas, I grew wise and learned to step aside and let the younger ones take on the mysterious search."

"Fine, I'll bite," Jason chided. I wasn't the only one who'd forgotten he was there, and all three of us jumped. "What's so important about this damn city?"

The man cocked an eyebrow toward him. "I trust this is another friend of yours, Ms. Mayberry?" he asked, his eyes still on Jason.

"He is," she said, flashing Jason a disapproving look as

though he'd shouted in a library before refocusing her attention on Leon. "As you were saying?"

He cleared his throat. "Ah yes, the Sumerians built the city-state of Ur. Records and speculation state that it was protected by enormous stone walls and beautiful, irrigated gardens and surrounded by thousands of homes. A true metropolitan oasis."

The man paused, lowering his voice so Kat and I both had to lean closer to hear him.

"However, a legend states that the city was *more* than just a city and that the gods built it and called it their home. It was thought they would frequently descend from the heavens, choosing to walk and share the lives of their people."

I licked my lips, trying to be patient but secretly dying inside. "So, what happened to it?"

He frowned. "War happened to it." The man's face turned solemn, grim. "King Sargon urged his daughter and High priestess, Enheduanna, to pray to the gods. If only he had greater knowledge, he could teach his people how to farm better, better techniques with medicine, and how to create stronger, sharper weapons. And lastly, he wished for more time on this Earth. She agreed, and for three days, she prayed to Inanna, not once leaving the temple's ritual room. Records are unreliable, but some state human sacrifice was performed to draw the goddess's attention. Finally, Inanna appeared.

"And while we don't know what happened, it must have worked. King Sargon's kingdom flourished for years. But when he passed his reign to his son, Rimush, he sought to prove to his father his worthiness and grew greedy as those in power often do. So, the legend says he disguised himself and followed his sister across the bridge without her knowing. He witnesses something because his scribes state that he returned with greater knowledge of war and weapons. However, his reckless invasions brought retaliations, and while under siege, a warring city-state destroyed the temple at the center of Ur."

"The sands of time did the rest," Kat added.

Leon took off his glasses and cleaned them with his shirt.

The revelations ignited my mind. His words were like missing puzzle pieces falling into place to fill the gaps.

"Archeologists have combed the desert, and several digs have revealed the remnants of walls and roads. Even items like pottery, tools, and religious artifacts have been recovered." He frowned, looking at Kat. "It's odd."

"What is?" Jason said, sounding beyond impatient.

I couldn't deny I was growing antsy, too.

"One was housed here at the museum until recently," Leon said. "And another at our sister museum in London."

"Until recently?" I pressed.

Leon's mouth twisted as if trying to chew a thick piece of meat. "Last month, the London Museum had a break-in. With all the priceless artifacts the thieves could've taken, only one item was listed as stolen."

"The stone," Kat supplied, her face grim.

The two shared a private look, and I wondered what else they weren't telling me.

Leon nodded before continuing. "Then, two weeks ago, our museum here shared a similar situation, and various pieces were either broken or missing. As this museum has been subjected to years of vandalism and looting, we figured it was another occurrence. That was until the curator at the London Museum called. She told me to check the Sumerian ruins archives. Sure enough, the only object missing was the stone."

"So, it wasn't a random break-in after all," Jason said, "Whoever broke in knew what they wanted and where. They only *made* it appear like a random robbery."

The man nodded.

"And the two in private collections?" I asked.

Leon turned and clicked awake on a computer screen. A numbered chart appeared on the screen, and he peered at it, his eyes scanning the lists of numbers.

"According to the auction logs, a private auction purchased them last Fall. No name was given, only a business."

"Let me guess," Jason said. "Kane United?"

Leon straightened and tilted his head. "Yes indeed. May I ask how you know?"

CHAPTER
TWENTY

The black car glided through the narrow streets as Assem drove us back to Kat's estate. I stared at the symbol in the palm of my hand. Leon and Kat had discussed some more the connections the stones had to the statue and what reason an energy company like Kane United would want with Sumerian artifacts, both coming to no single conclusion. I stared out the window as we passed by apartment buildings, mosques, and various sculptures I'd seen before inspired by the One Thousand- and One-Night's folk tales.

This trip had meant to give me answers, but instead, it had left me with more questions. However, much of what the curator said mirrored my dreams' visions: the altar, the colored stones, and Enheduanna. We also now knew someone at Kane United had taken the stones, but by whom specifically was still unknown. Also, unknown was what was stopping them from opening the gate this instant. I was chosen to prevent the gate from opening and them crossing the bridge, but what if I was too late already? Surely Enheduanna would contact me, but she'd only ever visited me in my dreams. If they opened it right now, would I be ignorant of it until I slept tonight?

I glanced at Jason as worry weighed like a pit in my stomach. His head rested against the back of the seat, and his eyes were distant as he stared out the window.

He'd walked out on us last summer, yet here he was, risking his life and career for something he didn't fully understand. And for what? Because I'd asked him to? Or had he seen enough to believe what I was doing mattered and might save hundreds of lives? He claimed that working for Division 12 allowed him to use his skills for the betterment of the world, but I knew he'd follow any order they gave him, even if he disagreed. That was part of his agency contract—command and a paycheck dictated where he went and what he did there.

Kat tilted her head, drawing me from my thoughts, and said, "When we return, I'll look closer at Leon's translation. Perhaps, with a little luck, we can determine what pieces of the coordinates are missing."

I nodded, wishing I had shared a fraction of Kat's optimism.

The sun hung low on the horizon when we pulled into the drive. The swirling dust had caused the sun to appear yellow and red. I stepped out of the car, and a gust of wind immediately stirred up the dust under my feet.

Assem shut the door and turned his head toward the direction of the setting sun. "The wind carries change this night."

I COULDN'T AGREE MORE.

Back in my bedroom, I changed out of my jeans and into sweats and a tank top. I ran cold water over my face and shut off the bathroom light.

I wandered into the hallway, heading to the kitchen for a late-night snack since we'd skipped dinner, and I caught Jason heading down the stairs.

I swallowed the lump lodged in the back of my throat, and he must've heard me because he stopped with his hand on the railing.

I met his solemn gaze. I knew what he was going to say. I'd known it the whole drive home from the distant way he'd acted like he was already cutting himself off from me.

"Ella," he said, not using my nickname. "I need to go."

Solid as a punch to the gut, the words solidified my fear into existence.

"Can you at least tell me why?" I murmured, peering down from the step above him.

Emotions shifted in his eyes, and he moved up two steps so he was only one below me.

"They saw us together. They know I'm helping you, and they know my connection to Kat. Our only shot at coming out of this alive is if I turn myself in. There will be bullshit to face, but once I'm back inside, I think I can find out who issued the contract, and then we'd have an idea *why* they're after you and the statue."

I clenched my fists, hating the resoluteness in his voice. "Fine, so say, by some miracle, they let you back in. Do you honestly believe they'll allow you access to that kind of information?"

His blue eyes flared, and he lifted his chin, studying my face. "I don't know. But I have to try."

He moved his hand to rest on mine, and his thumb stroked the inside of my wrist. I ignored the flutter of my heart, willing it to steady. Heat spread across my chest, radiating up my neck.

My world was spiraling, and the solid, steady beacon tethering me to the ground would soon disappear.

"Look," he said, his gaze holding me. "I've got a plan. But if I stay any longer, they'll be suspicious." He softened his voice. "You'll be fine. Assem said he would get you checked into a hotel and have some of Kat's security team stay with you. Then, when I know more information, I'll reach out, okay?"

The certainty in his voice did little to soothe the dull ache growing in my chest.

"Besides," he continued. "We've run dry, Elly. We're running blind, and I can't protect you if I don't know what I'm fighting. Going back in will also give me a chance to run a background check on Kane United. At least see if there's anything worth pursuing."

I swallowed, reflecting on his words.

I huffed a sigh. "Fine. When are you going?"

"Tonight."

I pursed my lips. It was pointless to fight him on this. If he thought the best option was to leave, I needed to trust him. "Alright. I guess, be safe and maybe try not to die?"

Jason laughed a husky and warm sound. "I never make promises I can't keep, but I can promise if I go down, I'll take several with me."

Then, before I had any time to react, Jason kissed me. The heat chased down my body from where our lips touched, and I gripped the banister as my knees turned to jelly.

The feeling of his kiss conjured a hundred forgotten memories. Memories I'd thought had left when he left. Memories to painful to remember. Memories, both real and imagined.

His hand cupped the back of my head, drawing me in closer. All the impossibilities that existed, the barriers and walls that prevented *this* from becoming more, crumbled. With his kiss, the world melted away until it was only...*us*.

That was until someone cleared their throat.

We broke the kiss, my back stiffening at the intrusion.

Assem, arching an impatient eyebrow, stood in the foyer, holding Jason's bag and a pair of keys.

Jason chuckled, his blue eyes still smoldering from the kiss. "Hell of a sendoff."

I pressed my hold fingers to my cheeks, attempting to tamper down the flush that had reached my ears.

There'd been an urgency to the kiss as if the world were on fire, and he didn't want to miss his chance before it engulfed us both. Well, he wasn't entirely wrong. Something terrible *was* coming, something that had wiped out one of the most powerful empires in the history of the world.

My hand gripped the railing as I watched him descend the stairs.

He took his bag and keys from a somber-faced Assem.

Jason's blue eyes found me still on the stairs as he opened the door. A hundred unspoken words transpired between us. Before he'd followed Assam outside, I took a mental image of him, hoping to burn it into my memory should this be the last time I see him.

Hot tears streamed down my cheeks as I darted up the stairs two at a time, abandoning the late-night snack. I shut the door to my bedroom, dove into the bed, and mercifully was asleep within seconds.

THE BRIGHTEST OF full moons hung in the midnight sky. Fluttering silk, scented with lavender and honey, caressed my face like the wings of a dozen butterflies. Warm sand pressed against my legs as I rose to my feet. A dress of shimmering, iridescent fabric draped my body, matching the color of the moon's pearl-like glow.

Enheduanna stood beside me. Her dress was red, although of a similar style. She craned her neck, gazing up at the stars.

We were alone in the center of a wide valley. Shifting dunes of sand glittered in the moonlight. Off in the distance, dark storm clouds boiled over shadowed peaked mountains. The distant rumble of thunder echoed after an occasional flash of lighting.

I copied her actions and looked up at the blanket of stars.

"When I was a very young child," Enheduanna said. "My mother would comfort me during a desert storm. Wrapping me in her arms, she'd tell me that although the thunder was loud and the lightning bright, the storms brought the needed rain. Our people depended on the rains for our crops. Even in terror, there is hope."

Enheduanna lowered her face, and her eyes met mine. For the first time, I gained a clearer picture of this woman who so frequently visited my dreams, dreams I had experienced enough to recognize almost instantly.

The smell was different here. Fresher. Newer.

From under the hood of her ivory-colored cloak, deep mahogany locks cascaded down her shoulders around her oval-shaped face. Her hazel-brown eyes were large, years of wisdom unmistakable, and adorned by long, dark lashes.

She reached out, placing a hand on my forearm. "You must not be afraid, Eleanora."

My heart lurched as she said my name.

"But why did you pick me?" I spoke. "I can't do this. Can't you find someone else? Someone that is a better fighter or stronger?"

A slight smile formed on her lips. "The storm approaches, whether or not you choose to face it."

"But I don't know *how* to stop the storm. How can I know when I don't even know where *it* is?"

"I've given you everything you need." She moved her hand down, taking mine and holding it up so the moonlight illuminated the scar's outlines. "The statue will give you answers to your questions. The rest you already possess inside you."

Enheduanna released my hand and turned her eyes on the storm once more.

"I witnessed the devastation the bridge caused. The fall of my father's kingdom. The death of thousands of Akkadians. The peace and unity to which my father had dedicated his life was destroyed within weeks, and the relentless fighting since then. There are things humans should not know. Terrible things. There is one who has almost assembled the key. You must not let it open again."

A flash of lightning blinded me, and the instantaneous crack of thunder rumbled in my chest. Bolt after bolt struck the ground, sending columns of sand into the air. I recoiled, shielding myself from the cascading sand and the violent barrage of lightning.

My palm tingled, the power releasing from me in my scared state. The vibrating molecules, frantic from the sizzling electricity, slowed their movement. The air grew thicker and denser, and the thunder's loud crashes muffled. Surrounding me, as if in a translucent bubble, was liquefied air. Wavering with the echoing thunder, it maintained its dome-like shape. I reached out, tempted to touch it.

Chemistry 101, you idiot. Liquified oxygen is cold.

I drew my hand back, but my eyes remained fixed, fascinated by its gelatinous movement.

A second later, a crash of lightning struck it. The bolt hissed directly above me, and a plume of steam erupted inside and out of the dome. Blinding me, I covered my mouth. The sulfuric stench of burned ozone and charred earth filled my nostrils. The thunder erupted instantly, and I fell to the ground, curling myself into a ball.

Enheduanna's gentle touch landed on my shoulder and lifted me up.

The storm had passed, leaving behind the cool air and an occasional distant rumble. The sun loomed low above the mountains, a hazy orangish-red.

"Your power is waning, Eleanora. You must recover that statue. The celestial alignment will occur in three days' time. You must be there to stop it."

Three days. It clicked into place like I'd known it all along.

"But what if I can't?" I whispered.

The woman met my gaze, her eyes full of sorrow.

"Should you fail to protect the bridge, and it is opened, there is but one way to close it." Her resolute gaze held mine. "You must sacrifice your mortal soul."

I blinked in disbelief. My mortal soul? Great. No pressure.

Enheduanna didn't smile. "If you fail, the darkness of humanity will be unleashed once again. Droughts, famine, and disease will spread. For another 4000 years, the world will suffer."

I awoke with a start, and my shirt clung to me, soaked with sweat. My heart still thrummed inside my chest, and I pressed my hands against my eyes, forcing my breathing to steady.

Three days' time. Your power is waning.

Palm side up, I focused my attention on the mark. I could sense the air above it, and immediately, the tingle trickled up my arm. The weight of the air grew thick and dense. As I peered at the air above my hand, everything behind it grew blurry, as if staring through a fogged window. The cold intensified, and I concentrated, forcing it to solidify into ice.

I strained to keep the air solid, but the air resisted the

magic's influence. Wishing to regain its natural gaseous state, it writhed and twisted. A bead of sweat trickled down my temple, refusing to give in. The skin on my palm burned as I focused.

A split second later, there was an audible pop as the air recoiled against the magic, snapping itself back to a vapor.

A pain originating from my shoulder radiated down to my hand as if I'd struck my funny bone.

"Shit," I muttered, clutching my arm. Well, I had my proof that Enheduanna was right. I was losing my power and couldn't waste any more time.

I needed the statue, or soon, the only power I had to stop the bridge from opening would be gone.

At breakfast, Assem and Kat had agreed to have me taken to a hotel an hour away and had given me a burner cell phone and assurances they'd call if they found out new information about the ritual, the statue, or heard anything from Jason.

Back in my room, I called my mom for a quick check-in. The call was partly to reassure me she and the rest of my family were safe thousands of miles away in California and partly because I needed to hear a familiar voice. The cryptic visits from Enheduanna had always left me shaken, but adding to it, Jason's choice to return to Division 12 yesterday had left my nerves beyond frazzled. I needed proof that there were people out there who would miss me should anything happen. It rang six times — probably because I was using a code to show my number as private — until Mom finally answered. The loud party on the other end and her shouting to tell me they were at a country club charity event told me everything was fine.

I gathered my toiletries from the bathroom and heard the phone buzzing on the nightstand.

I picked it up, and the caller ID stated I'd received a text from a private number. I clicked it open. On the little screen, the only illumination in the dark room was Taamir's terrified face.

I pressed a hand over my mouth, muffling a horrified gasp. My blood crystallized in my veins. This had to be real, but how? This phone number wasn't an hour old, and nobody but me knew it. Assem had told me to select a number when I'd activated it and not to reveal it to anyone.

I searched the photos for details, any clues to reveal where Taamir was or what had happened. His mouth was gagged, and his forehead had a nasty gash. I almost dropped the phone as it vibrated with another text.

It was another photo, but this one was of Rima, Taamir's daughter. Her innocent eyes were wet with tears, and she had a cloth wrapped around her mouth.

I fell to my knees, pressing the phone against my chest. "No. No. No." I desperately wished I could reach into the phone and save them. Tell them how sorry I was and that I'd make it right. Seething with anger, I keyed in a reply: "*Whoever you are, please don't hurt them. Tell me what you want, and I'll do it.*"

A second passed, and a new message appeared.

"*The statue. Send us a picture, and we'll tell you how to save them. They're safe for now. You have 12 hours.*"

I keyed in another message, filled with threats and promises to destroy them if Taamir and his daughter were hurt, but then I quickly deleted it. It was no use. They'd made it clear what they wanted, and anything I said might put them in more danger.

I left my room, hurried downstairs, and scanned the foyer, dining room, and office.

Finding them all empty, I breathed a sigh of relief and crept into the office. I needed the drawing Kat had created at the museum. It was the best chance I had to discover the location of Ur.

I rifled through her piles of books and journals, searching for the scrap of paper. There was a possibility Kat had taken it with her to her room or had it on her person. I clenched my teeth and jumped as the clock chimed on the wall, nine loud bongs.

My scalp prickled at the sensation I was being watched.

Pivoting on my heel, I shifted my body to face whomever it was that I would have to invent a reason why I was snooping in Kat's office.

Assem's statuesque and masked facade stared from the doorway. In his hand was the rolled parchment from the museum that Kat had drawn on.

"Oh, it's you, Assem," I said, smiling. "I thought I left a book in here, but I guess I was wrong." I started for the door.

Assem held out the paper to me. I stared at it, confused how he'd known that it was what I'd been looking for.

I cautiously took it from him, not completely convinced he wouldn't snatch it back. He peered down from his impressive height.

Assem's mouth curved into a wry smirk. "The winds have shifted. The storm is imminent."

My mouth went dry as his words echoed those from my dream. "Assem, I, uh," I stammered. "Thank you. A friend of mine is in danger, and I need to go."

His jaw shifted.

"I need to go home," I continued. "There's something there I need that I think can help."

Assem stuffed his hand into his pocket and withdrew his keys. Then, without waiting for me to continue, he'd left the room. I trotted after him, catching him as he swung open the front door.

"Oh, okay, now?" I said.

Assem's face looked grim.

I adjusted my bag and went out the door. The Mercedes had been parked to the side of the house, and we passed a few groundskeepers trimming bushes and raking leaves as we walked, but no one paid us much mind. Upon reaching the car, he opened the door, and I slid into the passenger's seat. He started the engine and pointed to the GPS on the dash. I keyed in Taamir's address, and the gravel crunched under our tires as we left the estate behind. A sadness clinched my throat. I hadn't said goodbye to Kat or Zhalika, thanking them for providing a haven for me these past few days, and I could only assume I'd never return.

TWENTY-ONE

The Mercedes engine hummed as the sun was sagging low on the horizon. It dipped behind the distant hills when we passed a sign informing us we were ten miles out of Deir ez-Zur. I had attempted to rest, but every time I'd drifted off, the horrifying image of Taamir's bloodied face and Rima's tears clouded my vision.

Restless energy coursed through me, and I flexed my hands and tapped my feet on the floorboards.

Finally, we took the exit between an enormous outcropping of rocks and onto the dirt road leading off the highway and to Taamir's house.

A swirling tendril of black smoke coiled up into the sky behind the house.

I shoved the car door open before Assem had put the car in park, stumbling across the gravel, and I grunted while springing myself from the car.

Assem shouted something about me needing to wait, but the thought of the statue possessed me. Assem's footsteps echoed behind me as I skidded to a stop when my small apartment came into view. Or what was left of it?

Smoldering piles of charred wood and broken stone were covered with fluttering shreds of carpet and cloth. My breath froze in my throat.

Taamir. I thought and spun, looking to the main house. It appeared untouched, with no damage that I could see. I darted toward the back door, pulling it open.

"Taamir!" I shouted. "Are you home?"

Heart hammering against my chest, I ran into the living room. Empty. I couldn't remember seeing Taamir's car in the driveway since all my focus was on the smoke plume in the back.

A soft whimpering came from one of the bedrooms, and I followed it. Larissa sat on the foot of her bed with her face buried in her arms, crying. Beside her, Maya lay on her side, asleep.

"Larissa," I called out, and the woman looked up. Larissa's bloodshot eyes peered up at me from under the loose locks that had fallen from under her headscarf.

"Ella?" she murmured, her eyes narrowing. "What are you doing here?"

An instant later, Larissa's embrace captured me.

"Praise be," she said, releasing me. She wiped the tears trickling down her cheeks. "They took Taamir and...Rima."

My throat was as dry as the sun-baked sands outside. "I know. That's why I'm here. I need you to tell me *who* took them."

"I don't know," she said, shaking her head. "We'd arrived home from shopping at the market, and Taamir and Rima had stayed home. Maya and I unloaded the car, and when we came inside, we discovered they were gone."

Her voice cracked, and she sobbed, pressing her face against my shoulder.

Sadness and frustration twisted and turned inside me as I

caressed the woman's back. Maya stirred, and Larissa went to sit with her daughter on the bed, pulling the young girl into her arms.

I couldn't fathom the pain she must be feeling right now, but I knew I'd do everything I could to make it right.

"Is there anything you can tell me about who took them? Maybe a smell, or you heard something? Did they leave anything behind?"

Larissa sniffed, stroking her daughter's hair. "There was one thing. A note on the table."

"A note?" I said, "Where is it?"

Larissa straightened and pulled a wrinkled piece of paper from her skirt pocket. "I thought it was one of Rima's art drawings at first. You know how she loves her markers, but it was different."

I took it from her trembling hand and read it.

Bring the statue, and they'll live.

Grand Aleppo Hotel, Room 209. 9 am tomorrow

I re-read it before flipping it over to examine the back. That was it. Two sentences.

The air in the room boiled, and my knees buckled. I sucked in a trembling breath and shoved the note into my bag. The note had been meant for *me*. Whoever had sent me those texts and knew I worked with Taamir had known I would come here and find the note.

I felt ill, feverish that my worst fear had come true. Two people I cared about were in danger because of me.

I glanced at Assem. "Stay with them," I said, and without waiting for him to reply, I jogged past him through the narrow doorway. I ran across the small yard and paced in a circle around the remnants of my apartment. Broken glass crunched under my boots as I attempted to climb over the charred wood and brick. If they'd felt the need to leave the note, it could only mean one very important thing: they hadn't found the statue.

I could only assume that after they'd searched Taamir's house and my own, they'd come up empty-handed and so enraged they'd decided to blow it up.

Assholes.

As I started sifting through the rubble in the fading light, Assem appeared with a flashlight. The light illuminated the fractured pieces of my simple life. Shattered pieces of pottery I'd found at the market. The smoldering remnants of my favorite woven blanket and a few tatters of my clothing. As I pulled free a broken piece of cabinetry, my heart leaped at the sight of the fridge's battered metal door. I knelt, wedging my fingers under the broken metal, and pried it upward, exposing the freezer compartment. Unable to see inside, I twisted my arm, straining to reach under the bricks and inside it. I worked my fingers along the smooth surface until they brushed the woven fabric of my sock.

Jackpot.

Still kneeling, I unwrapped the statue, breathing rapidly as I again succumbed to the power radiating from the statue's presence. I cupped it in my palms, absorbing the intricate details of the woman's face. My thumb caressed the marble-like smoothness of its edges, and the statue grew warm, the metallic surface illuminating as if lit by an internal light source. Glowing, it grew in intensity, the warmth radiating from where it sat in my hands, down my wrists and elbows, and into my chest. A stillness enveloped my mind, yet I was alert as if the world around me had pulled sharply into focus.

I flipped the idol over, examining it as the first stars appeared in the sky. Zig-zagging lines were etched into the base under Inanna's feet.

The artist's signature, perhaps, or some prayer to Inanna in

Sumerian? The markings fanned out in a spiral from a single prominent dot in the center, looking like roads leading to a focal point. The bridge's location. It had to be.

Surrounded by the wreckage of my apartment, it took everything not to jump up and down and howl like a jackal to the night sky overhead. Enheduanna had been right. I *did* have everything I needed; I just needed to look at it from a different perspective.

I held out the paper with Kat's drawing and felt Assem's ever-watchful gaze on me as I sat the paper atop the base. I twisted and turned it like a puzzle to reveal the full image. Finally, when all the lines matched, the center landed precisely on a point where Kat had written a single word: Palmyra.

I looked up, finding Assem's dumbfounded expression reflecting my own. My heartbeat drummed in my ears, and I folded the paper and stuffed it away with the statue into my bag.

"I need you to take Larissa and Maya to a hotel. Make sure you're not followed and give them your phone number." I told Assem, standing and brushing off the dirt and soot from my knees.

"That can be done. What about you?"

"Aleppo. I have to get Taamir and Rima back. Then," I hesitated, realizing what I was saying was beyond crazy. "Then, I'll go to Palmyra."

Assem blinked at my response and, thankfully, didn't argue. It's not like he could've stopped me if I wanted to. He was big and surprisingly quick, but as much as I'd hate doing so, Taamir and Rima's lives were at stake, and I'd use whatever means necessary to get to them.

"Very well," he said, left to fetch Larissa and her daughter from the bedroom. I went to the back of the kitchen and plucked Taamir's keys off the hook. By the time I was outside again, I saw the taillights of the Mercedes receding and Larissa staring mournfully out of the rear window.

I'll bring them back. I swear it.

Relieved that Larissa and Maya were safe for the time being, I threw my bag in the backseat, set the burner cell phone in the cup holder, and started the station wagon's engine.

I briefly played with the idea that I should call Jason and tell him everything that had happened and what I'd discovered, but reaching out to him would only put him in more danger. I had to believe he knew what he was doing, and I hoped he trusted me enough with what I was planning to do.

A quarter past eleven at night, very few cars shared the roadway, and even pushing the station wagon's tired engine to keep up a seventy miles per hour clip—it'd take me at least five hours to reach Aleppo. I pressed down on the accelerator. Dark thoughts plagued me, imagining what was happening to Taamir and Rima. Were they being tortured? Had they been given water? Food? Had they been separated?

I continued Northwest for an hour before I begrudgingly had to stop for gas.

I pulled into an empty pump. Even though it was still a balmy eighty degrees outside, I slipped on my hooded sweatshirt and a pair of dark sunglasses. I scanned my surroundings before climbing out and counted three other men using the pumps.

The station's attendant, an older man with thinning hair and glasses, strode over to me.

"Eh there, how much?" the man asked.

I lowered my voice. "Ten."

The man set the pump to ten gallons and then held out a hand.

I stuffed a crumpled bill into his palm, Twenty Syrian pounds—more than enough.

The man didn't move. Instead, he leaned an arm against the pump, watching me as I took off the cap and began filling the tank. Please, God, don't tell me he wanted to chit-chat. This was the only fuel station for a hundred miles, and obviously, he'd pulled the short straw to work the boring night shift, but I wasn't the only customer. Surely there was someone else he could bother?

"Your car?" he asked.

"My Uncle's," I lied.

The man revealed a toothpick, picking at the next row of crooked teeth.

The painfully slow pump rotated, ticking off the gallons. Five gallons, six...seven. Suddenly, there was a terrible grinding noise, followed by a gurgle, and the meter stalled.

Shit. My finger flicked on the trigger, desperate to keep the gas flowing.

"Uh, it stopped," I murmured, keeping my eyes down.

"It does that."

Sweat trickled from the nape of my neck, down my back, and under my sweatshirt. "Can you fix it?" I said, my voice wavering, hoping he was just odd and not dangerous. There was a chance I could walk away from this without incident.

My heart rate escalated, anticipating what he would do.

The man's smile broadened, and he took a step toward me. "For a price, I suppose I could," he sneered. His breath was hot and reeked of cigarette smoke and peppered meats.

My eyes frantically searched the other pumps. The other truck had left, and the car opposite me was empty since the driver had gone into the store.

The man stepped closer, his hand moving up to remove my sunglasses.

Fear and panic gripped me, and my hand shot up. The burst of power ripped through my arm, superheating the air between us. The man flew backward, his back hitting the pump with a loud bang. The metal on the pump hissed from the scorching hot air as the hose leading to it melted.

I stood frozen as the man lay unmoving on the ground. Uh, yeah, time to go.

I pulled the nozzle from the gas tank, not bothering to place it back on the holder, and wrenched open the car door. Inside, I jammed the key into the ignition, the motor groaned to life, and I stepped on the accelerator.

The car bounced as I swerved a hard right and re-entered the freeway. I glanced in the rear-view mirror, seeing the outline of the unconscious man.

You should've kept the change, dickhead.

The pump shimmered with a flame single tendril of flame before exploding.

I ducked my head between her hands on the steering wheel, the impact of the powerful blast jolting the car. An enormous red fireball floated upward, engulfing the wooden beams and rafters of the shaded lean-to above it.

I pushed the gas pedal down, desperate to put as much distance between me and the station as possible. A few minutes later, I checked the fuel gauge.

Half a tank.

I'd be on fumes once I reached Aleppo, but at least I'd make it.

When a sign warned me I was an hour from Aleppo, my hands tightened on the steering wheel. My thoughts warred with each other, torn with ideas on how to formulate a plan of action once I arrived.

I'd been to Aleppo only once and attempted to recall the city's layout. With a population of over four million, the city was a sprawling mass of multi-story stone buildings. A hub for international business offices, a diplomat, and a foreign relations headquarters. I recalled the Kane United office I'd seen there and knew it to be a subsidiary regional office that installed solar panels in the desert.

I slammed on the brakes, the tires screeching, and pulled onto the shoulder of the road. The truck that had been tailgating me blared its horn and swerved.

I ignored them, pressing my forehead against the steering wheel. I drew in a shuddering breath. What was I doing?

Taamir and Rima were in very real danger. I had to go to the address on the note. I had no other choice. It was their lives for the statue.

I slammed a palm against the car's dash, sending up a cloud of dust. I despised this feeling of being cornered, coerced into playing someone else's game. I gritted my teeth as I pulled back onto the highway. I'd do whatever it took to save them, even if it meant sacrificing the statue.

What came after that, I guess I'd have to find out.

TWENTY-TWO

Driving in the city of Aleppo is akin to catching slippery tadpoles from a pond, except instead of wriggling tadpoles, there are hundreds of cars. And instead of a mason jar in your hands, you have a white-knuckled death grip on a steering wheel and feel the years being sapped from your life with every intersection. Just when you think you have an opportunity to merge, a car slithers in beside you, taking said space. There honestly isn't a need for painted lines on the roadways since none of the drivers pay them any mind. Instead, swerving and veering every which way, they created new lanes between the torrent of cars. A cacophony of horns and engine gunning erupted as the deluge of cars, trucks, and motorcycles all shuffled through the flashing street signals.

I switched lanes feeling my blood pressure creep higher and prayed Taamir's car would make it to the hotel in one piece. I braked for a red light, reading the street signs, and then I spotted it. The Grand Aleppo Hotel is located in the government-controlled Eastern district, and the ten-story building occupies an entire street corner amongst the tourist-loving museums and galleries.

I entered the underground parking garage beneath the hotel and found an open parking space.

I hauled my bag onto my lap and debated whether leaving it in the car would be wise. Dread crept into my thoughts as it dawned on me that this person I would deal with wouldn't take kindly to waiting for me to retrieve it. It was my only leverage, but Taamir and Rima's life were on the line.

I stuffed the statue inside my bag and grabbed the burner phone from the center console. Assem had made me memorize his number. I sent him a text message:

Made it to Aleppo.

It was short, but what else could I say? I will text you again when, when what? When I've got Taamir and Rima safe, and I'm not dead? I liked to imagine a future where I walked away from this, but after the agents chasing us in the market, the destruction of my house, and now the kidnapping, that door seemed to be drifting close.

I buried my face, pressing my hands into the back of my eyelids. No. It was stupid to do this this way. It was all speculation until I had more information, and I could only assume they didn't want me dead. They only wanted the statue.

My breathing synced in rhythm with each stride as I climbed the stairs and through the door leading to the hotel lobby. I kept my head down, not daring to make eye contact with anyone.

Marbled pillars jutted up from marble floors, reminding me of the five-star hotels in New York. Multi-colored velvet cushions dotted the numerous chairs and couches scattered throughout the center, and palm trees in four-foot-wide pots projected up toward the diamond-shaped skylights at the stone ceiling's arching peak. I passed several boutique-style shops and a teal green tiled fountain cascaded over three obelisks of white marble. The smell of designer perfumes and oiled leather from handbags wafted my face.

Delicious smells of garlic and smoked meats wafted toward me as I passed several restaurants, and many of the tables were filled with guests. Their chatting voices, with a measure of accents, drifted out into the hallway. With the promise of the government's protection, the Aleppo Hotel recently reopened after being closed for three years. A man wearing a black suit strode past me. He held a room key in one arm, and another carried a basket with fine fruit wines.

I smiled to myself. It was doing *quite* well so far.

A middle-aged man with a trimmed mustache smiled as I approached the hotel check-in desk. He appraised my dirty jeans, t-shirt, and boots.

"May I help you?" he asked as if I were inconveniencing him.

"Yeah," I said. "I'm meeting someone here in room 212?"

The man glanced down at his notebook.

"Ah, yes. Here you go, Ms. Dawson," he said, handing me a room key. "Apologies, our elevators are currently under repair. The stairs are located around the corner and to your left. Please enjoy your stay."

I took the envelope, eying the man suspiciously. His rapid change in demeanor caused a chill to ripple down my spine. Whoever had booked the room had left this man more than a little rattled.

Great.

My eyes scanned the lobby as I strode toward the stairs. An assortment of people sat or stood among the upholstered chairs. A few engaged in discussion while sipping tea or coffee. A large clock — its polished chrome hands nearing the gold-foiled number nine — hung on the wall above the entrance doors.

I quickly took the stairs two at a time until I reached the second floor. Plush ivory carpet lined the wooden paneled hallways. The hallway was deserted, and I read the numbers on the doors until I reached 212. I held my breath as I slid the key in, letting it out when it clicked unlocked. My magic hovered right under the surface, ready and waiting. Pulse racing in my ears, I turned the knob and entered. No lights were on, and the curtains were closed. I closed the door softly behind me, every nerve fiber aware and waiting for someone to attack me. I stilled my breathing, listening.

An air conditioner hummed under the window on the far wall, and the double bed was made, appearing untouched.

Nothing. The room was empty. My defenses kicked into overdrive. Had I come to the wrong room? Maybe I'd skipped a floor?

I kicked open the door to the bathroom, expecting hands to reach out to snatch me, but found only a toilet and an empty shower. I knelt in the main room, searching under the beds and behind the curtains.

Still nothing. No bombs counting down. No men hiding like scary movie monsters with black masks and guns.

I paced from the bathroom and to the window again. The time on my phone showed three minutes past nine. What was I supposed to do now? I checked my messages. Nothing from them and nothing from Assem.

Was I too late? Had they meant no later than nine?

My body began to shake, and I was hit with a wave of nausea. I slumped onto the floor beside the bed and buried my face in my hands. Despair ripped through me, threatening to suffocate me. I'd failed them. I'd driven as fast as I could but missed the window, and now they were gone. My one chance, and I'd fucking blown it.

Tears, warm and wet, streaked my hands and cheeks.

A knock came at the door. At first, I thought I'd misheard the sound, muffled by the air conditioner, but then there was a second knock, this one more distinct.

I jumped to my feet, wiping the tears from my face. The door swung open, revealing a man about my age, his tall frame silhouetted against the hallway lights. He wore a blue turtle neck, ivory chinos, and loafers, looking like he would be more ready to spend a day on a yacht in Monaco than in the Middle East.

He slid off his sunglasses and flashed me a dazzling display of pristine white teeth against a clean-shaven jaw. While not un-handsome by traditional standards, he looked like someone who never had to endure hardship. While Jason's face was all hard lines and angles, his was rounded and softer. More boyish, then, man.

His deep-set hazel eyes, under pale blonde eyebrows, met my gaze.

"Good afternoon, Ms. Dawson. Terribly sorry to keep you waiting. I had another appointment that went over."

There was no way this was the kidnapper, but he seemed to know me. And he'd come alone. Underestimating me was his first mistake.

I narrowed my eyes, glancing over his shoulder at the empty hallway.

"I don't believe we've met before. My name is Derek." He held out his hand.

As if I'd fucking shake it.

"I demand to see Taamir and Rima," I spat.

"Of course," he said, sounding mildly offended. "I under-stand the importance of transparency in negotiations and expected as much." He picked up the TV remote from the table.

"I've discovered that adding visual elements during my presentations is a great motivator."

He turned on the TV, and an image appeared of a Taamir sitting on the cement floor of a small room. In his arms, he clutched Rima, whose braided pigtails were frazzled and partially undone.

My heart wrenched as if being squeezed by a vice. The man's eyes were on me, waiting to see how I'd react. I couldn't bear to turn away, fearing if I blinked, the image would disappear, and Taamir and Rima would vanish as well.

My words possessed a knife-like edge. "Don't hurt them."

The man ignored me and set the remote back on the table. "Now that I have your attention, I believe you have something for me?"

I tore my gaze away from the TV and glared at him. Loathing surged inside me, and for a moment, I considered raising my hand and engulfing him in superheated air. He was my only connection to Rima and Taamir, and if I killed him, it'd be signing their death certificates, too.

I reached into my bag, and his body tensed, worried I'd pull a gun from the bag instead of the statue. I revealed the idol of Inanna, the gold shimmering in the dimly lit room.

His eyes widened, and he licked his lips. "Give it to me," he commanded, holding his hand out.

I gripped it tighter and moved it closer to my body. "How do I know you'll let them go?"

The man stiffened as if my question had insulted him. "So long as you give me the statue, they will not be harmed."

A narrow beam of sunlight entered through a gap in the windows, and a shimmer on the side of the man's face caught my attention—a single bead of sweat clung to his right temple.

Something was making him nervous. His boss or partners, maybe? Or was it me?

"No," I said, lifting my chin. "I want to *see* them set free."

The man pulled a handkerchief from his pants pocket and patted his forehead. Carefully, he folded it into a square before tucking it away again. The process took only a moment, yet my heartbeats counted every painstaking second. I was playing a very dangerous game. However, I still had the upper hand as long as I had the statue in my possession. I prayed it would be enough.

"Very well," he replied, sighing. "Let's go."

Without waiting for me, he spun on his heel and was out the door. He whistled a melodic simple tune as I put the statue back into my bag. Once outside the door, two broad-chested men materialized at my side, and beefy hands grabbed my elbows. They dragged me toward the stairwell, and the hallway was suspiciously deserted. It was no use screaming or resisting. If I wanted to see Taamir and Rima again, I had no choice but to go where they went. And I could tolerate the manhandling as long as they didn't try to shoot me or stuff me in a trunk, I'd cooperate.

At the ground floor level, they shoved me away from the lobby through and out a metal door marked Keep Closed Except for Emergency.

The door slammed shut behind us, and with it, any chance of someone seeing me leaving with them. Derek led us into a narrow corridor and through another door into the underground parking garage. I spotted Taamir's car for a split second before a black hood was placed over my head.

"Is this completely necessary," I bemoaned. A hand tightened on my arm, and a sharp prick pierced the side of my neck. Instantly, my head swam from whatever drugs they'd injected me with. My wrists were forced behind my back and tied together.

They led me stumbling forward, from being unable to see to whatever sedative they'd give me.

There came the click of opening car doors, and a hand shoved my head down, positioning me into what I assumed was a backseat.

From under the hood's darkness, I heard an engine rev before feeling the swaying motion of a moving car.

My eyelids drooped, and my mouth felt like I'd swallowed cotton balls.

Right. Left. I struggled to make a mental map of where they were taking me. Accelerate. Stop. Right again.

The world swirled, and I lay my head back. Sleep lured me.

Another right, or was that a left?

The world faded. I frantically grasped at reality, trying to stay conscious. The final image I'd seen before they'd put the hood on me flashed in my mind. I'd seen the man with the baseball cap sliding into a silver Range Rover, and the license plate had read: KANE#1.

THE CAR'S ENGINE DRONED, and time blurred as I lingered in the twilight, drifting in and out of consciousness. My neck was stiff and ached from the awkward angle of my arms behind my back. The skin burned around my wrists where a zip tie dug them.

Eventually, the car slowed, tilting right, and the tires hummed from the roadway, shifting to the crunch of gravel.

Abruptly, the car stopped.

The doors creaked open, and I felt someone tugging on the strap to my shoulder bag. My mind shrieked at me to react, but my body refused to respond as if an elephant were sitting on my chest. My magic shuddered, and I sensed something about the drugs inhibited my ability to use it.

Hands clutched my arms, hauling me out of the car. The hood was yanked off. I squinted at the shock of sunlight as my chin leaned against my chest. Too weak to walk, they half-carried me with my boots dragging on the gravel through a gate between chain-link fence topped with barbwire. A metal sign reading: RESTRICTED AREA KANE INDUSTRIES dangled from chains affixed to a wooden post. We passed two small outbuild-ings, guards walking with dogs, and people in yellow hard hats milling about before a square beige stone building came into focus, and at least a dozen armed guards paced the flat rooftop.

Two men carrying assault rifles strode over from the main entrance.

"Mr. Kane wants her in the North Hall," one of them said.

My two captors directed me to a steel door, which buzzed with an internal mechanism before swinging open.

My heart thrummed, imagining this feeling as what inmates entering a prison felt like. The ceiling and walls were oppressive, and I could almost sense the hundreds of tons of stone and metal surrounding me. I staggered onward and worried if they weren't holding me up, I'd fall face-first onto the concrete floor. My breathing was labored, and I actively worked to stave off a full-blown panic attack. *Just breathe. It's the drugs they gave you.*

Cracks ran along the cement floor. Jagged pieces of stucco had broken off in the ceiling, exposing the twists of rusted metal piping. All the rooms had solid metal doors. One still had the faint outlines of PRESSURE TANKS stenciled in block lettering.

What *was* this place? An oil refinery or water treatment plant, perhaps. Whatever it was, it appeared it had either been decommissioned or desperately needed repair.

The men opened another metal door and tossed me inside. Unable to break my fall, I landed *hard* on my back, and pain exploded from my tailbone all the way to my shoulders.

"Assholes!" I bellowed, although my tongue felt too big for my mouth, so I was unsure if I'd said it aloud or in my head. The metal door slammed, cutting off my words. A clank of a bolt slid into position, and the sound of their footsteps faded as they walked away.

I was alone.

I rolled onto my side, the side of my shoulder aching as I used it to pry myself up into a sitting position. The only light came from a single window, at least ten feet up on the wall behind me. Scooting on my rear, I pressed my back against the concrete wall. I leaned my head against it and closed my eyes. My head swam as I suppressed a rising wave of nausea.

I closed my eyes, struggling to sift through my muddled thoughts. I needed to focus, concentrate on what I did know.

Derek *was* Mr. Kane. The statue was valuable enough to him that *he* personally met with me to ensure I had it. There was only one reason he wouldn't risk something this important being done by mercenaries like Division 12 or his personal guards.

He knew the power the statue had.

So why was I here now? Why didn't he take the statue from me when I'd been drugged and dump me in a ditch somewhere? I could only guess that Rima and Taamir were also being held captive here, so why hadn't he taken me straight to them?

What was he waiting for?

CHAPTER

TWENTY-THREE

Daylight filtered through the tiny barred window as I dozed throughout the afternoon and into the evening. At some point, I'd moved onto a thin mattress, covered myself with a wool blanket, and vaguely remembered a guard entering and freeing my wrists.

When the constant throbbing in my head finally became bearable, I slowly sat up. Cement walls on all sides met a low gray ceiling. It had been morning when they'd taken me. How long had I been here? Hours. Days? Dread twisted my gut.

Shadows cloaked the corners of the room, but I could make out the outline of a plastic bucket. I crawled over to it, not trusting myself to handle the change in altitude by standing. After relieving myself, I scrambled to where my boots were placed by the end of the bed and spotted my bag.

I leaped for it. A thud of pain ricocheted against the back of my skull, and I hunched over, covering my mouth as I tasted bile. The nasty lingering effects of whatever sedative they'd given me. After a minute, my headache eased, and I eased my way to my bag. I stuck my hands inside and discovered it empty.

I lifted the flap and dumped it over, still clinging to the hope that it had something that could help me and had been missed when they'd confiscated it.

A few almonds cascaded out, chattering on the floor.

I groaned and tossed it against the wall.

Both the statue and the burner phone from Assem were gone.

What was I going to do? I'd lost my only leverage. Did they plan on just leaving me here forever? The shattered remnants of hope ripped at my heart, catching the breath in my throat. I wanted nothing more than to lie on the dirty mattress, close my eyes, and wish all this was a dream I'd awake from.

Not a dream. A nightmare

But my resolve was too strong. I'd come here to rescue my friend and his daughter, and until I exhaled my last breath, I wouldn't stop.

My stomach grumbled, indicating that it'd been hours since I'd eaten.

A plate with a metal cover sat beside the door. I slid it toward me, the grind of the metal dish against concrete echoing in the small chamber.

I tore into the dry sandwich: Lamb and hummus and a hint of something pickled. I sucked in a slow breath, clenching my teeth and attempting to ease the bubbling rise of nausea.

I forced down the sandwich. Sweat stung my eyes, dripping from my scalp in the stagnant air. *Too* hot.

My heart raced as I feared I'd overheat in this concrete oven. Visions of my mummified and dehydrated corpse being found weeks later and danced before my eyes. Hadn't that happened to Ms. Gentry, our elderly neighbor in the trailer park? The police finally showed up after weeks of no one seeing her. She'd been found in my recliner; her skin wrinkled like a leathery raisin. Thankfully, she'd died of natural causes.

"As shriveled as a trout on the riverbank in July," the words of another neighbor replayed in my head.

Spending extensive time in the harsh deserts in the Middle East had taught me many fascinating things about the signs of heat stroke. They included such delights as excessive sweating, racing heartbeat, fatigue, and delusional thoughts. For example, my sudden recollection of a decade-old memory clearly indicated that I was in trouble.

My body was transitioning into survival mode. I refused to end up as human jerky like Ms. Gentry.

I reached for the bottle of water. It was warm, so instinctively, I focused on slowing the water molecules to lower the temperature. The magic came forth, and a frost spread over the bottle. The magic wavered feelings as if I were straddling a paddleboard battling the wakes of a cruise ship. The more I concentrated, the more it receded until it was gone.

A hollowness crept into me. I'd recharged at Taamir's. I'd felt the raw power from the statue, the heady rush of magic replenishing me. Had I been unconscious so long that the power had drained completely?

No wait. The gas station.

Shit.

I must have used more power than I realized.

With no other options, I drank the tepid water, draining the bottle in one long gulp.

I tossed the empty bottle to the side. My headache had returned to a steady pounding rhythm behind my eyeballs. I eased back to the mattress and rested an arm over my eyes.

The sounds of clicking locks came after, and the door opened.

Sitting up almost too fast, I steadied myself on the mattress.

Derek Kane stepped inside, and the door closed behind him.

His face was clean-shaven, and his expensive cologne permeated the room.

He eyed the empty plate. "I see you've recovered. Excellent. My apologies from before. I'm afraid our first conversation was rushed, and I didn't introduce myself completely. My name is Derek Kane."

I knew I'd recognized him at the hotel but had been so distracted by my need to find Taamir and Rima I hadn't realized how I'd known him.

Derek Kane was the oldest son of corporate mogul Anthony Kane and the founder of Kane United. Unless you lived under a rock, you knew who he was. His face graced the front of every trash magazine, dining in cafes in Paris, clubbing with supermodels in Miami, and he had a brief stint on a reality show called Born Rich: Tales of Billionaire Progeny, starring other adult children of the super-rich.

I wanted to stand, feeling vulnerable while seated, but I didn't yet trust my balance. "I know who you are," I said, keeping my voice low.

Derek grinned. "Good, and I know quite a bit about you, Ella Dawson." My name slid over his tongue as if he'd tasted something foul.

"It seems you and I have quite a bit in common. Both our parents chose to remarry, and while you remained with your mother, I was taken by my father after the divorce. My mother is too ill and deemed unfit to care for me." Derek raised his chin. His words seemed forced as if he were reciting them from a well-rehearsed script.

I grimaced. His mother's illness had been kept hush-hush, and all my knowledge had come from leaked sources. Although the divorce was never publicized, the engagement announcement to his new wife made media headlines for days. He'd met the "love of his life" and an heir herself to a multi-million-dollar corporation. But it meant that the two corporations would be unified with the marriage.

Millions had been spent on the wedding, including private helicopters to escort the guests to the secluded location. Soon after, they gave Derek a younger brother, Harrison Kane.

Amid rumors the company's refineries were in trouble in the Middle East, Derek had been put in charge. He had negotiated million-dollar contracts and secured partnerships with local businesses his father had been unable to accomplish.

However, I recalled seeing the news last summer report that Kane Senior had been diagnosed with terminal cancer. Kane United stock plummeted as nervous investors pulled out. In order to stop the hemorrhaging, he needed to pick an heir to the Kane throne. Everyone assumed the eldest, Derek, would be first in line to take over. However, too many a raised brow, Kane senior had chosen the youngest, Harrison.

Derek eyed me, waiting for me to respond.

"Take me to Taamir and Rima."

"I see we're done with the pleasantries," he said, clapping his hands. "Very well." He stepped back and waved a hand overheard. The door opened, and a guard stepped in. This one was smaller than the two that had taken me and had a neatly trimmed beard and a bulletproof vest.

"Bring the father and daughter, would you?" Derek told the guard.

The man's eyes flicked to me, and then he quickly nodded before leaving.

The door closed again.

Derek appraised me, and I ground my teeth together. My detest for this man grew stronger with every passing second he was in my presence.

I recoiled back into the mattress.

"I hate to admit it, but you were not easy to find." Derek

reached into his coat pocket and took out the statue. "And this," he paused, studying it. "Well, let's just say I've learned it has ways of protecting itself, revealing only to those it deems worthy."

So, that's how they hadn't found it in the freezer. Damn, I guess I wasn't as good at hiding things as I'd hoped.

"And then not only did you take it from me," he continued. "but the power inside it chose *you*. A photographer," he scoffed. "Who would have thought?"

When I didn't respond, he shrugged. "No bother. I've studied the legends enough to know that just because Inanna's power has been granted doesn't mean the gate can't still be opened."

Realization dawned on me, and a warmth filled my chest. It *had* been him that had stolen the stones. It was Derek who wanted to open the bridge.

The clang of a door opened, and Taamir and Rima were shoved inside while Derek moved back toward the door.

I jumped to my feet, ignoring the violent spinning of the room, and threw my arms around them. I choked back the tears, hugging them. Then, I pushed them back to examine their faces. Dried blood coated Taamir's temple and matted his hair. And Rima, although dirty and tired, appeared unharmed.

"I'm so sorry," I murmured. "I didn't mean for any of this to happen."

Taamir gave me a reassuring smile.

"You have the statue," I said, locking eyes with Derek. "Now let us go."

Derek folded his arms. "Unfortunately, you are no longer in a position to make demands. However, I intend to let you go," he paused. "In two days, once I've opened the bridge."

Without waiting for me to respond, he turned on his heel

and was out the door. The lock clanged shut, and we were left alone in what I now knew was a prison cell.

Rima, Taamir, and I sat huddled on the mattress for some time. Eventually, Rima rested her head against my shoulder, and their soft snores soon echoed off the room.

Taamir's face was bloodied and bruised, and despair clogged my throat. They'd tortured him. He *had* seen the statue. However, that was the extent of it. His ignorance regarding it could have been why they'd kept him alive as long as they did. Perhaps they'd held out hope that they'd break him, and he'd confess more intimate details about me. Names of other contacts, friends, or places I'd frequently stay. How much had he told them about me? Derek seemed to have extensive background on me, including my name and family. Could Taamir have been his resource? No, Taamir was a friend. He'd never betray my trust.

My stomach twisted when another thought occurred to me. Was that trust worth more to him than Rima's life? Had they threatened to harm Rima, he'd done what any father would've. He'd confess anything they'd wanted to know. And I could never resent him for it.

As the sun faded and fatigue slumped my shoulders and dulled my senses, I rejected the need for sleep. I didn't trust Derek as far as I could throw him, and there was a very real chance he had hidden cameras and would return and take Taamir and Rima the instant I let my guard slip.

I stood, letting Rima's head gently onto the pillow, and began to pace to keep myself awake. I was running out of time. In two days, whatever celestial or lunar alignment Derek was waiting for would happen, and the window to summon the Bridge of Vela would appear. And now, he had the key. I *had* to get the statue back.

But how? That was the problem. I needed my power to get the statue, but I needed the statue to get my power.

My thoughts sifted through everything Derek had told me. He said he'd studied the legends. But how much did he know? I had to assume, then, that he only knew what he'd found on his own, either from cuneiform tablets, books, or expert researchers he'd hired. I, however, had first-hand experience with Enheduanna. Well, as much as the spirit of a four-thousand-year-old dead priestess could be considered 'first hand'. Her soul, or whatever she was, told me things that weren't in the books Kat had or even at the museum, which meant there was a chance, however small, that I knew more than he did.

Enheduanna had warned me and shown me what would happen should the wrong person cross the bridge. Although Derek was an arrogant, entitled dickhead, he didn't seem to be harboring some burning desire to conquer a country or start a world war.

I was at a loss as to why he was infatuated with the bridge and his need to cross it.

I rested my head against the wall, savoring the coolness of the stone. I couldn't write off the idea that he *did* intend to use the bridge's well of knowledge for good reasons. However, something about that didn't feel right. He had access to money, lots of it. If he wanted to get his philanthropic rocks off, he could be like the rest of the bored and rich and start a charity.

I also wasn't convinced that he'd let the three of us go after he'd opened the bridge. That was total bullshit. We'd never walk out of here alive after everything we'd seen. If we wanted out, we'd have to *fight* our way out.

It was a long shot without my magic to aid me, but unless Enheduanna decided to make another appearance granting me unlimited magic, I was all out of options.

Taamir rolled over and draped a protective arm over a sleeping Rima.

I needed them to unlock the door, which meant I needed to get Derek's attention. Earlier, when he'd had the guards bring Taamir and Rima, he'd waved at something, indicating there *must* be a camera somewhere.

My eyes went to the corners for any irregularity in the wall and landed on a small black dot with a reflective lens about a foot above the door.

I walked closer and stared directly at it. "I need to speak to Mr. Kane."

Nothing happened.

What did I expect? A disembodied voice to reply? The doors to suddenly slide open?

My hands curled into fists. I couldn't falter now. Maybe they were on break and had stepped away from the camera. I spoke again. "Mr. Kane. It's about the Bridge of Vela."

I held my breath.

A minute passed, and I nearly gave up hope when the internal mechanisms clicked, and the door slid open.

Bingo.

CHAPTER
TWENTY-FOUR

A single guard stood in the doorway. I didn't hesitate and kneed him in the groin. He collapsed, clutching himself, and I swiped the pistol from his side holster.

I jabbed the pistol against his head. "Don't fucking move," I commanded as Taamir and Rima side-stepped around him.

The man's face paled, keeping his eyes focused on the floor.

"Tell me how we get out of here."

The man squinted his eyes shut.

"Tell me!" I pressed the barrel harder, and he winced.

"Mr. Kane would never forgive me."

"Mr. Kane doesn't have the gun pressed to your head, now, does he?"

The guard peeked up at me as if testing my conviction. I didn't want to kill him, but when those I cared about were threatened, I discovered a whole side of me willing to do things. Bad things.

"Two doors to the left, behind..." he started, but his words were cut off as a bullet whizzed by my leg, hitting the man in the back of the head. He collapsed face first, and blood pooled on the floor.

Startled, I dropped the pistol and spun around. Another guard with his gun drawn stood at the end of the hallway. "Don't move!" he shouted.

My pulse pounded in my ears as I raised my hands in surrender.

A second crack of a shot erupted from behind me, and I covered my head. There was a clatter of metal as the threatening guard dropped his pistol, and his hand immediately went to the left side of his neck.

Beside me, Taamir's hands shook as he clutched the pistol I'd dropped. His face was grim, his eyes set as he continued to point it at the second guard.

I seized the opening he'd given us and darted to the second guard, swiping his pistol as he doubled over, groaning. Blood gurgled from his neck and mouth, and his face was rapidly losing color.

Taamir lowered the gun and placed Rima behind him, and her small hands covered her ears.

Taamir and I exchanged a quick look. Our months of working together permitted us to relay our intentions without speaking, and he nodded before we started down the hallway.

Passing two doors, I took the third and exited the building. The morning sun just crested the tops of the surrounding outbuildings. Tall smokestacks rose high into the cloudless sky, although no smoke or steam erupted from their pointed tops.

I pulled Taamir and Rima with me out into the courtyard keeping an eye out for any patrolling guards.

Two had been posted far off to the right near the north gate, and I paused, looking to Taamir, and pressed my finger to my lips before signaling in their direction.

He followed my motion and then nodded. We ran swiftly but silently to the left. We'd entered through that gate at the north but could only hope there was more than one exit.

We doubled back. I halted Taamir and Rima while my eyes scanned behind the main building. Several jeeps were parked in a line and a gate big enough for vehicles to pass through not too far beyond then.

Seeing the place was clear, I glanced over my shoulder and motioned toward the nearest SUV.

"I'll go first," I said.

Taamir shook his head. "It'll be faster if we both go and can check them together." Then he directed a look at the pistol I still carried. "Rima," he said, getting his daughter's attention. "Stay with Ella, alright?"

Rima's bottom lip quivered, but the girl nodded.

I dashed toward the Jeep with Taamir and Rima hot on my heels.

I swapped the pistol from my right hand to my left before reaching into the open window to unlock the door. Taamir ran past my left shoulder, heading toward the second parked Jeep.

I pulled the door open and leaned in, my hand reaching toward the ignition. My scalp prickled as I held my breath. Warm metal brushed my fingers, and instantly, I turned the key.

In my entire life, I swear I'd never heard a more wonderful sound than when the car's engine rumbled to life. I angled Rima by my side and waved her to climb in.

She hesitated, looking to where her father was trying the handle of another jeep.

"I'll go get him," I whispered. "You climb in and then get down and hide."

The girl took a deep breath and then jumped in the front, clambering over to the back bench seat.

I stepped back, and Taamir was gone. "Taamir!" I called out.

My heart pounded when the seconds clicked off, and he didn't respond.

I moved to the front of the jeep, hoping to catch sight of him.

"Stop!" a guard shouted, sprinting from a door in the back of the building. He reached for his pistol.

I squeezed off three shots at him, both glancing off the side of the building before I'd emptied the clip.

"Go, save Rima," Taamir said, having materialized next to me.

The thin man sat crouched beside the Jeep's front tire, and his eyes appeared distant as he handed me the other gun.

"What are you doing?" I said, shaking my head. "Rima is in the car. Let's go!"

A sad smile formed on his face. "Tell my girls I will always watch over them."

The air evaporated from my lungs.

Taamir bolted from behind the Jeep, running full speed toward the guard. The guard's eyes widened in bewilderment as the thin man charged him. Taamir leaped, tackling the guard, and both tumbled to the ground.

Taamir swung at the guard, landing a few solid punches. Suddenly, there were two muffled cracks of gunfire. Time slowed.

The guard slowly shoved a limp Taamir off of him.

My boots skidded in the loose gravel as I ran around the front of the Jeep, leaping into the driver's seat. I smashed down the accelerator, launching it forward.

I ducked as bullets battered the driver's side door, and a searing pain exploded from my left thigh. A second pinged off the rear bumper, and I lifted my head again just in time to see us careening toward a very much locked gate.

"Hang on, Rima," I shouted over my shoulder. The words were barely out of my mouth before a horrendous crunch of twisting metal as we crashed through the gate. The glass on the windshield cracked from the impact, and dust swirled, obscuring my vision. I kept the gas pedal pegged and spun the steering wheel to the left, angling the car to what I thought was the direction of the road.

The tires bounced over rocks, and finally, the dust cleared enough just in time for me to smack into another wooden barricade, leaving it in splinters on the dirt road. I heard distant shouts and engines starting behind us.

My hands shook as I adjusted the grip on the wheel and directed the SUV off the gravel road and onto the pavement.

In the rearview mirror, Rima's small body lay curled in a fetal position on the floorboards. Her body shuddered as she cried.

I forced down the lump in my throat, still reeling from what had just happened. I couldn't allow myself to think about what had happened to Taamir. Not now.

I refused to let the anguish drag me down, immobilize me before I'd gotten his family safe. Which meant I had to get them as far away as possible. In the distance, cars zoomed back and forth in the shimmering heat waves above the highway.

I drew a sharp breath through my nose, constantly checking the rearview mirror to ensure we weren't being followed.

I took the on-ramp onto the highway, heading toward Aleppo. While I'd considered going to Kat's, the jeep was new enough that they probably had a GPS tracker on it and were hours away from finding it. The crowded city would allow me to ditch the car, and we could get lost among the businesses and apartments while we lay low, and devised a plan of what to do next.

The noon-day sun blazed overhead when I put the SUV in a public parking area.

I shut off the engine and leaned my arm over the seat.

"We're safe now."

The dark-haired girl looked up at me, her eyes wet with tears. "Baba..." she whimpered.

"I know, and I'm so sorry," I said, my vision blurring. "But right now, I need you to be brave, okay? I promised him to get you safe, and that's what I'm going to do."

Rima nodded, the tears cascading down her dirty cheeks.

Out of the car, I helped Rima step down onto the sidewalk. The girl's hand held firmly in mine as we walked for an unknown number of blocks. Finally, she complained about her legs being tired, and I led her to a busy intersection lined with businesses. People milled about, entering and exiting the clothing shops and neighboring restaurants.

"I don't know about you," I said. "But I'm starving. Why don't we get something to eat?"

Rima's eyes brightened, and her hand squeezed mine.

The door alarm beeped as we entered a restaurant. A young man with a white turban greeted us and motioned us to the corner booth near a window.

I shook my head and gripped Rima's hand, preventing her from sitting.

"Perhaps, a table in the back?" I asked.

The man tilted his head but then shrugged and led us to the back of the restaurant.

I breathed a sigh of relief as we were seated next to the opening where the waitstaff was shuffling trays in and out of the kitchen.

I ordered soup for myself, and when Rima said she wasn't hungry after all, I also ordered her soup.

After they'd brought it to us, I sipped the steaming bowl of soup, my stomach rumbling with every bite. Adrenaline had sapped my appetite, too, but I willed myself to eat anyway, knowing I needed to keep up my strength.

After some encouragement, I managed to get Rima to eat. The man returned to refill our water glasses.

"Do you have a phone?" I asked.

The man gestured toward a phone on the wall.

"Thanks," I said, pushing my chair back. Rima didn't look up, continuing to scoop and dump the soup into the bowl.

I debated who I should call. The police? The embassy? What if Derek's hooks were in all of them? Besides, what would I tell them? "Yes, hello, reality star and uber-rich playboy Derek Kane is chasing after me for an antique statue."

Yep. That totally didn't sound like an insane person needing less *or* maybe more drugs.

I picked up the phone. My priority right now was to get Rima somewhere safe.

I dialed Assem's number.

The line clicked as someone picked it up. "Hello," Assem said.

"Hi, it's me."

Silence.

"How are Larissa and Maya?"

"They are fine. Resting."

I released a breath, relieved they were okay. "Long story, but I need your help again. I have Rima with me."

"Where are you?"

"Aleppo, East Market Square. A little restaurant called Al-Mariza's."

A pause. "Stay there. I'll have someone get you in ten minutes."

The phone clicked, and he was gone.

TWENTY-FIVE

After hanging up the receiver, I returned to the table with Rima.

"I talked to my friend," I said. "He said your mom and sister are safe, and someone should be here soon to get you." I tried to keep my voice steady and reassuring. However, it sounded forced. The poor girl was traumatized and hadn't said a word about what had happened. I clung to the hope that she'd covered her eyes when her dad had been killed.

I knew that image would haunt me for the rest of my life. I'd never recover from the rage I'd seen reflected in Taamir's eyes in his final moments; his mouth curled into a snarl as he charged, sacrificing himself for his daughter.

And now he was gone, and his wife would be alone, and his daughters would grow up without a father.

The entrance door opened, tugging me from my thoughts, and a man and woman entered. Their eyes darted around the cramped room, seeing only a few tables occupied. When the man's gaze landed on us, he nudged the woman.

Her eyes flicked my way, and then they started walking in our direction.

My body tensed, ready to grab Rima and dart for the door should they try anything funny.

"Ahlan," the woman said. She must've been in her mid-fifties and wore a muted gray Hijab and a matching pewter-colored dress. The man was close in age to the woman, and he was a hair taller than her with dark brown eyes and a wisp of a goatee. Etched into the side of his face was a deep crimson scar. It cut a crescent path through his hairline from his temple to the corner of his mouth.

The woman's gaze fell on Rima. "I'm Sarine, and this is my brother, Sawan. Assem sent us to get you."

"Ahlan," Rima said and peered up at them.

"You say Assem sent you?" I said. "Do you have proof?"

Sarine nodded and looked down at the purse hanging at her waist. I held my breath as the woman rummaged through her bag and revealed a dog-eared Polaroid. She held it up for me.

A grim-faced Assem stood beside a younger Sarine and her brother with Kat's estate in the background.

"When our neighborhood was destroyed, we had nowhere to go. We are indebted to Ms. Dawson and Assem for their kindness." Sarine said and placed a hand on her brother's shoulder.

She shifted her attention to Rima and flashed her a warm grin. "Your mother and sister are excited to see you. We will bring you to them."

Rima raised her eyebrows at the mention of her mother. Her usually rosy cheeks were sallow, and dark circles were beneath her round eyes.

My chest pinched at how haggard her young face appeared.

Rima gave me a questioning look, and I nodded and smiled reassuringly.

Rima climbed out of her chair, and Sarine stepped forward and pressed the girl against the folds of her skirt.

I wondered if she'd had kids of her own. If so, where were they?

"We have a car out back. Come," Sarine said.

I stood and immediately winced from the shock of pain radiating from where I'd been shot through the Jeep door.

Sarine cocked an eyebrow and glanced at the blood stain on my thigh. She pulled out a few crisp bills from her purse. "Here. There is a pharmacy a block to the West." Then added, "Allah keep you safe."

I pocketed the cash, tempted to go with them. But I couldn't. Not yet. I was the bridge's guardian, and nothing had changed about that, even if I no longer had my abilities.

The bridge would be vulnerable tomorrow night, and I had to do everything I could to stop it.

"Please take care of Rima. I have something else I need to do."

Sarine furrowed her brow and reached into her purse again. "Assem warned me you may say as much." She handed me a flip phone. "He told me to give you this if you decided not to come with us."

I took it and tucked it in my back pants pocket.

Sarine and Sawan flanked either side of Rima and escorted her through the restaurant. At the door, Rima shot a bereft glance at me before being whisked outside. I swallowed, my throat cinching, at the sight of the young girl's sorrowful face.

I fought against the threatening tears.

Not yet. I told myself. Taamir's death would have been for nothing if I gave up now. First, I had to stop Derek from accessing the bridge. Only after would I allow myself to mourn Taamir.

～

I PAID for our meal with some of the cash Sarine had given me. A steady ache had grown in my thigh muscle, and I limped into the drugstore. The small shop was surprisingly crowded for late afternoon, and I had to wait in a line before handing the man at the cash register a twenty for a roll of gauze, bandages, a bottle of peroxide, and a paper pack of aspirin.

"Do you have a restroom I could use?" I asked when he gave me back my change.

The man nodded and pointed toward a hallway in the back.

The door to the bathroom was barely visible between shelves stacked with boxes of shampoo and baby wipes. The space was tiny, the tile floors cracked and broken, and I gagged at the brown stains on the toilet seat. At least the sink worked, and there were enough paper towels to place on the floor where I could sit. I double-checked the door was locked before tugging my jeans down below my knees.

Dark crimson blood oozed and dripped down my leg as I carefully lowered myself to the floor. Gently, I examined the edges, feeling for a bullet fragment. Although the skin was sore, I breathed a sigh of relief when I felt nothing hard lodged inside. I rummaged through the paper sack and pulled out the peroxide.

I poured it over the wound, and I gritted my teeth from the sharp stinging sensation as it fizzed.

Someone knocked.

"Just a minute!" I grunted, sucking in a breath as the stinging slowly subsided.

I dabbed the wound a few times with paper towels, then covered it with gauze and secured it with a bandage. I hoisted myself to my feet using the sink as leverage and pulled my pants up again, careful not to tug at the edges of the tape.

It wasn't professional by any means, but it would have to do.

Already, Derek could be in Palmyra with the stones and the statue.

I tossed two aspirin in my mouth before scooping a handful of water from the faucet. Finally, I tossed the garbage into the wastebasket and pulled open the door.

A woman stood beside a fidgeting toddler. They ushered me into the narrow hallway. My leg was tender, but I managed to keep at least a semblance of a normal gait.

Now that I'd ensured I wouldn't bleed to death or suffer a horrendous infection, I needed to find somewhere quiet and away from prying eyes or ears so I could contact Jason. My eyes scanned the busy street and spotted a cafe on the corner. I found a secluded corner table in the back. A few people ordered coffee from the register, but as it was afternoon, most chairs were empty.

I flipped open the phone, and scalp prickling, I dialed Jason's number.

It rang once before he picked up.

"Hello?" he said, his voice sounding wary due to the phone displaying an unknown number.

"Hey Jason, it's me."

"Jesus Christ, Elly! Are you alright? Kat said you left without warning, and I've been trying to call you. Where the hell are you?"

The guilt of worrying Kat gnawed at my gut. When all this was over, I prayed she'd forgive me.

"I'm sorry," I said. "I'm fine. Have you talked to Assem?"

The restaurant door chimed, and a pair of young men entered.

"Assem? Kat hasn't seen Assem either for three days. Kat said he'd messaged her he was taking a few days off. But she was worried 'cause he never takes time off."

I bit my lip.

The two men had moved to the corner instead of finding a place in line. I met their gaze briefly before a waiter asked if they needed a table. The hair on the back of my neck stood up.

"Elly?" Jason chimed in my ear.

I turned my back to them and whispered into the phone.

"Someone contacted me after you left. Taamir and Rima were taken, and they wanted me to bring the Inanna idol. I had no choice, Jason. Assem sent someone to take Rima, but..." my voice faltered. "Taamir didn't make it."

"Holy shit," he said and paused. I could almost imagine him pacing the floor as he held the phone. "Taamir, really? Jesus, Elly, I'm sorry. But what were you thinking?" His words simmered with anger and frustration, and I detected a hint of hurt.

"You were gone, and there wasn't time for me to call you. Please, I need you to listen. The man who took them was Derek Kane. The Derek Kane. He had me too, but we were able to escape." I paused, eying a group of teenagers that had entered.

The two men had moved to a table and shook their heads as a waiter offered them water. Their eyes settled on me briefly before they resumed looking over the menu.

God dammit I was being paranoid. There was no way they could know who I was. We'd escaped three hours ago. There was no way they'd searched the hundreds of stores, markets, and apartments that separated me from where I'd left the SUV.

Still, I knew I was overstaying my welcome.

"Hey, Jason, I gotta go." A wet hot tear trickled down her cheek, and I wiped it angrily away. *Don't fall apart now.*

"You're in way over your head. I need you to tell me, right fucking now, where you are."

I sniffed, easing backward toward the rear of the restaurant.

My hand tightened on the phone. He'd returned to Division 12, and for all I knew, they were listening in on this very conversation. If I told him the truth, Division agents would swarm upon me in less than an hour. There was no way they'd let me walk out of here. I'd be detained in a black site location or worse, Jason would insist they send me back to the US.

Kane had connections everywhere and had hired Division to find the statue and me.

I couldn't change it.

"I'm in Aleppo," I said firmly. "Waiting at a coffee shop for Assem to come to get me."

Years of negotiating my way into restricted military areas had taught me the best lie was the one buried in the truth. I had to convince Jason I was safe and that he could back off but vague enough to slow down anyone they sent after me.

The phone clicked, and at first, I thought Jason had hung up.

Jason sighed. "Okay, good. Have Assem bring you to Kat's. I'll meet you there, and then we can figure all this out."

Feeling the weight of the two men watching me, I hurried out of the employee entrance in the back.

TWENTY-SIX

The second I'd clicked the phone closed, I'd stepped into the narrow back alleyway.

Not wanting to risk drawing attention by bursting into a run, I increased my stride to a fast walk. My blood hummed inside my ears. The honking horns and yelling drivers set my teeth on edge.

At the corner intersection, I took a chance and sprinted to a large group of shoppers that had started across the road.

As I stepped onto the curb, the scents of roasting meats and herbs floated toward me from the street cart. A motorcycle sat against a light pole, and its rider, a teenage boy, shoved pieces of Falafel into his mouth, standing beside two friends beside him.

I side-stepped out of the group and leaped onto the bike.

It'd been years since I'd ridden a dirt bike, but by some miracle, I managed to kick-start it on the first try. The engine spurted and emitted a gasping wheeze of smoke as I revved the throttle. The bike launched forward and wobbled for a few feet before I found my balance again. The boys shouted at me as I sped across the intersection, weaving among the stalled traffic.

I hunched down, pressing the bike to go faster. I'd been interested in motocross when my daredevil boyfriend, my freshman year of college, had invited me to ride at his parents' mountain property. His parents had even built him a custom practice track among the acres of pine trees. He'd loaned me an extra bike, and we'd ridden through the forest trails, often stopping along the way to help me adjust my riding gear, which usually ended with it coming off.

I hunched down over the handlebars, and the small engine whined as I laid on the throttle. Cars buzzed along the busy roadway, and I weaved in and out, with no plan on where I was going, only that I needed to find somewhere, I could lie low until I figured out how I'd get to Palmyra or get the statue back.

A horn honked, and I glanced over my shoulder. The grill of a dark blue Tahoe bore down on me, uncomfortably close. I changed lanes. The windows were tinted, but I could faintly distinguish two people in the front seat. The window rolled down, and a man in sunglasses pointed a pistol at me.

Dammit. They'd found me.

I swerved before he could shoot, the motorcycle's handles vibrating as I bounced down an offramp. There'd be no hope of losing them on the highway. The only advantage of the nimble bike was to disappear among the narrow streets. Air whooshed in my ears, and the SUV's engine roared as the driver gunned the engine, following me.

The hot air beat against my cheeks, causing tears to stream from my eyes. A giant orange and red sign in the center of the road warned me of the ongoing construction. The pavement had been cleared away, leaving a gap where a new underground sewage pipe was going.

Panic seized me as I imagined careening into the thirty-foot-wide pit, and I clamped down on the foot brake, locking the rear tire. The bike slid out from under me, and I was tossed from it, tumbling over the roadway until I landed on a pile of dirt and crushed asphalt.

My diaphragm spasmed as I struggled to breathe. Dust coated my tongue, and my gravel sharply bit into where it clung to my blooded arms and hands.

A car door closed, and still dazed, I twisted my head to look toward the sound. I grimaced as excruciating pain felt like it would split my skull in two.

"Jesus, she might've broken her neck," a man's gruff voice said.

"You better hope not, or it'll be your neck that's broken too," another man said.

A shadow fell across my face as a form crouched over me. I felt a needle pierce my neck again and sputtered angry curses at them even as my eyelids drooped. The tires of the cars crossing the overpass thumped steadily, and try as I might, violently thrashing to stay conscious, the drugs pulled me under.

TWENTY-SEVEN

Hushed voices tugged at the corners of my consciousness, my ears picking up the fragmented bits of conversation.

"She's been asleep for an hour," a woman said, her tone weighted with concern. "Should I alert Mr. Kane?"

"No, Suzie. He's on a conference call and made it very clear not to interrupt him," another woman replied.

An involuntary moan came from somewhere nearby, and it took a moment for me to realize it'd been from me. The backs of my lids felt like sand, and I attempted to rub them, but my hand caught. Handcuffs tethered my left hand to the seat, and I gave it a hard jerk, and the sharp metal dug into the tender skin of my wrist.

"Son of a bitch," I cursed. My free right hand moved up to my neck, feeling the telltale bump where they'd injected me, once again, with a sedative. I hated how this was becoming a habit and wondered if I'd heard of any permanent side effects from repeatedly dosing someone.

As my mind cleared, memories bombarded me: the coffee

shop, her phone call with Jason, the stolen motorcycle...the crash.

My skull pounded, and I lay against the headrest, attempting to stop the spinning.

A low, constant drone filled my ears as I examined my surroundings. A strip of yellow lights illuminated above was embedded into an ivory molding. Polished wood veneered tables with gold trim sat between groupings of smooth, leather recliners. A series of oval windows were the final tip-off.

I was on a plane. Or, more specifically, a private jet, judging by the lack of crying babies and ample legroom. And it wouldn't take a leap of the imagination to guess who this was. My mouth went dry.

"Oh, you're awake," the first woman chimed, and the pretty blond, her hair in a tidy bun, strode over to where I was seated.

"Mr. Kane wanted me to make sure you're comfortable. Would you like anything to drink? Water or tea, perhaps?"

Idly, I wondered how much a stewardess for a private plane made. Did she get extra to be cheerful, even when dealing with someone who had been taken against their will?

"Water, please," I croaked.

The woman nodded, left, and returned shortly after. She set a glass with ice cubes and a water bottle on the glossy marble table in front of me.

The attendant flashed me an awkward smile and unscrewed the lid of the water for me.

I'd thank her if I weren't currently a fucking hostage.

I eagerly drained the bottle, forgoing the ice.

The attendant took the empty bottle. "Anything else I can get you, Ms. Dawson?"

"Yeah," I grumbled. "You can tell me why I'm here and where the hell we are going?"

The woman's eyes widened. "Why, you're on Mr. Kane's private jet," she said as if it were something I should've known.

"Fine. Great. And where exactly are we going?"

Again, the woman seemed perplexed by my questions. "I was sure Mr. Kane had told you? We're on our way to Palmyra."

Palmyra. A surge of panic flooded me. Then that meant he'd used the statue and somehow figured out the location of the entrance of Ur.

Derek was many things, but he didn't seem stupid or reckless. If he was ignorant of the dangers, maybe I could warn him. Attempt to reason with him by explaining the risks of activating the bridge and persuade him not to open it.

The woman continued to stand expectantly. She'd assumed I had known our destination, which meant she didn't know I'd been drugged.

And the handcuffs? She probably had seen it all and guessed it was some role-play bullshit or kink Mr. Kane dabbled in.

"Another water, Ms...?" I said, trailing off.

The woman smiled, and I noted her maroon lipstick, the exact shade of her pencil skirt and blouse.

"Suzanne," she said.

"Suzanne, I'd love another bottle of water if you've got one?"

Suzanne nodded and took a bottle from an overhead compartment.

"When will we arrive?" I asked as she placed an opened water bottle on the table.

"The captain just informed me we should land in about thirty minutes."

I nodded and sipped the water. The fog lifted from my thoughts as the water flushed the drugs from my bloodstream.

"I need help with the trays back here," another woman called from the back of the plane.

"Excuse me," Suzanne said, half curtsying, and darted off.

A small ceramic pot with a blooming white orchid sat on the table before me. All the oval-shaped window shades were closed, and I maneuvered myself against the window. Then, lifting the shade, I peered into the darkness. No city lights appeared below. We were either above cloud cover or over the middle of the barren Syrian desert.

I guessed the latter.

"Not much to see out there, is it?"

Derek Kane strode toward me from the cockpit, the burgundy curtain behind him still ruffling. He'd changed into navy blue slacks and a white button-up shirt with the sleeves rolled up to his elbows and was missing his baseball cap.

He settled in the diagonal seat to me and lifted the glass he'd brought, rattling the ice cubes.

Suzanne materialized beside him. Deftly, she took his empty glass and placed a square black napkin on the table in front of him, followed by another identical glass full of an amber liquid.

"Would you like one?" he asked, noticing my attention.

I didn't move.

He shrugged and winked at the stewardess before lifting the glass to his lips.

His eyes met mine, staring at me over the rim of the glass as he sipped.

Still half full, he set the glass down and eased himself back in the seat, his eyes never leaving mine.

Anger seethed through my veins. "Where are you taking me," I snarled.

Derek chuckled. "The dumb act is really getting old. We're going to. Palmyra."

"Why?" I said, my teeth clenched. I was walking a thin line, but I needed to get him talking, or I'd never know how close he was to summoning the bridge.

Derek laughed again. "Come on now. I've no patience for games. It's where the gates to Ur are, of course." He raised an eyebrow. "But you already knew that, didn't you?"

I remained motionless and didn't reply.

He sat back again, using his finger to trace the rim of his tumbler. "That statue of yours, the one you stole from me." He shot her a threatening look before continuing. "It was indeed the missing piece to the map. The final key to locating the lost city."

I bristled. "You have the statue and found the entrance to Ur. Why am I here?"

This time, Derek didn't laugh. Instead, his face twisted and contorted into something sinister, something *corrupted*.

Well, shit. I'd given him the benefit of the doubt, and it'd come back and bit me in the ass.

He adjusted himself in the seat, regaining his composed mask. "The stones of Ur are common knowledge, but the role of the statue of Inanna had remained unclear. That is until recently." A smug, self-satisfied grin formed on his face, and I'd never wanted to punch someone so badly in my life.

"I procured a set of cuneiform tablets—ones that have never seen a museum's shelf—that contain the ritual components to open the bridge. A part of Enheduanna's personal collection. My team located them among the ruins of Giparu, where a disciple of hers assembled the exact procedure to call forth the Bridge of Vela. Including the use specific use of the Inanna idol and its guardian."

Undiscovered tablets. That explained why he'd been sponsoring so many archaeological digs. He'd been searching for the ritual.

I'd seen the visions of the devastation it could cause. Somewhere in his research, they must've seen the warnings and learned of the records of how the Akkadian's fall from power had been awash with centuries of bloodshed.

He tipped back the glass, swallowing the remains of the whiskey.

If he did know, he didn't seem to care.

Suzanne brought him another as if waiting out of sight for his glass to empty.

"That's where you come in," he said.

I ground my teeth together, knowing already what he meant.

"It seems the cuneiform tablets specifically state that the idol of Inanna and the stones aren't enough. There must be a mortal embodiment of the goddess to open it. While Enheduanna was a priestess and used herself, you, my dear Ella, are the key."

The blood in my veins turned to ice.

No, that wasn't it. They were wrong. I wasn't the key to opening it; I was the key to keeping it *closed*. Panic's icy claws sank into my gut, and I refused to break eye contact with him. He wouldn't get the pleasure of seeing how the revelation affected me.

Enheduanna had warned me that if I were too late, I'd have to trade my soul to close it. What if my soul had to be sacrificed either way? What if she'd lied to me and convinced me I'd still be alive afterward?

That was it then. No matter which path I chose, if I walked into Ur, I wouldn't walk out.

"So," he said, "I need you to stick around a little longer than I'd planned. But no matter, you'll get a front-row seat to the show when the bridge is opened."

"You can't!" I blurted out, desperation clinging to my words.

"If you open it, thousands will die. We're not mean to see the world of the gods."

An indignant look darkened his eyes before he regained his composure. "I can, and I will."

"You must know what will happen if you do," I pleaded. "I've seen its destruction. It's too dangerous. You can't possibly think the benefits will outweigh the risks."

Here was my chance to make him understand. My life depended not only on it but the lives of countless others.

He rolled his eyes. "Stop being so dramatic. Of course, I know all about the risks. But it is one I'm willing to accept. Humans would still be pounding sticks and rocks if that bridge had been opened. Overnight, the world's collective knowledge exploded in a matter of years. One can only guess what treasures behold those who dare to look inside."

"King Sargon only wanted to look inside, too," I quipped. "And look what happened after. Hundreds of years of famine, droughts, and raging floods. A civil war that has lasted for thousands of years—"

"King Sargon was a fool!" Derek bellowed, cutting me off. "Blinded by his insatiable hunger for immortality, he'd delved into the knowledge he was too ignorant to understand."

"And you think you're any better?" I snapped.

Derek's jaw clenched.

I'd struck a nerve. Good.

He didn't respond for a moment, and when he finally did, his words were measured and careful. "My intentions are unlike those of the idiot King. The world cannot sustain the rate of energy consumption for much longer. Fifty years at most, and we'll be back in the dark ages. Unless we discover a new, renewable source of energy."

He paused again as if letting his words sink in. "I believe that the bridge will hold such information. With me leading

Kane United, I can guarantee the world will be enriched by the gifts I bestow it for many years to come."

Turbulence rocked the plan, and my stomach somersaulted.

Derek clutched his whiskey glass, cursing.

The captain's voice spoke over the intercom with an Australian accent. "We're decreasing altitude and will be landing shortly. Please buckle your seat belts as we will be experiencing a few bumps as we descend."

Mr. Kane climbed out of his chair. "Great chatting with you, Ms. Dawson." He rubbed his hands together. "Lots of fun, exciting things are coming. I look forward to talking to you again very soon."

He retreated to the front of the plane again and pushed the curtains aside before disappearing behind them.

I gave a pitiful tug at the handcuff on my left hand, and my lip curled with disgust.

Oh, he'd find a new alternative energy source alright, and then Kane United would lock in its patent down so tight, it would ensure record profits for decades.

No matter how much he denied it, he was no different from King Sargon. While the King of Akkad wanted his dynasty to last forever, Derek wanted his family's corporation to.

TWENTY-EIGHT

The plane bounced violently as the wheels touched down, ushering a painful protest from the wound on my leg. For a white-knuckling thirty seconds, while the pilot navigated the landing, I recognized the irony that *this* would be how I'd perish before ever getting to sacrifice myself to close the bridge.

Since the airport in Palmyra had been defunct for years, I imagined it was more like an abandoned stretch of road than a maintained tarmac. After Derek had left, I'd passed the time by trying to use my magic and burn the leather on the armrest, but since it was the right hand that had been cuffed, anything else was out of reach.

It was pointless anyway, and the attempt to summon my power resulted in a rebounding hollow pang as if I'd pulled the trigger on an empty gun. It wasn't until that moment that I realized how much I'd depended on my new ability.

I'd survived without it, of course, up until this point in my life. However, it felt as if I'd only begun to scratch the surface of my capabilities. My focus and strength were only just beginning to intensify. It wasn't until I didn't have it that I became more aware of how much I'd grown to covet the familiar magic tingle, crave it even. How easily it had come to me. I'd been able to possess, while not particularly wield, this new power so easily.

I'd been made well aware of the dangers involved should I lose control of it. And even after the short practice session with Jason at Kat's estate, I'd still slipped up at the gas station, which had cost me dearly.

Should I, by some miracle, restore my magic, I needed to be more careful with how much I used it, saving it for when no other options were offered.

The plane lurched to a stop, and my wrist strained against the cuffs.

"The captain will secure the cockpit and stairs," Suzanne said, standing. "We'll be de-boarding here shortly. Is there anything I can get you while we wait?".

I forced a tight-lipped smile. "How about a key for the handcuffs?"

The stewardess stiffened, and she let out a nervous giggle. "Um, I...I don't think Mr. Kane would like that. Besides, I—"

"She doesn't have the key," Derek said, cutting her off. His face was relaxed as he stepped up to us. Less than a day until he could open the gate, and the dude was acting like he had all the time in the world. Maybe it was the residual magic or the urgency from Enheduanna in my last dream, but deep down, I could sense the pull of the impending moment—the mental tick, tick, tick, as the minutes sped by.

A mixture of relief and appreciation washed over Suzanne's face, and she moved to the back of the cabin.

"However," he continued, "You'll be pleased to know that the handcuffs will no longer be necessary once we are off the plane. They were merely an assurance that you wouldn't try anything stupid, like attacking the lovely Suzanne or trying to force your wait out of the emergency door without a parachute."

I pressed my lips together. "Believe me, they both crossed my mind."

Derek plastered a fake smile on his face. So leering and smug it made me want to gag.

"As we are now safely on the ground and surrounded by hundreds of miles of nothing but rocks, dunes, and an occasional oil well, I can assume you understand any attempt you make to escape would be a terrible idea."

I lifted my chin, not responding.

"Good," he said. "I will have Garrhu and Naibro escort you off the plane to where we will keep you until you're needed."

He left again, striding to the back of the plane. Minutes passed, leaving me to grow more and more restless. From this angle to the window, I could make out a cracked asphalt roadway that was painted with faded yellow striped lines.

I'd never been to Palmyra for two reasons. One, because while it had once been a hot tourist location, drawing in crowds from around the world to visit the two hundred acres of extremely well-preserved ancient Roman ruins, the war had left the town and many of the heritage sites in shambles. And two because the surrounding area was littered with inactivated land mines and leftover traps from when ISIS had controlled it.

That, and it was in the middle of freaking nowhere. Okay, three reasons.

During the conflicts, the Syrian government had struggled to maintain its security, but it soon had become all but abandoned.

Which meant it was isolated and accessible only to those with the necessary connections and resources, like the son of a billionaire.

The engines cut off, and a side door was lowered. The smell

of jet fuel wafted into the cabin. Two guards in combat vests, black and gray camo suits, and full-faced helmets concealed the men inside. They hurried over to me. One held an assault rifle at the ready, while the other used a small key to release my handcuffs.

I felt the metal slip from my wrist and rubbed the tender skin where the cuffs had left red abrasions.

The one guard gestured at me with the rifle. "Go," he barked.

I hurried to get ahead of him, eager to be off the plane. The other man stepped beside me, and a gloved hand gripped my forearm.

Fresh, cool night air washed over me as I stepped down the short flight of stairs and onto the tarmac. A dozen spotlights hooked to generators beamed onto the pavement, illuminating a dozen figures silhouetted against the oppressive darkness of the desert beyond. I could make out nothing beyond the ring of lights, and we could have just as likely been on the moon as in central Syria.

The waving outlines of the Milky Way blazed across the center like a winding starry river, and millions of stars and planets glittered in the clear night sky. I wished I could dive into them like an ocean and escape whatever fate awaited me.

I felt a tug on my arm. "Let's go," the man said, tightening his grip.

"Nice night, isn't it?" I said.

"Go," the man said again, tapping his finger on the trigger. I scoffed and marched onward across the cracked pavement. Apparently, he wasn't much of a stargazer. As we neared the derelict airport terminal, a dozen men with guns at their hips stood in a semi-circle beneath one of the awnings and adjacent to two of the spotlights. A table had been erected. Derek leaned over it, sifting through piles of papers on the table.

His mouth was moving, but the rumble of the generators drowned out anything he was saying. A taller man stood across from him, with his arms tucked behind his back. At first, his face was hidden in shadow, but as the guards led me closer, steel-blue eyes reflected in the light.

He raised his eyes from where he'd been pointing at what I now saw was a map, and a soft gasp of surprise escaped me.

I blinked, and my body stiffened in shock. Were the after-effects of the sedatives they'd given me making me hallucinate? There was no way.

The man flashed me a crooked smile. The same smile that in the past had made me forget I needed to breathe and question whether I could stand.

"Jason!" His name tore from my throat. "Jason! Please help me!"

Still watching me, he lifted an amused eyebrow and nudged Derek beside him.

Derek kept his eyes on the maps — ignoring Jason — and ran his fingers along the roadway. "Oh yes," he said, "I believe you two have met. Unfortunately, I'm afraid Agent Price is not available right now."

I jerked against the iron fist holding my arm, struggling desperately to break free. "Let me go!" I shouted, throwing all my weight against the man.

Derek straightened and gave the smallest of nods.

This time, I felt the guard release me, but the sudden lack of resistance threw me off balance. My feet slipped out from under me, and I sprawled onto the ground. My hands slapped the hard asphalt, still warm from the day's heat, and my cheek burned where it met the sensitive skin of my face.

Men's laughter permeated the air, and a surge of anger blazed white hot inside me. Then, before I could pick myself back up, a hand seized the back of my neck and swiftly lifted me to my feet.

Jason stood beside me, his hand firmly clamped at the base of my head. He locked eyes with me. His gaze was hard, cold, and devoid of any emotion. Fear stretched like a shadow in my mind. "No, Jason," I pleaded. "Please, I'm sorry for everything. You don't have to do this."

I desperately searched his gaze, praying to catch a glimpse of the man I knew in there, the man I loved. The man I still loved. He squeezed my neck and forcefully tilted my head away. "Get her out of here," he said, shoving me toward another guard.

"No!" I begged. "You can't help him. You don't understand. You can't cross the bridge!"

The lights blurred, going in and out of focus as betrayal and confusion clouded my thoughts. The guard half-dragged me into the dark recesses of a building. I stared at the ground, watching the pavement transition to sand. All the fight had left me, and I felt numb as they carried me up the stairs and into a travel trailer. It smelled of burned toast and kerosene. I was thrown onto a bed with a green and orange striped comforter and curled into a ball. They didn't bother drugging me. They knew the betrayal of Jason would be enough to subdue me. Derek had won. I had lost.

I closed my eyes, unsure if I ever wanted to wake up again.

TWENTY-NINE

An explosion erupted all around me, and the concussion of the impact threw me forward on a dune. Grit and sand clogged my nostrils while gunfire ricocheted off the stone pillars and arches surrounding me. I remained flat on the ground as the rain of bullets streaked overhead. Finally, when the gunshots had ceased, I stood, my ears still ringing, and observed the miles of dunes stretching out from me. The desert landscape dipped, cresting down to form a valley with a glittering river at the bottom. Beside me, soldiers trudged through the sand with rifles held aloft as they slid down the shifting dunes toward the river. Houses and buildings dotted the sandy bank, and a defending army of hundreds positioned themselves behind spiked walls and barricades.

The invading army lowered their rifles, shouting their battle cries as they charged down to the awaiting army. Cracks of rifle fire echoed off the valley walls.

Enheduanna appeared beside me. Her deep-set eyes gazed out onto the battle raging below. A light breeze fluttered the thin white gown around her feet, exposing the smooth, tanned skin of her legs beneath.

From this distance, only small shapes of the attacking soldiers scurry amongst the stone houses; however, the blood-curdling screams of soldiers and villagers carried up to where we stand. A flash of yellow light, brighter than the sun, illuminated the village, followed by a strange popping noise. A heartbeat later, the buildings were blown apart with a tremendous explosion.

My fists balled at my sides, filled with a rage I had no basis for. I don't know this city or recognize the uniforms the soldiers wore, yet I'm furious, seething by the senseless acts of violence.

I whipped my head to Enheduanna. "Why are you standing here? They're slaughtering them. We need to do something." I shouted over the clamor of shouts and guns firing.

Worry furrowed the space between Enheduanna's brow. "I know."

"Then why don't you stop them? You have to stop them," I protested.

Enheduanna looked at me, and the air evaporated from my lungs at the horror that had become her face. The left half was its usual perfection—smooth jaw, rose-blushed cheeks, with dark, thick curls framing it. But on the left, shreds of tattered skin hang from protruding cheekbones and a black hole where her left eye should be.

"This is what you must see. *This* is what will come to be should the Bridge of Vela be opened. Exposure to the world of the gods corrupts even the purest of hearts. Overtaking them by greed and the insatiable need for power, the world shall fall. Cities and states will be destroyed, and millions of innocent lives will be lost. Countries will battle each other, each escalating their assaults by wielding weapons not of this world. Their destructive power will be beyond anything anyone has ever seen. The knowledge of the gods is not meant to be shared with humans, and devastation for years will plague the lands."

The weight of her words permeated the air like a living thing with inky black wings and soulless eyes—the vision of the corrupted. Enheduanna was showing me a memory, *her* memory of the last ruling King of the Akkadian empire. Her brother. He was no longer recognizable as a man but had transformed into a disfigured, grotesque creature possessed with an infinite desire to conquer and claim.

The warring town had caught fire in the valley, and flames from collapsed buildings spiraled like pillars into the night sky.

Enheduanna sighed. "But there is more." Suddenly, we were swept from the desert, and the world shifted. When my vision returned, my body swayed as I regained my balance. Enheduanna and I were standing in the street in a suburb. Rows of giant maples loomed over houses with white picket fences and painted shutters. Bright pink roses bloomed around the base of an ostentatious craftsman with yellow bricks and a gray roof.

I gasped. "This is my mother's house. We're in California."

"Yes," Enheduanna replied.

"Why are you showing me this?"

"I need you to see that *this* time will be different. When King Ramush crossed the bridge, the destruction was contained only in the Akkadian empire. I begged Inanna to hear me and grant me the power to close it before the devastation spread beyond the borders of my kingdom. I can no longer sense Inanna's presence, and my form exists only as a memory I imbued into the statue. This time will be different. Like an incurable disease, there will be no stopping the spread."

Something wet and warm brushed my hand, and I looked down. I cradled a woman's body in my arms. My mother's lifeless eyes stared at me, red blood oozing from her mouth.

"No!" I said, grief choking the words. My chest constricted with every shuddering breath, and I clutched my mother closer, burying my face in her hair. I breathed in the smell of her; lilac and sweet violets.

"Please," I begged. "Please, god no."

The vision disintegrated, and I was propelled forward as the weight of my mother's body disappeared.

I stared through a blurred vision at my hands, reeling from the shock of the emptiness and overwhelmed by the intense emotions the sight of my dead mother had evoked.

"You are the Guardian, Eleanora," Enheduanna said. "You must stop it from opening, or all I have shown you will come to pass. By the time I realized the mistake, it was too late. But you still have time."

The world faded away again, and I felt myself cast into the void, weightless and adrift in the cold blackness of the night sky.

Knives stabbed the sides of my temples as I awoke. My heart ached from the vividness of the lingering emotions the dream had instilled in me. I opened my eyes and stared at the wood-paneled ceiling of the single-wide trailer. The memories of the day before rushed up to greet me as if they were delighted that I was awake and eagerly waiting to bombard me.

Good morning. Remember how you're destined to die, or the world ends? Oh yeah, and your ex-boyfriend betrayed you, and don't forget you watched your friend die.

Coffee?

Mood thoroughly darkened, I grumbled and sat up. A rooftop air conditioner hummed, and I could feel the cold air blowing from it. Not cold, but cool enough that if it wasn't for the blazing sun shining through the curtains, I could still imagine it being night. My eyes burned, and the taste inside my mouth was a mix of cotton balls and sand. I wetted my lips. They were cracked and dry, so I stood, searching for a glass of water.

The trailer couldn't have been more than twenty feet long, and the mustard yellow and brown curtains revealed it was an eighties vintage. I found a chipped mug in the cupboard and filled it from the small sink, finding it had water. I gulped down two glasses, then rummaged through drawers for anything to eat. I found two granola bars and a packet of instant oatmeal. I devoured all of it, not bothering to cook the oatmeal, and instead ate it dry with a spoon.

My stomach partially appeased, and I returned to the bed. My thoughts were a jumbled mess, and I lifted my hands to rub my face, hoping to clear my mind. A moment later, I realized that Derek had kept his word about the no handcuffs thing.

I leaped from the bed, possessed by the sudden need for fresh air. The door was five steps from the bed, and I gave it a shove. It didn't move.

"Son of a bitch!" I said and punched the door. The aluminum frame flexed and dented but didn't budge.

I spun around, going to the window above the kitchenette. Bars had been bolted on the outside, and even though I managed to pry the glass open, there was no way I could climb out.

That bastard had locked me in.

I groaned and flopped back on the bed. I pressed my face into the pillow, reeking of mildew, and released all the pent-up frustration and anger. I screamed until my throat ached and my lungs burned.

I was mere feet away from the entrance to Ur and the gate itself, and yet I could do nothing. Even now, I imagined Derek standing beside the altar, aligning the stones and calling down the Bridge.

I'd failed.

Warmth spread along my leg from the wound on my thigh. I sat up, wiping the wetness from my cheeks. The leg of my jeans, now stained a brownish red, was ruined. I pulled them off, forgoing modesty at this point. If they had hidden cameras, so fucking be it. I marched to the bathroom. I attributed the headache and fatigue to the blood loss, and I would only grow weaker unless I did something.

The bathroom held a roll of toilet paper, a hand towel, a toothbrush with most of the bristles worn, and a small bottle of peroxide. I grabbed another towel from the kitchen and found electrical tape in one of the drawers.

Back on the bed, I peeled off the remnants of the bandage. The skin surrounding the cut appeared blanched from the lack of air, curling up at the edges where the bullet had torn through it. To keep my mind off the pain as I cleaned it, I sorted through the whiplash of seeing Jason with Derek.

It all made sense now. How quickly they'd found me after I'd spoken with Jason on the phone. How Derek had known where I lived. Known about Taamir and his family and would do anything to protect them, even trade the statue.

The hardness in Jason's eyes surged to the front of my mind. It had been that moment that any doubt he was still on my side had evaporated. I'd witnessed his cold, indifferent stare, and the harshness of it had seeped into my bones, eviscerating every ounce of hope that he still cared about me.

A severe twisting pain arose in my chest as if a hooked dagger were prying out my heart.

I'd trusted him. Believed him. And once again, he'd betrayed that trust. How long had he been deceiving me? Had he been lying to me the entire time after I'd called him asking for help? Had he manipulated me into revealing my magic, the statue, and knowledge of the bridge? Had any of the last three days been real?

A lump formed in the back of my throat as I recalled the memory from our night together at Kat's. Our bodies are entangled. His hands caressing me, his mouth on mine, his blue eyes full of passion and longing.

I scrubbed my hands over my face as a wave of nausea rolled through me. How could I have been so blind?

Had he even been ambushed when he'd met with this supposed contact? He'd come back wounded, but had it all been planned? An act to keep up the appearance he was on our side?

I stood, pacing the camper like a tiger waiting to go on stage at a circus. The part that bothered me the most was *why* he'd done it. Had Derek hired Division 12 long before I'd found the statue? Or was Jason hired on his own? Derek knew about Jason and mine's history, so either he had discovered it on his own, or Jason had told him.

I knew where Jason's loyalties lay. He'd chosen Division 12 over me before, so how could I have possibly fathomed he had changed?

I secured the washrag over the wound, cinching a hair too tight, and tore off pieces of electrical tape to hold it.

I gritted my teeth. Fine. Jason wouldn't help me close the bridge. I'd have to do it on my own. And if he chose to stop me, well, I'd have to show where my loyalties were then, wouldn't I?

Muffled voices came from outside the door, and I barely had enough time to get my jeans buttoned before the door swung open. Hot air wafted from outside, and two men entered.

Jason entered, followed by one of Mr. Kane's guards.

My breathing became shallow, and seeing only red, I lunged. "You son of a bitch!"

The guard maneuvered between us and caught my flailing

arms in his iron-like grip before I'd so much as managed to touch Jason.

My chest heaved as I stared at him, hating him with every cell in my body.

I thrashed, breaking their hold. "Let me go."

"Want me to sedate her?" the guard grumbled, peering down at me while I cussed and spit.

Jason shook his head. "No, Garrhu, I don't think that'll be necessary. She just needs to get it out of her system."

I lowered my arms and raised my chin in indignation.

"Done?" Jason said, arching a brow.

Hot tears pricked the backs of my eyes, but I blinked them away.

"Leave us, Garrhu."

"Mr. Kane gave orders not to leave her alone with you."

"I'll be alright," Jason said, turning to him. "You can wait outside the door."

The man opened his mouth to protest, but Jason's forceful gaze caused him to close it. He huffed a sigh and retreated through the trailer door. His broad shoulders were too wide for the narrow frame, so he was forced to turn awkwardly sideways to leave.

The door slammed shut with a resounding bang.

I dropped my gaze, staring at the peeling linoleum, and my hands were fisted so tight my nails dug into the skin. I couldn't stand to look at him.

"Elly," he said flatly, and my nickname carried none of the tenderness.

"I'm sorry about this. Truly I am. I didn't want it to go down this way. Everybody reports to somebody, and you, of all people, should know that. I report to my commander, and he to Major General Rodriguez. Mr. Kane has a contract with Division 12. Kane United is one of our biggest clients. Our reputation for discretion regarding our clients proceeds with us, including when something of interest needs protecting. They know we stand by our contract of secrecy."

"Fuck you," I spat. Sure, it was a weak response, but it made me feel better, anyway.

Jason huffed a sigh. "We'd been sent to retrieve the crate in the parking garage for Mr. Kane. But you got to it before us and then, without thinking, decided to open it. Do you realize that none of this would have happened if you'd controlled your impulsiveness?"

I chewed the inside of my cheek hard and tasted blood. Hoping the bright burst of pain would numb the sting of his words. He was right. I was impulsive and reckless, and it'd nearly gotten me killed. But he was wrong about one thing. Deep down in my very core, I knew I'd been destined to find the statue, and there was nothing I could've done to change it. No matter my actions, one way or another, it would have ended up in my possession.

"And even more so," Jason continued. "You triggered the idol to awaken and infuse you with its magic. And now, you've caught yourself up in the thick of this goddamn mess. Mr. Kane won't let you leave."

If Derek had sent him here to try to soften me up because he thought he could use our history as some kind of leverage, he'd thought wrong.

Fool me once, broken heart. Fool me twice; just broken.

I felt the weight of Jason's gaze on me, and cautiously, I moved my eyes up to his. "Why are you here? Does it get you off to give me a lecture? Guess what. I don't care anymore. If I die here, so be it, but the second I get my powers back, I'm going to seal the gate. And I won't stop no matter who gets in my way," I paused, grinding my teeth. "Even you."

If he had any opinions on this, they were hidden beneath a

mask. "Fine," he said, snarling. "You want to know the truth? Derek thought you were only a threat, but now he says the statue is worthless because of *you*. They'll have to use you instead as the key."

"I don't fucking care," I said, turning away to stare out of the dust-coated window. I knew, but his words caught me off guard, and I snapped my head back. "The statue is what?"

Jason tilted his head. "I said, it's nothing but a hunk of metal."

For a fleeting second, my heart skipped a beat. He must have seen the change on my face because he added. "What the hell is wrong with you? This means you'll be strapped to the altar along with the stones."

I wasn't listening, my mind racing ahead. I despised Jason and every second he was in my presence, but I needed to keep my temper in check and him talking if my plan was to work.

"The ritual," I said. "How much longer?"

Jason crossed his arms, his left brow raising slightly.

Shit. I'd asked one question, and he was already suspicious.

"Tomorrow night. They're preparing to blast the opening to Ur today," he said, apparently concluding that it didn't risk anything if I knew.

His confidence was founded. It was true; dozens of highly trained mercenaries surrounded me, and thousands of acres of barren land riddled with mines separated me from civilization. I couldn't have been *more* trapped if I'd been in a maximum security prison.

"All you have to do is cooperate, and this will be much less painful for everyone," he said, moving to the door. He tilted his chin and flung open the door, exiting into the harsh afternoon sun. The door shut, and I dashed to it. I lifted my foot, ready to unleash my fury, when I heard Jason speaking to someone outside.

I pressed an ear to the thin wall of the camper.

"...think she'll cooperate?" someone asked.

"Yeah," Jason said. "She's smart enough to know when she's caught. And if she tries anything funny, I'll put her down myself."

I slapped my hand against the peeling wallpaper of the trailer wall. Digging into the very depths of my being, I desperately tried to summon my magic. Fury caused the blood in my ears to roar, and I screamed vicious curses at the universe, enraged at the cruel unfairness of my helplessness.

No stirring of magic, no tingle, nothing. My magic was as gone as though it'd never existed.

THIRTY

Feeling defeated, I slid down the wall. I tucked my knees under my chin and traced the outlines of the eight-pointed star, wondering if Enheduanna had misjudged my capabilities, my strength. It'd taken everything I had to get here and survive, and now...now I had nothing left.

An enormous bang resounded, shaking the walls of the trailer. I jumped to my feet and rushed to one of the square windows. I tore open the curtains and was forced to grab a nearby moldy dish towel to wipe away the years of grime.

Massive granite pillars projected up into the air from symmetrical platforms and cast long shadows in the afternoon sun. Iconic stone columns supported domed porticos and arching roofs. Once a great city of Roman temples and colonnades, most structures had collapsed due to time or destruction from the civil unrest. The remaining structures were scattered amongst piles, broken blocks, and rubble. The Citadel was to my left, perched atop a hill of raised bedrock overlooking the ruins. The ancient stronghold, dubbed Palmyra castle by many, was fortified by thick and high walls and had historically been surrounded by a moat with a drawbridge. The recent Syrian defensives and occupation by terrorists had left several of the walls collapsed.

A plume of dust and smoke pirouetted upward at the base of the hill, and movement caught my eye. Men darted about like scurrying ants, running to where the explosion must've blasted a hole in the ground. Humvees roared past the trailer, sending clouds of dust spiraling in their wake.

In the chaos, I thought I glimpsed Jason, wearing his Division 12 fatigues, but he quickly disappeared into the multitude of people and trucks. Something had gone wrong with whatever they were blasting, and the whole picture was one of utter pandemonium.

I seized my chance and reached for the door. I gave it a sharp jerk, and it rattled on the hinges more than it had before, and I suspected the concussion from the explosion had vibrated something loose.

I took a step back, inhaled a deep breath, and, channeling every martial arts movie I'd watched, hit it with a powerful kick. The door bowed outward with a satisfying crunch of splintered plywood.

Sweat dripped down the sides of my forehead. I licked my lips, tasted the salt, and kicked it again. The wood gave more, and there was a crack as I snapped off whatever lock had held it.

Tentatively, I pushed open the ruined door, and it slammed the side of the trailer. Sweltering desert air tinged with smoke greeted me as my eyes darted from side to side.

At least a dozen canvas tents had been erected around the trailer, and boxes, shovels, ropes, and axes were scattered around the camp.

The generator attached to the camper hummed, and in the closest tent, no more than ten feet away, I could make out silhouetted figures moving inside.

An empty Jeep was parked far off to the right, and I placed a foot on the first step, preparing to run to it, but I snatched it back when a group of three men jogged from the tent beside me toward a larger tent to my left. Their clothes were dirty, and their cloth headbands were grimy with sweat.

Two carried pistols on their hips, and judging by the tree trunk-sized biceps of the third, he could do just as much damage as the ones with guns. I retreated behind the doorway, pulling the door with me. My heel caught a twisted piece of the metal doorframe, and it groaned as I stepped onto it. I held my breath and squeezed my eyes shut, hoping they hadn't heard. Should they happen to look my way, there was no way they wouldn't notice the giant boot-sized hole in the trailer door.

When no one shouted, I kept my back pressed against the inside wall and carefully pushed open the door. The group of guards had made it to the tent and were ducking inside.

I couldn't wait any longer. With the coast as clear as it'd ever be, I leaped out of the trailer and sprinted like a demon toward the Jeep. I skidded into a squat beside it as a group of workers carrying shovels and ropes hurried past. They piled into a cargo truck. The transmission groaned as they forced it into gear and drove to where the plume of smoke had thickened and blackened.

In the distance, panicked voices shouted orders to one another.

As much as I harbored the desire to steal the Jeep and leave this whole place behind, my purpose forced me to stay. First, I needed the statue, and *then* I could get the hell out of here. Besides, how far could I get without them catching me? Even with some of the security preoccupied because of whatever had happened with the explosion, there were still plenty nearby that would notice a Jeep just heading out.

The ceremony was tomorrow, which meant I still had time to stop it.

I darted around to the back, then bolted to one of the empty smaller tents. Wooden crates had been set outside the entrance, and I read the stenciled labels reading: CAUTION EXPLOSIVES.

I threw back the flap and was immersed in the cool shade of the interior. My eyes swept around the room, searching for any sign of the statue. Two round tables were pressed against the left side of the room, and to the right were stacks of folding chairs and shipping crates. Maps and charts had been spread out on the tables, and I rushed over to them. The silhouetted figure of two men marched past, and I froze, hearing the foot-steps just outside the tent. Heart racing, I eased down to a crouching position behind the table. I slowed my breathing, straining to listen.

"Get the other truck," a man's voice said. "and bring it to the West entrance. The supports collapsed after the blast and need it to clear the rocks."

"Yes, sir," the second said.

Footsteps drew closer as a man entered the tent. From his position, I was hidden but would readily be exposed if he chose to move closer. He sighed as he sat at the table by the entrance. He must've been in his late fifties, with salt and peppered hair under a black hat and thin mustache. He wore the Division's standard black and gray fatigues. He scanned the room again before pulling his pistol from its holster and plopping it down on the table. Then, he leaned forward and rested his face in his hands. A minute passed, and I thought he'd perhaps fallen asleep in that position until a scratching hiss followed by a beep came from him. The man let out a long, exasperated sigh and slowly sat up. He reached to his left, unhooking a walkie-talkie from his belt.

He raised it to his mouth and pressed the side button with his thumb. "This is Craig, over."

The walkie hissed, emitting two more beeps before another garbled voice came.

"Agent Craig. They need you to look over the transfer report in the supply tent."

"Now?" he grumbled.

"Yes sir," the other voice hesitated. "Mr. Kane needs to know how much C4 can be requested and delivered today without raising red flags at the border."

Craig sighed and closed his eyes. I could almost see the weariness wafting off of him. How long had he been in Division 12? And surely in the military before that. I imagined this was what Jason would look like in twenty years. Tired, worn out, and...alone. I didn't miss the satisfaction that thought gave me. Assholes deserved to be alone.

"Alright," he said. "I'm on my way."

He stood and walked toward the tent opening. My eyes flicked toward the pistol, still sitting on the table. My pulse ratcheted up a notch as I watched him leave. I waited only a few seconds before springing to my feet. After two strides, my hand had closed around the pistol's grip. Although not as big as Jason's, it was heavier than I'd expected. I dropped the clip, checking for bullets.

"What the hell—" the guard's alarmed voice caught my attention, and he stood wide-eyed from the tent entrance,

I slapped the clip back into place and lifted the gun, aiming it at his chest.

The man threw his hands up and backed up a step. "Whoa, whoa. Now, let's talk about this. You don't want to do anything stupid."

"Tell me where the statue is," I said, leveling him with my gaze.

Bewilderment flashed over the man's face. "What are you talking about? What statue?"

I took a step closer, keeping the pistol trained on him. "Don't play dumb. Just tell me. Where is he keeping the bronze statue of Inanna?"

The man's eyes grew wider still, but he chewed on the corners of his mustache. A worse liar than a heavy-handed fruit vendor, he'd be terrible at poker.

"I know you know where it is. Take me to it, now." Although my hand was steady, I hoped he missed the slight tremor in my words.

The man nodded. "Okay, I'll show you. Just get that damn gun off me, will ya?"

I didn't move.

The man sighed and, keeping his hands up, gestured with his head. "Over there, in the safe."

"Open it," I said, motioning him toward it with the gun.

The man hunched down and walked to the safe. He knelt awkwardly, not wanting to turn his back on me, and his hand shook as he keyed in the numbers on the keypad.

The safe beeped, and he pulled the door open. I tilted my head to the left to peer over the man's shoulder as he withdrew a small box. About the size of a wooden cigar box, he set it on his knees and opened it. The statue lay tucked inside among foam padding.

"Hand it over," I demanded.

The man stood, cradling the box in his hands, and held it out to me. Then, holding the pistol with my right hand, I held out my left toward him.

He shook his head. "Lady, you think I'm an idiot? I'm not touching the damn thing."

I reached my hand inside the box, removing the idol. A current of energy flared from the statue, causing the muscles in my arm to involuntarily tense. My left hand clamped down, constricting hard around it as if I'd touched a live wire. In an instant, a brilliant yellow flash blinded me, and I stumbled backward.

Ancient magic surged into me, and I threw my head back, succumbing to the powerful force and letting it overwhelm my senses.

The pistol fell from my grip and thumped as it hit the dirt. Suddenly, I was weightless, floating hundreds of feet in the air with the stone ruins of Palmyra below me. From a bird's-eye view of the entire camp, the white canopied tops of the tents were grouped in clusters of four and five and bordered by digging equipment, trucks, and security guards patrolling the roads and footpaths that made the perimeter. A dust cloud hovered around the base of the hill, and people were carrying wheelbarrows of dirt and rocks as they attempted to clear the entrance.

My body moved toward it as if floating in space, closing in on where I'd focused. Panic constricted my throat from the growing fear I'd be seen if I got too close. However, nobody looked up even as I hovered, not twenty feet above them, as if I were invisible. I peered down at the ground, and my lack of shadow confirmed my theory.

Well, this is something new.

I moved again, and this time I drifted toward the cliff face. I cringed, bracing myself for the impact, but at the last second, I'm veered to the left and taken around to the mountain's Eastern side. To my right, I glided past the citadel's enormous rock walls and towering pillars.

I sank lower to where the citadel and the mountain meet, and my feet landed gently on the ground, and I stood before a tall archway all but hidden with overgrown thorny bushes. This place was on the opposite side of where they had blasted. Derek had his crew looking in the wrong place.

One-foot-tall cuneiform letters were carved in the stone

arch big enough to park a bus under, but I hadn't the foggiest idea what they said. Probably a warning to turn back, or you'd die.

If only Kat were here to read them for me. A dull ache radiated from my breastbone as I thought about the old British lady who smuggled wine and called everybody dear. I hoped she and Zhalika and everyone else at the estate were alright.

I passed under the archway, striding to where the lower part of a rocky hill was carved smooth. As if pushed, I reached to touch it, running my hand on the stone's sand-paper-like surface and detecting the nearly imperceptible grooves of an eight-pointed star.

I pressed my lips together and aligned my right palm over the symbol. Magic trickled from me, and I heard a low grinding sound buried deep somewhere inside the hill.

I dropped my hand, stepping back. The wall shuddered as if Derek's crew had set off another detonation, and slowly, it slid inward, revealing a dark tunnel leading underground.

Suddenly, an earth-shattering pain burst from the back of my head and jolted down my spine. The vision disintegrated.

CHAPTER

THIRTY-ONE

My eyes snapped open, finding myself face to face with a pistol and one pissed-off Division 12 agent whom I had recently been on the opposite ends of a gun with.

He loomed over where I lay sprawled on my back in the tent.

"I've got her, Mr. Kane," he shouted over his shoulder, his eyes not leaving mine.

From the corners of my vision, Derek appeared beside the middle-aged agent. "Very good," he said, taking off his sunglasses. He squatted beside me and took the statue still clasped in my hand. I wrapped my fingers around it. Derek stood, and before I knew what was happening, he stomped a booted foot onto my forearm. I cried out as the tendons and muscles of my arm burned in pain. Tears streamed from the corners of my eyes as the statue tumbled from my hand.

He removed his boot, and I gasped, clutching my arm to my stomach.

"Thank you," he said, picking up the statue. The agent kept

the gun pinned on me as Derek found the foam-lined box on the table, tucked the bronze figure into it, and closed the lid.

"It is clear now you were growing restless in your quarters. The crew informed me we still have a few hours before they reached the doorway. Perhaps you'd like to join me for dinner?"

I glared at him from where I still lay on the tent's floor.

"Would you please escort Ms. Dawson to my tent, Agent Craig?"

"Yes, sir."

The agent hoisted me to my feet. I felt the muzzle of the pistol on my back and instinctively arched away from it as he shoved me to the opening in the tent. Derek strolled beside me, sliding his sunglasses into his shirt pocket. The sun dipped low, casting the horizon in pinks and yellows to silhouette the citadel.

My eyes lingered on the hilltop, remembering the vision the statue had given me. The visions had always come to me when I'd been asleep, so what had changed that I now had them when I was awake? While I wasn't one to look 'a gift horse in the mouth', or in this case, 'a statue in the hand', — I was thankful the magic had shown me where the *true* entrance to Ur was. However, the random blacking out was a bit of an inconvenience.

The agent's hand tightened on my arm, drawing me through the entrance of another tent. A polished wood table sat in the tent's center with a woven rug beneath it. A server with dark skin carried a tray of fruits, nuts, cheeses, and thinly sliced meats.

The agent cinched my hands behind my back, and I felt the cold bite of handcuffs on my wrists. White-hot anger boiled inside me. "I thought you said no handcuffs."

"I did make that promise. However, when you destroyed a piece of my property, that voids the contract." He stuck a grape into his mouth, looking smug, but the tone in his voice was less controlled than usual.

I'd struck a nerve. Kane Junior didn't like his stuff broken.

He motioned to the chair to his right. "Please sit."

I felt the weight of his eyes from where he sat at the head of the table as I moved to the empty chair. Agent Craig pulled it out for me. The chain connecting the handcuffs jingled as I awkwardly arranged myself to sit in the chair.

"It would please me if you'd eat," he said, chewing on a slice of apple. Derek gave Agent Craig a nod, and he forked a few pieces of cheese and meat onto my plate.

I stared at it.

Derek laughed. "Go ahead. I assure you it's not drugged or anything." And as if to prove it, he stabbed a block of cheese and popped it in his mouth. He made *mmming* noises. "See? Now eat."

My mouth watered, and I couldn't remember the last time I'd eaten anything. I hesitated, unable to move my hands.

He laughed again, placed his elbows on the table, and rested his chin on his hands, watching me.

Contempt for this vile man spilled out of me when I realized what he wanted me to do.

I'd starve before he'd get to watch me eat like a dog.

"You know," he said, rolling up a slice of meat and cheese. "I wish you'd see this as an opportunity like I have. You've seen firsthand the turmoil here. This terrorist cell attacks this one. This government shifts so another can take its place." He twirled his finger in the air. "On and on, the cycle never ends. Fighting over oil, water, land." He scoffed. "Don't get me started on the squabbling over religion. Whose god is the true god? For centuries, armies destroyed one temple to erect another."

He placed the meat and cheese in his mouth and chewed. My stomach grumbled *loudly*.

"The instability," he continued, wiping his hands with a cloth napkin. "Has hampered any significant growth to the region. If the right catalyst were ignited, per se, a substantial and permanent change would occur."

I eyed him warily, watching his jaw work as he chewed. He pointed a fork at me.

"You *do* see it, don't you? The benefit to this region if peace were achieved. Only then could true change begin. The land and people can heal and advance to a brighter future."

I straightened my shoulders. It was all bullshit. It had to be. Guys like him didn't want peace; they wanted money. Wars were cash cows, at least to the investors who knew how to leverage them. And yet, what he said aligned with what Enheduanna had warned me about. A small part of me wondered if there was an inkling of a possibility that Enheduanna had been wrong. Maybe *this* time, humans were ready to embrace the knowledge of the gods. What if the progress in four thousand years had made us more prepared this time to face whatever lay on the other side?

Derek picked up another piece of cheese from my plate and held it to my lips.

I turned my head away, my resolve unwavering, even as a gnawing came from the pit of my stomach.

He shrugged and dropped it back on the plate. "You can't tell me you haven't thought about it? Wondered what mysteries lay on the other side? Help me do this. We can open the Bridge of Vela together, and then we'll both have the answer. A truth we can share and alter the course of humanity. We could bring enlightenment to a world that has stagnated for far too long."

"You're wrong," I said.

Derek chuckled. "Am I? Even now, you doubt yourself. I know all about the stories and the legends of high priestess Enheduanna.

"Enheduanna has shown me what will happen if you open the bridge. What is on the other side *will* corrupt us. War and famine will ravage the world until we're back into the dark ages."

"She showed you?" He twisted his mouth incredulously. "Jason told me all about how you went to the museum and read the tablets, but what do you really know about the daughter of the mad King of Sargon? Do you know how many works of Enheduanna are held in private collections? Artifacts that have never seen a museum shelf?" He smacked his lips. "We'll just say a lot. And with the right connections and the right amount of money, those artifacts can change hands. My team learned all sorts of exciting things from them."

I didn't move. There were *more* tablets. Had Kat told me that, or had she kept that little tidbit to herself so I wouldn't worry we were only working with half the picture? I gritted my teeth. She'd never do that. Which meant he was either lying or Kat hadn't known.

"Those tablets you read," he said, folding his napkin on his lap. "They had her poems and a few other meaningless records, but they didn't tell you that she was *just* as power-hungry as her father. She'd entice and lure young women with false promises to join her temple. They surrendered themselves to her, dedicating their lives to serve."

He took a sip of water from his glass, and I noticed that there wasn't one for me. I assumed they were worried I'd try to break the glass and use it to injure myself or him.

He leaned back in his chair and crossed his legs. "Do you know *how* she harnessed the magic in the stones and the statue?"

I didn't reply.

"She forced them to kill themselves," he said, smiling as if he were proud of this fact. "A ritual suicide to bind their souls into the stones. Locked inside for eternity, she tricked them, used them. She was jealous at how powerful her brother had become, and acting out of nothing more than spite, she'd sealed the bridge. Cutting off his access to insurmountable knowledge."

He reached down next to his chair and set the small black box on the table. "I've spent a fortune hiring researchers and scientists on this passion project of mine. My top archaeologist was quite intrigued by this statue." He clicked open the latches, took the statue out, and placed it on the table between them. "It seems it harbored Enheduanna's soul and the ancient power she'd wielded." He sighed and leaned back. "But it seems not to possess it anymore. I'd assume you had a little something to do with that?"

A knot formed deep in the pit of my stomach, staring at the tiny bronze statue only a foot away from me. Of course, he knew about my powers. Jason had told him.

His lips twisted into a smirk. "Your silence is answer enough. It is a disappointment, to say the least; there may be a way yet to proceed with the ceremony without it. It will, however, require your help and, from what I understand, would be in your best interest to retain a residual amount of the power should you hope to survive the ceremony. Leon believes that your body will take the place of the idol."

Leon. Leon was helping Derek. But for how long? Jason had to have known as well. An icy coldness sank into my stomach. Who else had betrayed me?

Kat? Assem?

"And although the instructions for a four-thousand-year-old ritual are unclear." Derek laughed dryly. "He does feel, with your full cooperation, you can come out of this without any permanent bodily harm."

Sacrifice your mortal soul.

The words echoed in my head. I had read them myself. But now they were saying it wasn't so? I felt disoriented. The truths I'd clung to were fading, like when the bridge had disintegrated under me in my vision.

An explosion from outside the tent erupted, and the dishes on the table rattled. Derek held his glass to keep it from spilling over. The earth rumbled beneath my feet. An image flashed in my mind's eye of a vast network of catacombs spreading for miles below where we sat. An ancient city buried in the sand.

Another blast shuddered the table, and I cringed, my nails digging into the palms of my hands. I imagined the ground giving way and the table, chairs, and the whole tent being sucked into the chasm below.

Unbothered by the blasts, Derek waved a finger at the attendant. The man approached and bent, whispering in Derek's ear.

He stared off into the distance, listening. I fidgeted with the handcuffs digging into my wrists. The temptation to call forth the power was there, but it wouldn't affect the metal. The chair was wood and would catch fire with a nudge from my magic; however, what would that do besides fill the tent with smoke and most likely piss Derek off more? And possibly burn my ass.

My tongue swept the backs of my teeth. Moreover, what if he was right? What if this was the last of my magic, and I needed it to survive the ritual?

I couldn't risk it. Not yet. I needed to save it, only using it if I had to.

Derek's jaw shifted, and his words were edged with venom. "Please send Leon in."

Beads of sweat trickled down my neck and back as the tall, lanky museum curator entered carrying a stack of books. His hair was matted, and he had dark bags under his eyes like he hadn't slept in for weeks. His eyes went to me, and I glared daggers at him.

"You called Mr. Kane?" he said, his eyes moving to where Derek sat.

Derek didn't look up from his plate. "Yes. It seems my demolition crew has notified me that although they've breached the main door, they've discovered only an empty room upon clearing the rubble. It is not the entrance you informed me would be there."

Derek chewed slowly and swallowed.

Leon's face blanched. "Please, sir," he stammered. "My calculations were—"

"Your calculations were wrong," Derek snapped.

"If only I had a bit more time to examine the tablets—"

"You're out of time, Mr. Weber." Derek stood and threw his napkin onto his plate, and the man cowered, hugging the books to his chest.

Derek reached under the table and pulled a snub-nosed pistol from where it'd been hidden underneath. He held it up, pointing it directly at Leon an arm's length away. Leon squeezed his eyes shut.

Derek's thumb moved, pulling the hammer back. "I have no patience for inept people to be around me. Time is no longer on my side, so please enlighten me on how to get into Ur."

"Sir, I don't—"

"You have three seconds."

My heart thundered against my ribcage.

"Three, two..."

"Stop!" I shouted, jumping to my feet and knocking over my chair.

Both men looked at me.

Derek's finger tapped the trigger. "Is there something you'd care to say?"

"Don't shoot him," I said, moving my hands behind me.

"While I commend your admirable nature, I'm afraid this is

a necessary action. I've no tolerance for employees that no longer serve my purpose."

"Please..." I pleaded. "Please, you can't shoot him."

Derek scowled. "Do you have a reason why I shouldn't?"

I swallowed. Although I seethed with bitterness toward the spineless man, his pale face and whimpering instilled a sense of pity for him. Although he had, without a doubt, betrayed me, it didn't mean he deserved to die.

I took a deep breath, gathering my courage. "He doesn't know the location of the entrance to Ur, but I do."

THIRTY-TWO

"Is that so?" Derek replied, lowering the gun slightly.

I nodded, even as the hairs on my neck prickled. I could barely convince a convenience store owner to give me a discount on computer accessories, and now I was bargaining with a man who literally made multi-million-dollar business deals. This was a dangerous dance I did not know the steps to.

"Yes," I said, my voice surprising me with how steady it sounded. "I'll tell you once you let him go."

His finger relaxed on the trigger, to my relief, and he lowered the gun completely. A sheen of sweat glistened off the curator's face, and Leon peeked open an eye.

As if weighing the truth of my words, Derek pursed his lips.

My insides squirmed. What if I'd promised him something I didn't have? The statue had triggered a vision of Ur, but what if it had been wrong? What if it was only a memory locked inside from thousands of years ago, set on replay? What if it had collapsed further in the tunnel and would lead him to another dead end?

"Very well," Derek said. "Get out of my sight."

Leon whispered a quick "Thank you, sir." And hurried out of the tent.

Derek set the pistol on the table and turned to face me.

"Let us finish our dinner then, hmm? And you can tell me what you know."

The attendant righted my chair, but I remained where I was.

"As you were saying, Ms. Dawson?" Derek said.

I lifted my chin. "The entrance to the West is a decoy." I paused. His dark eyes were intense, peering at me from under narrowed brows.

"The true entrance is hidden on the East side of the citadel."

Derek tilted his head. "Is it now?"

A statement more than a question, I didn't respond.

"I suppose you'd be willing to show me the location?"

I nodded.

"Excellent. Let's go."

A guard immediately entered from outside with an assault rifle slung over his shoulder.

"What? Now?" I said.

Derek flicked an annoyed look toward me. "Yes, now. We're on a rigid timeline, and every second is wasted if we're looking in the wrong place." He paused and pressed his lips together in a tight-lipped smile. "I wish you'd had more of an appetite, but I am pleased with how our dinner conversation went."

A BREEZE HAD PICKED up since I'd entered the tent, and as we exited, I squinted my eyes, the stinging sand buffeting my face and bare arms. They load me into the backseat of an idling Humvee. The opposite door opened. Jason climbed in, wearing camo combat gear and his pistol in a front holster. Both doors slammed shut, snuffing out the howling wind.

Jason nudged me with his elbow. "Finally decided to cooperate, eh Elly?"

I stared at my dusty boots on the worn rubber floor mats and didn't look up. "Screw you."

Jason chuckled, a deep rumbling sound in his chest.

"Derek tells me you're going to show us the location to Ur?"

My stomach tightened. I didn't owe him an answer.

"Don't be like that," he said, hanging a hand on the roof handle. "You know this is part of the job. And until Division 12 is no longer on Mr. Kane's payroll, I have to follow their orders."

"Fuck their orders," I snapped, twisting my head up to face him. "And fuck you."

He smiled, but it didn't reach his eyes.

I turned away, staring out the dark window as the Humvee bounced on the dirt road.

"Here's our stop," Jason said when a few minutes had passed. Then, he leaned over to open my door.

I squeezed my eyes shut and held my breath. Not daring to touch him. Smell him. He disgusted me. The man I thought I knew was nothing more than a spineless, self-centered asshole.

When I heard his door open and close, I opened my eyes and slid out of the passenger side. We had stopped at the East entrance to the citadel, and it stood more than a hundred yards off to my right. The wide base—perched atop the towering hill — was lit by a few spotlights.

Three black Humvees were parked side by side. Hands still bound in front of me, Jason led me to where a group of men were standing. Mr. Kane peered through a pair of binoculars in the direction of the citadel, his elbows resting on the hood of a truck.

"Care to take a look?" he asked.

No. I bit my tongue, resisting the urge to spit in his face.

"They are only binoculars." He said, holding them to me. "What could it possibly hurt?"

I glared at him, pouring every ounce of hate into my eyes. What did it matter now? This was a one-way ticket for me. My hands still bound, I jingled the cuffs.

"No worries, I can hold them for you."

When I didn't move, he placed them before me and rested them against my eyes. The desert landscape of rocky mounds and scrubby bushes took on an eerie green-blue from the night vision filter. Mr. Kane's hand pushed my sight up to the base of the mountain toward the Eastern side of the citadel. A dozen or so men scurried about, rolling wires for the explosive detonators. A sharp whistle erupted in the still of the night, and the men broke into a run, disappearing to the right as they evacuated the area. Sticks of TNT were wedged along the perimeter of the wall. My pulse quickened when I spotted my vision's familiar pillars and engravings.

"Perimeters clear, sixty seconds," a voice scratched on a nearby walkie-talkie.

I stepped back.

"Not yet," Mr. Kane said and held them in place. "You don't want to miss the show."

I pressed my face to them, and he directed my head to one of the pillars. The sight of a man seated in a chair seized the air in my chest, and icy claws sank into my skull as I recognized the man.

Leon.

His eyes were wide with terror, and he struggled in the chair, straining at the gag on his mouth. Sticks of C-4 explosives had been strapped to the legs of his chair.

I spun toward Derek.

"Someone's still up there!" I shouted at the guards around me. "What is wrong with all of you?"

I lunged for Derek, but Jason's firm grip closed around my upper arms, still tethered behind my back.

"Let me go," I snarled. "They're going to kill him!" I thrashed against his hold, but he held tight.

Jason's face fell into shadow, and he reached up until he'd seized both my arms.

"We had a deal," I said. "You promised you wouldn't hurt him!"

"Yeah, I know," Derek said. "But wouldn't you agree Enheduanna would appreciate the sacrifice?" He shrugged and held the radio to his mouth. "All clear."

"You fucking asshole!" I spat, lunging against Jason's grip.

But it was no use. A second later, a series of pops came from the hillside, followed by a thundering explosion. Gravel and dirt rained down from above them, pinging off the metal hoods and roofs of the trucks.

A sudden, unnatural rush of wind swirled the sand around our feet, and I looked up. A dust storm, ten miles wide, was enveloping the citadel. Angry flashes of lightning illuminated the boiling clouds high above it.

Before I could make another attempt to break free, everyone moved at once, re-entering the vehicles. Jason pulled open a door and shoved me inside with the vehicle already in motion. We wound our way up the curving road, and my pulse throttled my ears. I'd underestimated him and assumed he had a shred of sanity left in him. How could I have been so stupid to think he'd be reasonable? That any deal I thought I'd made, he'd stand by? I wouldn't make that mistake again. If I was to play his game, I needed to be more than just a pawn.

A massive black cloud of roaring dust and sand darkened the starry sky as it glided across the desert. As wide as the horizon, the dust storm reached high into the night sky, blacking out the stars. In the Midwest, they had tornadoes, and in the

South, hurricanes. In the Middle East, there were Haboobs. The first and last time I'd laughed at the ridiculous name was before I'd experienced one.

The spine-chilling way the storm approached, a silent march of boiling dust and dirt. Until the headwinds began, there was a light breeze, a gentle warning to seek shelter. Soon the billowing cloud encompassed you, and everything around you disappeared into swirling sand. Dry lightning crackled as the particles of sand discharged the electrical currents. Should you find yourself unprotected, the needle-like pain of high-velocity sand stings your face. It streamed into your eyes, ears, and nose—until every breath was agony.

And, now, we were driving straight toward one.

The trucks stopped, and again, Jason pulled me out into the night. The air was tinged with sulfur from the explosions. A haze of dust still hovered, and several men coughed as they dug away at the broken pieces of stone.

Jason pushed me toward the entrance. A splintered piece of wood lay at the base. A powdery dust coated a sticky red puddle of blood around it—all that remained of the chair and Leon.

Bile rose into my throat, and I covered my mouth.

"Over here!" a man called out from the pile of rubble.

Derek strode forward and clambered to the entrance. Jason led me along, and I stumbled as he urged me over the shifting rocks until we stopped into the rock wall in front of a ten by ten square void. A musty breeze arose from somewhere deep inside, causing the lingering cloud of dust to flutter.

We'd found the entrance to Ur.

THIRTY-THREE

"All right, gather the gear, gentlemen. Time to move out." Derek said, calling out orders.

The truck's doors slammed, and I heard the zipping of backpacks and flashlights clicking on and off from behind me. A crew of a dozen men clambered up toward the entrance; their arms were burdened with lanterns, rope, shovels, and canteens. A man carried a small black box to Derek, and he waved a hand up to stop him. The man lifted the lid while Derek held an open backpack, and they placed the eight palm-sized stones inside it.

My skin prickled. If he had the statue, I'd bet all the money I had it was in that backpack, too. I *needed* the statue. No matter how slim the chance, it was my only hope to stop him.

"Time to go," Jason murmured behind me, pressing his hand into my lower back. With my hands bound behind me, I struggled to maintain balance as I scrambled down the other side of the shifting rocks. Derek took the lead, followed by three men, then Jason and me behind them. The remaining crew were brought up in the rear.

Through the opening, we entered the dark tunnel. Narrower

than the entrance, the smooth path sloped downward, descending deeper into the earth. Beads of moisture sparkled as the flashlights bounced off the chiseled rock walls. My thigh soon ached as we walked over the difficult terrain.

The tunnel descended slowly. I lost track of how many times it doubled back, feeling as though it would never end. Finally, when I'd lost track of time, the tunnel widened, and we entered a cavern over a hundred feet across and twice as high. Stalactites hung from the dome-shaped a hundred feet up, and eerie hues of green and yellow mineral deposits coated the walls and floors. An emerald green pool sat in the center with a glass-like surface since no breeze disturbed the air. A white sand beach encircled its perimeter, and the tunnel continued on the opposite side of the pool.

The underground cave must've been formed centuries ago, unbeknownst to the world where it remained hidden under the Citadel.

Derek motioned for us to halt. Labored breathing reverberated off the rock walls as men lowered their packs and paused to catch their breaths. Derek unrolled a piece of paper and called a man to bring a flashlight to him.

Derek thrust a finger at the map, then barked an order at the man beside him. "What the hell are you waiting for? Go," he said, sounding like an indignant teenager.

The rough-looking man nodded and darted to the milky-green pool. He pressed the butt of the rifle to his shoulder as he stepped toward the pond's edge and peered down into the water. The slightest hint of a ripple waved across the surface. I blinked, not believing my eyes. No way did anything live in there.

The man exchanged a nervous glance with Derek and a few other nearby men before kneeling.

He set his gun to the side, where the rust-colored cavern

floor transitioned to pure beach-like ivory sand, and reached out slowly as if grabbing something near the surface. The surrounding ground shuddered as if another blast had been detonated deeper underground.

I shouted at him to stop, but it was too late.

The intensity of the vibrations grew, and the sand spiraled up like a writhing dust devil until it reached the ceiling.

Two men started walking over to him, but a signal from Derek sent guards with grim faces to block their path.

The man's screams echoed off the chamber as the sand hissed. I stared unblinking, unable to look away. The dust swirled, picking up speed, and the hiss morphed into a buzzing as if it were a swarm of angry hornets that had had their nest kicked.

Only a faint outline of the man could be seen through the ever-thickening dust cloud. The ground shook violently, and the sand accumulated around him, burying his feet, legs, and chest until he let out one last terrified scream before burying his head. As if turning to quicksand, the cavern floor opened and pulled him under. The swirling sands dissipated, and all that remained was a slight red indentation beside the pond.

"Jesus fucking, Christ," Jason breathed next to me.

A cold, tingling numbness spread across my body, and I swallowed. I was at a loss for what I'd just seen. Enheduanna's advice covered nothing like *that*.

Derek shifted his feet and scratched the side of his neck. He gestured to the map and murmured something to the Division agent next to him.

I pursed my lips. He was playing it cool, but this had surprised him too. And the control freak definitely didn't like the unexpected.

Like, say, photographers stealing artifacts from crates.

"Alright then," he yelled and rolled up the map. "Don't go

near the pond of water unless you want to end up like that guy." At once, the workers and guards streamed to the right, giving themselves a wide berth from the green water, and I heard a few of them mutter quick blessings for protection.

Derek stuffed the map into his backpack. "Looks like we'll have to figure out another way past it."

"How are we supposed to do that?" A man protested from the group, and a couple more shouted their agreement.

Derek placed a hand on his hip and surveyed the cave walls. "There," he said, pointing to a narrow ledge to his right no more than two feet across. It ran along the length of the wall, maybe ten feet from the edge of the pool.

"We can use the rope ladder to reach that ledge," he said. "We'll have to leave the heavier packs, but we can travel faster without them." He glanced at his watch. "We've got three hours. Let's go."

The men threw their backpacks into a pile on the ground without hesitation. Two men moved to the opposite wall and, using what looked like crossbows, shot spikes with ropes attached to them into the wall about six feet above the ledge. They unfolded a metal ladder and used the ropes to hoist it up.

Derek made them climb up first, and then once he confirmed that nothing else weird was going to happen, he followed.

I had no time to resist as Jason shoved me toward the ladder's base. I stepped on the first rung, and it swayed under my weight. I studied the spikes lodged into the wall high above me, well aware that there was no reality in which this would pass any OSHA inspection. Carefully, I made my way up it and heaved myself onto the ledge. It was wider than I'd realized, allowing two people to stand shoulder to shoulder. From this view, the lantern light glinted off the turquoise water in the pool, revealing a black-painted, eight-pointed star in the middle. A delicious chill made goosebumps race up my arms.

Once the entire group was up, we started along the stone edge. My hands rested against the wall, a reassuring presence more than anything because it wasn't like there was anything to grab onto if my foot slipped. I stepped lightly, deliberate with each step, and eyed the water lapping at the edge of the pool twenty feet below. Sweat soaked my shirt by the time we reached the other side. The men hammered in new spikes, and another ladder was tossed down.

After descending safely on the other side, Derek waved us onward, and I could sense his growing impatience. Jason held a flashlight in one hand and his pistol in the other, and I often had to half-jog to keep pace.

We continued further in the tunnel, and I noticed cuneiform scrawled along the rock walls. I squinted in the dim light, struggling to decipher the angular shapes.

"These are messages," a man next to my shoulder said. "The citizens of Ur left them."

The older man's face was wrinkled, and only a thin strip of gray hair remained on the back of his head.

"You can read Cuneiform?" I said, keeping my voice low as they walked.

"A bit, yes." He nodded toward the left wall. "Nothing too complicated, but enough." He shot a look toward Derek and the two guards with rifles flanking him. "Enough to keep me alive."

I scowled, annoyed at how these people had ended up working for him. What suffering had they already faced to see him as a better choice?

We came across a mark bigger than the others I'd seen. A foot long, the first two symbols were triangular, while the third was several bisecting lines.

I gestured to it. "What does this say?"

"It says the rain has come to their village." The man shook his head, and his mouth twisted. "But not a good rain, a rain of *death*. Flooding their fields, washing away their livestock."

"A great flood?"

The man nodded. "Many of these writings are records visitors left behind as they sought the city. Most likely desperate for help when their prayers to the gods were unanswered."

"They believed the gods would be here, didn't they?"

"They were here. At least, that's what the legend says. Ur was the one city where the gods would visit. If you were lucky, you might even catch the attention of one and receive their blessing."

Jason shot me a warning look, and I glared back but stepped away from the older man.

The light from the lanterns and flashlights bobbed along the walls and ceilings as we walked, and soon, there was a sound of running water growing louder. Finally, the tunnel walls fell away, and Derek stood in front, lifting his lantern. The light streamed into the darkness of the cavern beyond, illuminating the outlines of rounded peaks of stone buildings, squat stone walls, and carved pillars—an entire city preserved under the earth. In the center, an immense tower loomed, and a series of domed arches projected high into the air above it.

"Ur," the word spilled from me.

CHAPTER

THIRTY-FOUR

"Welcome, gentleman," Derek said, and then after directing a look at me, added, "And lady."

My stomach twisted. We'd found it. We were here, standing at the entrance to the great city-state that generations of scholars and researchers had been searching for.

Suddenly I was keenly aware of the thousands of tons of rock and stone perched precariously above me, and I shut my eyes against a wave of vertigo. So many questions flitted in my head. How had this city been formed underground? Or had it been constructed above ground and the citadel erected over it? My brain couldn't comprehend the magnitude of what it would take to bury a whole city.

Derek marched on, leading us down a footpath that descended along a series of switchbacks. The city sprawled for at least half a mile. With no support structures rising, I couldn't imagine how the ceiling hadn't collapsed after all these years.

At the bottom, the road curved into the city's center, leading them between the buildings. I stole a glance inside the square openings that had been windows. Shadows obscured their dark interiors, and I suppressed a shiver. The entire place was deathly quiet. No dripping water. No rustle of bats. Nothing. What had happened here? There had to have been some natural disaster. Earthquakes were still common in Syria. Could that have been the cause of how a city ended up beneath thousands of feet of sand and rock? My throat constricted. Had people been living in the city when it happened, buried alive with it?

Visions of mummified corpses and desiccated skeletal remains assaulted my vision, and I inhaled a deep breath, shoving away the dark thoughts. From my periphery — the darkened recesses where windows and doors had been — clawed at my vision, tempting me to peer closer.

I kept my gaze on the backs of the men ahead of me, ignoring my increasing unease.

I scanned the faces of the workers, and the whites of their eyes shone in the dark. They stumbled into each other, shying away from the houses and buildings.

A rectangular temple stood atop a high podium at the city's center. Massive round columns supported a portico chiseled from rare marble and granite with silver inlays spiraling up each pillar.

The tile roof was a dark burgundy, and the edges of the triangular pediment rising above the columns were painted silver.

We trudged up the wide stone staircase. My thigh burned with the exertion, but I couldn't slow down if I wanted to. The thrill of being here drove me, and I swallowed the pain.

A plinking sound caught my attention, and something small bounced off my arm. I slowed, looking upward. The cavernous roof—well over a hundred feet high—was shrouded in darkness, yet sand shimmered down like drifting dust particles caught in the light. It spattered around me, filling in the cracks and crevices of the stairs.

The men ahead murmured exclamations, but my feet were already moving.

My leg protested; still, I gritted my teeth, taking the steps two at a time.

As if triggered by the shouts of the group, the trickling sand shifted from a light patter to a torrential downpour. Lightning fast, it piled up, forming knee-high mounds around my ankles.

A man close to my age, with glasses and a still baby-smooth face, shouted that he could no longer move. The snow-white sand covered his legs up to his thighs, and he struggled, hands writhing to keep from being buried.

I raced the remaining steps to his side, and sensing Jason's presence beside me, we each grabbed an arm and yanked. The man groaned in agony as his body twisted and was pulled free.

The man collapsed on the ground, panting. Bile soured the back of my tongue when I saw from the ankle down nothing remained but bloody stumps where the man's feet had been.

"Holy shit," Jason said.

The man howled in pain, and I stood in a daze, conflicted about what to do. I needed to help, but how? I winced, feeling a sharp sting on top of my ear. Then another struck my left wrist clasped behind my back as if I'd been stung by a bee. Jason cursed and slapped at where sand had touched the exposed skin between his glove and jacket.

I craned my neck up to the origin of the falling sand, but Jason grabbed me by the shoulder and dragged me to the entrance. "Don't look at it. We have to get under the roof!"

The mortally wounded man shrieked to help him, and my gut knotted with guilt for leaving him behind as Jason's firm grip forbade me from returning.

Other guards and workers crowded together, hurrying under the protection of the portico. Only steps away from safety, a Division agent had fallen. He pried off his helmet and frantically clawed at where the skin was peeling on his neck. His face contorted, and I could almost hear a sizzle as the sand disintegrated his body.

The deadly grains of sand had reached a steady downpour. It covered the ground at least a foot thick in most places but formed dunes higher than my head in others. It felt like we were prisoners in an oversized hourglass.

Tick. Tick. Tick.

Derek closed the space to stand in front of the door to the temple.

"Alright, now what?" he said, looking at me through the group. Several injured moaned, and there was a thump as one collapsed. A lead ball formed in my stomach, and I didn't dare look in that direction for fear of what I'd see.

Derek cleared his throat. And I moved closer, examining the intricate details of the grand temple. More than six feet across, a square stone door sat recessed in the wall. Cuneiform ran along its top, just under the roof line.

My fingers probed the outline, studying the edges of where the door met the wall. Derek instructed two of his two guards to do the same and waved over another man, who withdrew a crowbar. He shoved into the where the two pieces of stone met each other and heaved.

He might as well have been prying open Fort Knox's doors for all it budged.

A man hissed as the toes of the heel of his boot melted away. "May Allah protect us," he whispered, cramming closer to the mass of two dozen bodies. The toxic sand had begun to overflow the tall mounds and creep in under the roof.

"We're all going to die unless you open this," Jason said, having to shout at me over the swishing sound of spilling sand.

"But I don't know how," I shouted back.

"Well, you have about thirty seconds to figure it out."

I sucked in a sharp breath and rubbed the tender skin on my wrist where the sand had touched me. A memory from my first vision of my handprint in stone elbowed its way to the front of my mind.

"I have an idea. Take these off," I said, spinning my back to face Jason and thrusting my bound hands at him.

A momentary hesitation flickered in his eyes as he looked at Derek, who nodded. Jason pulled a key from his shirt pocket, and the handcuffs fell from my wrists.

I dashed to the tall door and pressed my hand on the marble. My lower teeth tore into my bottom lip as I closed my eyes, trying to block out the panicked cries of workers and guards yelling orders.

I focused on remembering how that first vision had felt. How the rock-hard, solid stone had softened, melting under my touch. I willed the bonds to weaken and grow malleable like clay. It was not the powerful surge I'd expected. Nevertheless, a trickle of magic tingled my palm, feeling like a feather was brushing against it. My hand sank into it like wet mud. I plunged my hand deeper, burying my arm up to my elbow, unsure of what it was I knew I'd find. A gasp escaped my lips as my fingers caught hold of a metal ring. A dozen sets of eyes bore into me as I gripped the object and twisted.

. A deep rumbling resonance shook the ground beneath our feet, and I withdrew my hand. Gray liquified marble dripped from my fingers, splattering like opalescent paint onto the granite floor, and a harsh grating came from the door as it slid open.

Boots pounded the floor as everyone jostled through the door before it had fully opened. Jason pressed a hand against the small of my back and forced our way through. Shifting sand formed swirling eddies around our feet, and the soles of my feet grew hot like I was walking on hot coals. The sand stopped, however, at the threshold as if an invisible barrier prevented the sand from entering.

～

FOR A MOMENT, only the panting of men breathing and an occasional whisper of settling sand punctuated the silence.

A lantern blazed to life, and then another, radiating a bluish hue of light over all of them and capturing the scowl on Derek's face.

My heart battered against my ribcage as I wiped the sweat from my forehead, still too stunned to digest what had happened. My dreams blurred with my memories of Enheduanna, her visions becoming mine.

A handful of glowing flares were tossed into the darkness of the temple's interior, revealing a great hall with eight ten-foot-tall doors evenly spaced around the perimeter. In the center sat the stone altar. The same one from my dreams.

A Division agent began barking orders, instructing men to inspect the perimeter for any more traps or places the acid sand could get in. Derek sent two extremely hesitant guards to the altar.

They side-stepped up to it, their gazes sweeping every which way, anticipating the floor giving out or the roof collapsing. I didn't blame them for being scared. This place was one giant death trap.

Upon reaching the side of it with their limbs and heads still attached, Derek joined them, along with six other men. They stood around the rectangular granite slab, and he dictated to them where to place the stones. "The crimson goes to the left, the emerald on the far side," he said, looking down at the iPad in his hands.

The pressure of a hand brushed my wrists, and I spun. "No. Wait. What are you doing?"

However, Jason was quicker and stronger than me and caught my other wrist, flipping me back around. "Orders," he said in my ear, and the cuffs clipped shut behind me. His hands remained on my arms. "Where do you want her?"

Derek looked up and saw that I'd been handcuffed. "Over there," he told Jason, nodding to the East wall.

With my hands behind my back... *again*, Jason escorted me across the room and stood behind me.

Voices filled the room as everyone did their tasks, set up work lights and tables, and plugged in generators. A Division agent tried to get a walkie-talkie to work but was met with static and silence.

Jason's thumb gently caressed the mark on my palm.

I stiffened.

Wait. No. I'd *imagined* I'd felt it. My brain and nerves were fried, and I was still jittery from the adrenaline rush.

I felt it again, and my stomach fluttered. My body was obscured from the view of Jason, but I kept my face from betraying my bewilderment. What was he doing? Trying to distract me? Did he want me to react? Cause a scene? My temper flared, and suddenly I was too hot. How dare he wait until we're down here to do this. He had countless chances to reveal himself, and he decided to wait until the last fucking second? I jerked my body forward, breaking his hold, but refused to look at him.

Derek must've interpreted my step closer as interest. "You can't help yourself, can you?" he said, waving me closer.

Now that Jason had given me a sign, a message he was on my side, I was conflicted. But what I was supposed to do with that information, I hadn't a clue. However, I did know that if I didn't comply with him, he'd be suspicious. So, I adjusted my shoulders and walked to the altar to join him, leaving Jason behind.

The stones on the altar were a rainbow of colors, from ruby to emerald to dark cobalt blue. Inside them, an iridescent orb pulsed steadily.

Derek positioned himself next to me. "I've traveled the world and seen things that would blow your mind, but never could I have imagined seeing a human soul. It is quite distressing if you think about it. A person's soul being trapped for eternity."

I swallowed the walnut-sized knot that had formed in the back of my throat. These were the souls of the priestesses. They really had sacrificed themselves. But had it been willingly?

A final amber-colored stone was placed, and the indentations where they sat glowed a single pulse before fading to dark.

The balding man I'd spoken to before who could read the cuneiform approached the table. "The stones need to be placed in an exact sequence, or the ceremony won't work,"

Derek shot him a glare and thrust the iPad at him. "There's nothing about an order on this. Tell me what is the correct order."

The man cringed, shaking his head. "I don't know. Leon had researched that part."

I averted my eyes, sensing Derek's frustration seeping from him.

Guess you shouldn't have killed him, numbnuts.

Derek stiffened. "Fine," he said, looking toward the eight men awaiting his orders.

We were running out of time. Even without a view of the stars, I sensed the impending celestial alignment. The acid sand was meant to be a trap, a barrier to force those who entered the temple to open the gate or be unable to leave.

It was already clear the walkie-talkies didn't work, so there was no way cell phones would. We'd be trapped underground forever, well, not forever. We'd die of dehydration first. Five days, give or take.

I had no choice. "I know the order for the stones," I said.

Derek lifted his brows. "Now, why am I not surprised? I'm glad you decided to support the effort instead of fighting it." He waved his hand in the air. "Enlighten us."

I moved to the altar's edge. The voices in the room hushed as the workers and guards stopped whatever they were doing to watch me. I reached for the stones, moving a red with an orange and swapping the green with a yellow. Then, I inhaled deeply and closed my eyes, forcing myself to recall the image of the altar from my dream.

I opened my eyes and pointed to the stone — one that was the blackest shade of midnight —on the star's farthest tip out of my reach. "Move that one to the left. Switch it with the purple."

The older man shot a worried glance at Derek and scrolled through the iPad as if confirming what I was saying was right. He didn't need to look. I knew it was, just like I'd known how to find and open the door to get here.

He nodded, and the man shifted the positions of the stones, doing as I had instructed.

A hum echoed in the room like a distant train was moving within the walls. The stones began to pulse brightly. This time, the pulsing transitioned to a steady, vibrant glow. All of our faces were washed in the glow of a rainbow of colors. Soon after, the moss that clung to the cracks of the walls illuminated, glowing with an otherworldly fluorescence. A blazing light, as if the noonday sun had appeared, flooded the room, chasing away the shadowed corners. The cuneiform engravings on the altar glowed, the flux of light tracing the lines of the words and symbols.

Derek's lips curved into a smug smile at the same time as despair settled onto me like an icy shroud.

The stones were set.

THIRTY-FIVE

I'd done it. My eardrums hammered with the sudden quickening of my pulse. The altar was ready. I knew what was to come next.

"Come now," Derek said. "Don't look so glum." He raised his hands like an orchestra conductor calling for attention. "*This* is how we can shower enlightenment upon the world when these hidden truths are finally brought into the light."

I chewed the inside of my cheek, staring at the magically charged altar. My focus shifted in and out, not quite ready to believe that this was happening. This wasn't a dream I would soon wake up from and find myself on the couch in my apartment.

This was real.

Like unicorns and aliens real. Magic, older than anything I could comprehend, existed.

"I will bring new insight to humanity," Derek said. "Just think of what it could hold. A cure for all diseases, renewable energy sources, space travel."

I opened my mouth, but he continued before I could speak. "Come. We'll cross it together and share in our discoveries. Your silly photos will never change anything. It'll never be enough. But *this* will."

His words were like daggers, tearing at my most intimate fear and displaying at my feet like a gutted fish. I curled my hands at my side, feeling the taut skin of the scar.

From the recesses of my mind, I felt the tingle of the magic, faint like an echo of a memory.

A guard pushed me forward, but I dug in my heels. Wildly, I searched the room, searching for Jason among the faces, but he was nowhere to be found. Where had he gone? Maybe he'd found another way out, and somehow, we'd escape before the ritual.

"My patience is waning," Derek groaned. "Quit fighting. You will open the gate for me."

Another guard drew a pistol and trained it on me. I hardened my jaw, not taking my eyes off the altar, but I didn't move.

Hands reached under me, lifting me onto the stone table. I struggled, kicking and thrashing as they set me on the altar on my back and bound my feet at the ankles.

Desperation closed my throat, and my breathing became rapid and shallow. Leon — the only person who'd known how to perform the ceremony while sparing my life — was dead.

"Please!" I protested and flailed my head around, struggling to find anyone to help me in the sea of faces. "You don't have to do this!"

The hands were strong, pinning me down. Then, suddenly, a blue light shot forth from an opening in the ceiling high above me. A grinding noise, metal upon stone, reverberated in the large room. My eyes danced wildly around, searching for the source of the noise. Dark, ethereal figures emerged from the shadows along the base of the walls. Cloaked in darkness, they glided like ghosts toward the altar. A guard nearest my head glanced behind him, and his gasp was cut short as the faceless specter faded through him. The color in the man's eyes melted into inky blackness, and he fell to his knees, his chin resting on his chest as if asleep.

Derek's face remained an expressionless mask, showing no reaction as the men were possessed one by one. When the last one tried to escape, sprinting toward the closed door, the wraith swerved, quickly changing its path as it followed him. He skidded to a stop at the door. Desperately, his head snapped back and forth, deciding whether jumping into the flesh-melting sand would be better than having his body by an undead shadow.

The specter advanced with an otherworldly speed. The man spun, eyes wide with terror, and pressed his back against the stone. Frantically, he reached for his pistol and unleashed a series of shots in rapid succession. Like a flock of ravens swooping through clouds, the bullets pierced through the creature, leaving trailing wisps of shadow and smoke before colliding into the opposite wall.

When the clip was empty, the man stared at the gun in shock, as if it'd betrayed him, and hurled it at the wraith. It continued unfazed, and he covered his face as the creature disappeared into him.

An icy breeze swept toward me as the man stood. The pupils of his eyes were clouded in darkness, and he strode purposefully toward the altar and resumed the place he'd abandoned and placed his hands on the stone.

Derek stood a little taller and puffed his chest.

"You have no idea what you've done," I said. "Whatever is inside them will never leave them."

Derek furrowed his brows incredulously. "Like I care? They're a means to an end."

To my left, I caught sight of Jason maneuvering himself to the back recesses of a dark corner. His eyes met mine and softened. It couldn't have been for more than a millisecond, but I'd seen it, nevertheless. His jaw twitched, and he vanished behind the cluster of workers, all staring at the altar and me.

The possessed men's darkened eyes stared blankly down at the stone between their hands. The figures chanted beside me in traces of Arabic mixed with an ancient dialect I could only guess was Sumerian. As the chanting grew louder, the stones around me brightened. Under my shoulders, the altar trembled, vibrating with their chants.

Their voices carried upward, raising the stones' energy toward the ceiling's peak. The single star intensified from the opening where the night sky was visible. A vibrant red, its bright tendrils lengthened, growing brighter. The air in my throat went dry as the light cascaded down. My eyes followed its path as it descended and landed on my chest. I braced myself for a shock of pain but was startled by a soothing sensation as the magic caressed me as if I'd sunk into a spa. It coaxed me to remain still, and the epitome of relaxation seduced me.

I would have laid there for eternity.

"Bridge of Vela," Derek said from beside me, and his voice sounded distant, as if he were speaking through a pane of glass. "I, Derek Kane, eldest son of my father, command you to lower your gate and allow me to cross."

As he finished, the altar underneath me rumbled. The light grew heavy, pressing down upon my chest and abdomen, but I relished the feel of it. The raw energy created rippling sensations of heat from my head to my hands, my stomach, my legs, and my toes. I shivered, intoxicated by the magical head rush.

I was tethered to the world of the gods. I could *feel* everything.

Every molecule. Every atom. Every blade of grass brushed against the soles of my feet. Every trilling songbird. Every food and drink. Every alluring scent, from groves of blooming lilacs to damp earth after a rain. I also knew its name.

Šamû, city of the gods. Paradise.

I closed my eyes, surrendering to the clarity of it all—the ecstasy of awareness.

"Elly," Jason's voice whispered in my ear, his voice infused with fear.

No, that's wrong. There's nothing to be scared of. It all makes sense now. He needed to understand that.

"You have to stop," he said again. "You're going to die."

The vision faded, dissipating into a mist, as my eyes snapped open. A glowing sphere of crimson swirled inches above my chest. I blinked, disoriented from the intensity of what I'd seen lingering in the back of my eyes. Everything in the temple appeared hazy as if looking through a mist.

Derek stood at my feet, his face bathed in the ruby light. He stared intently at the sphere projecting from me. Faint outlines shimmered on its iridescent surface as the bridge solidified, ascending toward the night sky.

Swiftly, Derek climbed onto the altar, straddling my legs. I followed his gaze up. At the top of the bridge was the city of the gods. I could see the velvety green of hills dotted with a steepled castle of ivory and gold. A primal desire gnawed at my gut, aching to go there.

As Derek stepped lightly onto the bridge, black spots speckled me from a flare of jealousy. I should be up there, not him.

I clenched my fists and attempted to move but discovered the bridge's weight pinned me down. A crack of gunfire sliced the air, and I turned my head the hair's breadth I was able to.

Jason held up his favorite pistol—the one he'd bought when they'd been together, and everything had been right in the world—and pointed it at Derek's back. "Stop, right fucking now," he said.

Derek's right foot hesitated as he glanced over his shoulder at Jason. An unfiltered look of intense loathing and vile hatred shot toward him before he defiantly placed his shoe down. "It's too late."

"Now, Elly!" Jason said, his eyes briefly flicking to me before firing another shot. This one pierced the back of Derek's right shoulder, and he arched forward from the impact. He bellowed as he fell onto his knees, his hand clutching his shoulder.

"You have to close the gate!" Jason shouted at me.

I strained at my invisible bonds, but it was impossible. My diaphragm burned as I heaved to draw a full breath, but with each desperate breath, the pressure of the bridge bearing down on me intensified. I was suffocating. Dying. My ribs ached as I gasped for air.

"Get up. Fight it," Jason pleaded and fired off two more ear-splitting rounds.

Acrid smoke from burning buildings stung my nose.

You are the Guardian.

Rivers running red with blood from centuries of warring armies filled my mind.

Protect the Bridge.

Cries of anguish from millions of people facing dark futures rang in my ears.

Save the world.

The familiar tingle of magic awakened like an ember in a hearth. I wriggled my hand free and pressed it into the stone. My body arched as the power exploded from inside me. The intense burst of pure magic penetrated the three-ton stone below me, and the low creak of flexing stone shifted into a violent ripping sound as if the earth's continents were splitting in half.

The bridge's weight eased long enough for me to gulp in a ragged breath. The stone protested against the strain of my muscles, the matter refusing to yield to the magic until, finally, there was a snap as the molecules separated, rupturing the stone, and the altar with me still on it exploded.

A thousand granite shards flew into the air, colliding with the pillars. Terrified shouts and thudding footsteps filled the room as the workers scrambled to escape the falling rocks and stone onslaught.

I tumbled to the ground and fell onto my side. I tasted the copper of blood on my tongue. A red powder coated my face and arms as I sat up. Dust hovered in the air as guards dragged injured workers to the exit. The eight men that Derek had used for the ritual lay dead on the ground next to the shattered pieces that had been the altar.

"Elly!" Jason shouted and was by my side. His arms wrapped around me as he lifted me to my feet. I coughed, my throat raw as if it'd been scrubbed with a wire brush.

Jason half-carried me toward the door. "Jason," I murmured. At least, I think I said his name. I blinked, trying to clear my thoughts and free myself from the daze of the power of the bridge.

"You can't leave me here!" Derek bellowed from where he lay on his back, with his left leg twisted in an unnatural position.

Jason's strong arms held me as we hobbled over the scattered, broken rock to the temple door.

The sand was gone from the gap in the door, revealing the dark shapes and outlines of the city. "We can't leave him," I said, pulling back.

Jason jabbed a finger at the ground. "Screw him. He wanted in here so badly he can die here. Besides, I can't carry both of you."

Derek moaned as two workers ignored his pleas and darted to the door.

My teeth pierced my lower lip, meeting his steel-gray eyes. How could I have ever doubted him? This was Jason. *My* Jason. "Please," I said. "There have been enough deaths."

The muscles in his jaw worked even as the hardness in his gaze softened. "Fine," he growled. "Wait here." He stashed his pistol in his chest holster and left me just outside the door, leaning against a stone pillar.

The stone door shifted as if whatever had been holding it open had been removed, and it started to slide shut.

Shit. "Uh, Jason," I shouted. "Hurry, it's closing!"

Jason didn't look back and skidded to a stop beside Derek. He hauled him upright and wrapped an arm around his waist. Derek's broken leg dragged uselessly behind him as Jason carried him.

Thirty feet. Twenty. Exertion reddened Jason's face, and he grunted, heaving them toward the exit.

The door was half closed. Only a three-foot gap remained.

They weren't going to make it.

Panic appeared on Jason's face.

I staggered forward, screaming for Jason to run, as the door shuddered shut.

Three feet of solid stone stood between Jason and me. I unleashed the fury and frustration I'd been harboring for months. Years. My pathetic attempt to change the world photos, only to watch the suffering continue.

A sharp pain stabbed my left shoulder as I raised my arm and rested my hand on the door. Sweat broke out across my forehead as I focused, seeking out the voids in the rocks. I searched the molecules, isolating the weaker bonds that, with enough pressure, would break. The rock groaned in protest as a crack streaked through the door's surface, spider-webbing over the stone. Molten rock smoldered like lava in the crevices, hisses of steam sputtered, and smoke swirled in the air. I bit my lip and pressed further, feeling the heat from the superheated rock warm my face like I was too close to an open oven.

In a split second, the stone gave way, surrendering to the magic, and it burst. The shock wave flung me like a rag doll backward as the three-ton door evaporated into a fine gray mist.

I crashed hard on my back at the top of the stairs. The base of my skull smacked the ground as I lay sprawled on the ground. The world whirled, and I stared up at the drifting ash. Like pewter-colored snowflakes, they settled on my face and arms before the black spots in my vision coalesced into darkness.

CHAPTER

THIRTY-SIX

Someone shook me, and I moaned as the jarring movement flared the pain in my shoulder.

I worked my tongue, feeling like I'd chewed on a burned marshmallow, and opened my eyes.

Jason hovered over me, his face filling my vision. His eyes narrowed as he placed a hand under my neck, cradling me. "Are you alright?"

Every part of my body hurt. With my good arm, I felt the back of my head and found a hard lump. My stomach lurched at the shock of pain. "Yeah," I murmured. "Just fucking peachy."

Jason smiled, and his face visibly relaxed. "Good, let's get the hell out of here."

As I stood, the ground shifted, or at least I thought it did, and I braced myself on Jason's shoulder to stay on my feet.

The workers and agents that had accompanied us down here had fled ahead of us. As Jason and I made our way out of the ancient city, the shadowed buildings silently watched us pass. It was slow going, but finally, we stepped out into the cool desert. The fresh breeze of the morning air was heavenly as it dried the sweat clinging to my shirt and back. The first rays of the sunrise painted the horizon in vibrant hues of tangerine and apricot. Jason carried me to the Humvee and carefully helped me inside.

"Yeah, I got her," he said to someone nearby. "We need more medics. There are quite a few hurt, and I suspect some more still down there. I want this whole place secured."

Jason's voice faded in and out. My eyelids felt like lead, and finally, my head slumped against the headrest.

A WEEK HAD PASSED before they finally let Jason and me leave. Division 12, along with the United States and Syrian governments, had thoroughly questioned us. Jason had Commander Jackson's backing when they tried to fire him for breach of contract and insubordination. But in the end, they marked a strike on his file and forced him on a temporary leave of absence while they finished their investigations. It was all smoke and mirrors. Jason was far too good an agent for them to terminate.

However, his six-week hiatus was a boon for me. We weren't healed, far from it, but had decided to approach the second attempt at our relationship with more perspective. We both agreed to take it a day at a time, be more present when we could be together, and adjust when we couldn't.

Derek Kane had been airlifted to Damascus. Although he faced multiple surgeries to fix his leg and months of physical therapy, it was assumed he would fully recover.

Kane United's high-profile law team quickly shielded him from severe consequences. However, he'd need to testify before a congressional hearing in the coming year.

After we'd relayed our information, we'd puzzled the investigators when they'd been unable to recover the statue. The eight stones, too, had disappeared.

The mark on my palm had also vanished when I'd severed the bridge's connection. And Derek's fall after I'd broken the altar had shattered the idol in his backpack.

Division 12 had taken the fragments and claimed they'd protect them in a top-secret holding facility. That was bullshit, but there was nothing I could do about it. Besides, the statue was nothing now, just busted-up pieces of bronze and gold.

A helicopter carried us to Cairo, and an agent had left a cell phone for me to use. I called my mom and told her I was coming home to surprise Cara at her bridal shower. The conversation lasted an intense twenty minutes but ended with her crying happy tears, so I guess it was a win.

Jason emerged from the cockpit of

"Everything good?" I asked.

The blades whirred to life, and Jason pulled the door shut. "Almost," he said, his blue eyes dancing, and pulled my face to his.

I inhaled sharply, caught off guard, and a warmth spread across my chest and up my neck to my face. I'd stayed at the Damascus hospital for two days to recover, and while sipping milkshakes and hospital pudding, Jason had explained everything to me. All that had happened after he'd left Kat's and how he'd discovered that other agents there were allied with him, ready to defy Division in order to thwart Kane. Then, when he'd found out Kane had me, the agents on his side pulled strings, so he was placed on Kane's security detail. Everything he'd done was so he could guarantee proximity to Kane and protect me.

Still, it'd taken several days, along with three bouquets of flowers, a balloon, and a stuffed elephant, to convince me to forgive him.

The phone beeped in my hand, but I ignored it, refusing to end the kiss.

Soon, however, the vibrating became too insistent, and

Jason released me. His blue eyes danced with the lingering effects of the kiss's intensity.

"You going to get that?" he said, his voice husky.

I sighed and saw that it was Kat requesting a video call. "It's Kat," I said, then flashed him a cheeky grin. "So, behave."

Jason sat back, crossed his arms, and grinned. "I never make promises I know I can't keep."

I pursed my lips but clicked it to accept the call. Kat's bright, cheery face appeared on the screen. Her gray hair was braided on the sides of her temples, and coral-colored lipstick tinted her lips. "Ella, dear! How are you?" Kat said—the sounds of the stables filtered through the speakers on the phone.

I smiled. "I'm doing okay. It's been quite a week."

"I don't doubt it. And your shoulder?" Kat's eyes went to the sling on my left arm.

"Sore, but I'll live." I rubbed it gingerly. The doctors concluded the dislocation had been from when I'd fallen down the stairs, and I didn't argue with the theory. Confessing the truth that it had been from when I'd atomized a stone door would undoubtedly encourage them to send me to a psych ward.

The truth was, I still didn't understand how I'd accomplished that. That day's events seemed hazy, as if I hadn't experienced them myself but had watched them play out on a movie screen.

"How are the girls?"

"Take a look for yourself," Kat said. The screen shifted, and Kat's face disappeared. Taamir and his wife stood beside the wooden fence of the arena. His two girls squealed with delight as they sat astride a plodding horse being led by one of the stable hands.

A sob choked in my throat. Although my heart soared at the sight of the happy family, it was bittersweet. Their lives were forever changed because of the statue, and I doubted I'd ever accept the guilt. I promised myself I'd check on them from time to time. Not just because I cared about them but because I owed it to Taamir.

"How's Assem?" I asked.

The phone panned back to Kat's face and she flashed a smile. "Oh, you know Assem. Unflappable that one. He'll be happy to know you're alright. Did the International Society of Foreign Aid reach you yet?"

I nodded. "Yes, thanks for connecting me to them."

The ISFA had been quite interested in my experience and requested my attendance at their next month's annual meeting. They'd assured me that a few diplomats and wealthy philanthropists would all be there, giving me an opportunity to rub shoulders with the movers and shakers of the charity world.

"Don't mention it," Kat said. "And the package I sent you?"

I patted the unopened cardboard box on the seat beside me and nodded.

"Good," she said, and the video feed flickered.

The helicopter droned as it ascended.

"We're taking off, Kat. I might lose our connection. I'll call again when we land, okay?"

Kat nodded, and the screen went dark.

During my conversation with Kat, Jason had dozed off. With his arms still folded, his head slumped to the side of the bench. It was a three-hour ride to Cairo, where I'd board a plane to New York. I planned to spend a few days there before flying to Sacramento, where Jason would be my plus-one at the wedding.

I set the phone down and reached for the box. After sliding a finger under the tape, I lifted the lid. A note with Kat's handwriting lay on top, and I pulled it out to read.

Thought you might need this.
K

I reached inside, under the newspaper, and found my laptop and, atop it, the memory card. I chuckled to myself, not wanting to wake Jason.

In my hurry to leave, I'd forgotten my stuff at Kat's, including weeks of irreplaceable photos I'd taken.

I rested the little memory card on my palm, and an electric tingle trickled down my arm to where the scar had been. An outline of the eight-pointed sun flashed brilliantly for a split second before fading.

The statue may have been shattered, but my life as a Guardian of Vela was far from over.

THE END

THANK YOU FOR READING

Thank you so much for reading and taking a chance on this book. If you enjoyed Bridge of Eternity, I'd love if you'd leave a review. Readers like you are everything to me! This is only the beginning of Ella's journey and I can't wait to share what awaits the Guardian of Vela!

ACKNOWLEDGMENTS

Ella's story has lived inside me for years, patiently waiting while life happened and I worked on other stories. The path to get it finally to out into the world could have been done without the amazing support and encouragement from my friends and family.

Thank you to the Llamasquad and my writing partners, for their never-ending emotional support, world building brainstorming sessions, and beta reading. Katy Lapierre, Susan Wallach, Catherine (Cat) Bakewell, Cyla Panin, Adrielle Blaas, Mary Roach, Lillie Vale, Lenore Stutznegger, Rochelle Smit, Nicole Aronis, Ashley, Erin Madison, Trisha Kelly, Gabriela Romero Lacruz, Makayla Sophia, Alaysia, Marina, C.T. Danford, Lisa Matlin, Janis Johnson, Katie Knightly, Megan Lynch, Rachel Greenlaw, Sarah Van Goethem, Melissa Bowers, Sabrina Kleckner, and Sarah Rowlands. You guys are the best writing friends an author could ever wish for!

Thank you Katelyn Uplinger, for your constant encouragement, and cheerleading me, and making me laugh every step of this journey. I cherish you friend!

Thank you JoAnna Illingworth for writing and publishing the Black Umbrella. I enjoyed it so much and reading it was the final inspirational push I needed to finish Bridge of Eternity and release it to the world.

Becca Crandall your encouragement and guidance for the past two years helped grow my skills (and confidence) as a writer ten-fold. Words can never express how grateful I am for our partnership.

To Morgan and Isaac Huether, Brandon Raines, Kyle Jones, and Chris Carpenter, you crazy kids mean the WORLD to me. Your friendship and support helped me through the all the times of doubt that my writing would ever see the light of day. I look forward to laughing many more times until my face hurts, exploring many more dungeons and slaying many more dragons with you.

To Amy Harris and Nina Leishman, you two have cheered me on since the very beginning when I first started this writing journey. As devoted reader friends, you both were constantly in the back of my mind as I wrote Ella and her story. I hope I did you proud.

To my husband, Michael thanks for reminding me to drink water and eat food while I locked myself away in the office or hours or days at a time working on this book. Thanks for listening to me while I droned on and on about how cool a fictional man was.

To my kids, Kian and Megan, I love you both to the moon and back and thank you for letting me bounce cool action scene ideas off of you and talk at length about Mesopotamian mythology for months.

And BIG thank you to all the readers! All of your support, pre-orders, posts, reviews and comments I receive bring me untold joy. Thank you from the bottom of my heart.

-Amelia

ABOUT THE AUTHOR

Amelia Cole is an adult contemporary fantasy writer. She has won various awards for short stories and has been featured in an anthology. She lives in the Pacific Northwest with her husband and two children, on a small farm. You can find her on Instagram, TikTok, and Facebook @ameliacolebooks

www.ameliacolebooks.com

COMING SOON BY AMELIA COLE...

November 2023: BREAKER OF MOUNTAINS Vela Series Book Two

SPRING 2024 : Vela Series Book 3

www.ingramcontent.com/pod-product-compliance
Lightning Source LLC
Chambersburg PA
CBHW070745160726

48004CB00001B/52